Unbridled Passion!

Drew stopped and stared longingly into my eyes. "With you here, my darling, this is truly paradise." He pulled me into his embrace and lowered his mouth to mine. As Drew's lips moved caressingly a heady thrill spiraled. At last, I thought, melting against him. Then disappointment once again settled in . . .

Books by Irene M. Pascoe

THE CURSE OF BELLE HAVEN
DARK TIDES

DARK TIDES

IRENE M. PASCOE

DIAMOND BOOKS, NEW YORK

For Del, my hero.

DARK TIDES

chapter 1

I KNEW THE horrors of the past four years would haunt me forever, and that I must accept what I'd seen and heard and go on with my life. But I hadn't expected ghastly visions to torment me in sleep, to shake me awake with my body bathed in cold perspiration. Night after night it was the same. And I wasn't certain if I had set sail from San Francisco because I was trying to put as much distance between myself and the painful memories as possible, or if I was running to the man I'd met mere months ago.

From my shipboard bunk I frowned up at the ceiling. In the past I'd always known my mind, always known the path I wished to follow. Only then I'd had a home and a family. Now both were gone, and I felt lost without a foundation upon which to rebuild my life.

"We can change that," Drew Phillips had murmured when he'd proposed to me on our last evening together. That was in the spring of this year, 1865. Now it was November and I was on my way to be with him and his family. Not to become his bride, though, as he hoped. A part of me wanted to think that maybe one day marriage between us would come to pass. One day when I felt whole again and not just this shell of Rachel Montgomery.

The thought of seeing Drew brought a smile to my lips. How well I remembered his smile, so easy and infectious. It had been a balm to my battered emotions, and even the exhaustion that had gripped me back then seemed to fade in his presence.

Another heavy swell tossed the ship and I was nearly pitched off my bunk. This wasn't my first time at sea and I was used to rough water. But the voyage across the Pacific Ocean had been miserably turbulent and the handful of other passengers and I on board this merchant steamer had, for the most part, kept to our quarters. For that reason this trip had also been lonely, but that was soon to end. Within the next two hours we would be making port, the journey would be over, and I hoped that in this new land my heart would heal and my life would once again go forward. Equally important, I hoped—no prayed—the plaguing nightmares would end.

I left the bunk and navigated across the heaving plank floor to the porthole and glanced out. My mind was so intent on Drew that all I really saw was his well-chiseled face. He was handsome beyond compare, but it wasn't his dark good looks that attracted me. I was drawn by his devil-may-care attitude, his intelligence, and the intriguing shadows I'd seen flicker across his features on two or three occasions when he thought I wasn't looking. There was more to Drew Phillips than met the eye. At times I'd had the strange feeling he was harboring a deep, dark secret. In all likelihood, though, the shadows were reflections of the profound sorrow he and I had shared with scores of other Americans.

We'd met in a makeshift Union Army field hospital during General Sherman's march across Georgia. While under the general's command, Drew had suffered a near-mortal wound from a Rebel blast. For two days he'd drifted in and out of consciousness. I was cleansing and re-dressing his wounds when he'd at last come around. He'd gazed up at me, wonder struck, and whispered "Angel." For a disoriented moment he must have thought he had passed to the great beyond. In my work-stained clothing and with smudges of fatigue beneath my eyes I didn't see how I could have been mistaken for an angel.

Drew had blinked, and when he'd looked up again, his next words were, "You're beautiful." The death and suffering I'd witnessed had left me too numb to give even a passing thought to my appearance. In fact I was grateful that no one else heard the compliment, for military nurses were not allowed to be attractive. At least not according to Miss Dorothea Dix, who had established the Female Nurse Corps as part of the army's Medical Department. If I hadn't donned a Mother Hubbard, hiding the gentle curves I'd been blessed with, and pulled a mopcap over my thick hair, she would not have certified me for duty.

As I'd moved from one field hospital to another, following the troops, my only concern for myself had been to remain healthy so that I could continue with my work. And Drew's further compliments scarcely registered in my mind. "Your hair is the color of the sun," he had whispered, lifting a bandaged hand to caress the blond tendrils that escaped my side combs. "Soft as silk. And your eyes are as clear and blue as the water back home."

It wasn't until sometime later that I learned "back home" was the tropical island of Maui, in the Hawaiian chain. And it certainly never occurred to me that I might one day leave the mainland for that far-off place.

A huge wave flung a heavy spray over the grimy porthole, and I braced myself as the ship rocked perilously. There was no blue to be seen in the island waters today, or in the brooding sky. By the time we cast anchor just offshore Lahaina, the wind had dropped to a heavy breeze and rain was pouring down.

Drew had told me that the valley on the leeward side of the island was normally hot and arid, but even when gusting kona storms blew in, the air was still fairly warm. With that in mind I slipped on the summer-weight mantle, which matched my plum-colored percale. As I was adjusting the hood over my upswept hair, a brawny crewman, wearing a slicker over coarse clothes, came to help me with my bags.

Back when I'd served briefly on a hospital ship, I'd mastered negotiating narrow stairs during harsh weather and I reached the deck of this vessel unscathed. However, my seagoing confidence fell to the pit of my stomach and refused to rally when an unexpected wind gust propelled me to the rail and I saw the rope ladder that had been thrown over the side. Below, bobbing like a cork in the choppy water, was the small passenger boat that would take me ashore. "Isn't there any other way off this vessel?" I sputtered.

"This ain't a passenger ship," the crewman tossed back, and urged me onto the rail. "Jest hold on tight to the ladder. You'll be safe. I'm right behind you."

His reassurance brought me some comfort, but it too quickly vanished when my right foot slipped as I began my descent. "Careful," a man from the boat below shouted as I clung to the

swaying ladder with a death grip. Salty air dried my mouth and
my skirts whipped and ballooned. Still, I had no fear they would
be blown skyward, for the beating rain kept them in place. Another minute in the torrential downpour and the garments would
be plastered to my body.

I closed my mind to the spectacle I surely made, flapping in
the currents as I struggled to keep from becoming airborne and
plummeting to the deck below, or worse yet into the deep, dark
water. I hadn't been this frightened since the war when shells
whizzed by the hospital tents. The only blessing, if one was possible in this hair-raising circumstance, was that I was too preoccupied to notice if anyone was laughing at me.

By the time I reached the bottom of the ladder, I was shaking
visibly. I nearly collapsed with relief when a sailor helped me
into the passenger boat, then showed me to a bench in a covered
area. It was cramped, scarcely large enough for me and my three
bags. But what did that matter? I was still alive! This place was
dry, and since I was the only passenger who had disembarked for
this island, I wouldn't have to share the tight quarters.

I caught my breath, and after thanking the crewman who'd
helped me off the merchant steamer, I settled back for the short
but rough ride over the water. From where I sat all I could see
through the windows was the long line of ships anchored offshore.

When we came alongside the dock, a sailor hoisted my bags.
I ducked my head against the elements and followed him from
the boat. For weeks I'd looked forward to my arrival on Maui,
to seeing the lush landscape and volcanic mountains Drew had
described. But all I managed to glimpse on my flight to shelter
in one of the buildings at the head of the wharf was a stretch of
white sand and the wind bending coconut palms to submission.
If this was paradise, it was a far cry from what I had imagined.

For sinking moments I was struck by overwhelming loneliness
and the sense of not belonging. Back on the mainland I'd been
excited by the prospect of being among people whose culture
and language were foreign to me. Now I felt at a complete loss
and I couldn't even remember the dozen or so Hawaiian words
Drew had taught me. Drew! I glanced around the official-looking
office we had entered and issued a small prayer that he was here
to meet me. There were several men working at scattered desks.

All of them were Caucasian and dressed in American-style clothing. But there was no Drew. Despite the prayer I hadn't expected he would would be here. He knew I was on the way, but one Pacific storm after another had delayed my arrival. Since Drew had said that was a likely possibility and we might miss each other, he instructed me to go straight to his office in town. Or if my ship anchored after nightfall, a room would be waiting for me in his family's hotel.

"You'll be taken care of right proper here, miss." The sailor put down my bags. Overhead, the rain drummed on the tin roof.

"Thank you." I looked out the window at the wharf. On this late, stormy afternoon activity was light. At least all I saw were a few barges being unloaded. Without thought my attention drifted to the forest of masts and spars rising from the dozens of ships moored offshore. In a heartbeat I found the one I'd just left and an unexpected lump stuck in my throat. That vessel was my last tie to home! True, ships sailed to the mainland regularly. Still, San Francisco was over two thousand miles east, and Ohio, where I was born and raised, again that much farther.

Shoulders drooping, I swung about. I was the only woman in the office. As I stepped forward, shaking the rain from my mantle, a balding man rose from his desk and came my way. He acknowledged me with the Hawaiian greeting, "Aloha." I was thankful that his next words were spoken in English. "May I see some identification, please?"

I nodded and fished in the drawstring bag I'd secured firmly over my arm. He scanned the document I'd handed over. As he returned it to me I inquired, "Where might I find the Phillips Land Development Corporation, sir?" An eyebrow went up and his sagging features took on a curious expression. Did he think I was a woman of means, here to invest in property? All I had to my name was the small inheritance from Father and the pittance I'd managed to save from my twelve-dollar-a-month nurse's pay. The ordinary cut and quality of my apparel was visible proof of my station in life. Most women, and perhaps even some men, would deduce that immediately. This male, however, might be wondering if I was a poor relative seeking a handout from the wealthy side of the family. In any case whatever had piqued his sudden interest in me remained unclear. But at least he answered my question politely and without further delay.

"It's just a few doors up on Front Street," he said, "near the corner of Lahainaluna. But it's much too blustery and miserable for a woman to be on the streets. May I send a message for someone to come fetch you, Miss Montgomery?"

His warmth and thoughtfulness brought a small smile to my lips. "That's very kind of you, but since you say it's not far, I can manage."

"If you're sure . . ." His voice trailed off.

"I am." Bad weather wasn't even a minor inconvenience compared with the ship's rope ladder.

"In that case you're welcome to leave your bags until called for."

"I'd appreciate that," I said, accepting his kind offer. I was about to ask where I might purchase an umbrella when it occurred to me that an umbrella in the occasional heavy wind gusts would either be flipped inside out or trap air that could surely carry me aloft. So once again I adjusted my hood and stepped out into the elements. And once again I became a spectacle of flapping as I struggled against the currents.

Hindsight told me I should have stayed on the mainland until early spring, when the weather was more hospitable. But Drew had insisted that I come at once. Actually he'd pressed for me to join him even before the war ended seven months ago. "It's almost over, Rachel," he had pointed out. From all I'd heard and seen I'd known that was true. Still, to leave behind the wounded was something I just couldn't do. Not then, or even after the Confederacy fell at Appomattox. And I will never regret that I continued to serve until I was no longer needed. When that time came, I returned to Ohio, packed my family treasures, and sold the only home I'd ever known. My widowed father had died just weeks before the onset of the war, and my two brothers perished defending the Union. Now the loss of my family was an ever-present weight on my heart.

A sharp rush of air brought me back to the moment, and I noticed, as I passed shops and other establishments constructed of wood and stone, that I seemed to be the only one out braving the weather. The locals undoubtedly had the good sense to remain home or behind the closed doors of their businesses. At least the air was warm, and for that I was grateful.

With my head bent once more against the wind, I didn't see

the man crossing the threshold before me and I ran into him, almost sending him sprawling. "I'm sorry," I murmured. I was even sorrier when he breathed in my face and the putrid odor of whiskey and tobacco assaulted my senses.

"Sorry, too," the unkempt man slurred on a hiccup, and leered at me with a lopsided, licentious grin. As I quickly scooted past the swaying obstacle he bellowed after me, "Wanna drink, missy?"

I didn't have to look back to know that he'd just staggered out of a grogshop. From what little I'd managed to see of Lahaina's principal thoroughfare, there were plenty of them. But then, Drew had told me this thriving town was the winter port for whaling vessels, and sailors swarmed ashore to indulge themselves. He'd even admitted that his family owned two of the more prosperous taverns, as well as a lumberyard, hotel, mercantile, and prime parcels of land.

At last I was at Drew's office and I heaved a sigh of relief when I saw that it was still open. As I stepped through the doorway of the stone building, I prayed he was in. After six weeks of near isolation in my quarters on the ship, I dreaded the thought of another evening alone. The gray-haired man behind the desk in the outer office looked just like the conservatively dressed bankers back home. He lifted his head from the papers strewn before him and regarded me over the rim of his spectacles. Behind him were three closed doors. "Is Mr. Drew Phillips in?" I inquired, and held my breath.

"No, I'm sorry."

The dread deepened, then I remembered that Drew and his brother ran the family businesses jointly. "Jordan Phillips, perhaps?"

The man shook his head. "He and Mr. Drew left the office together. May I be of service, miss?" he asked, clearly noting my dismay.

"I'm Rachel Montgomery—"

Before I could say another word, a smile brightened his face and he came to his feet. "Miss Montgomery, it's a pleasure to meet you. I was told you would be arriving soon. Allow me to introduce myself, I'm Jacob Winston, chief clerk and accountant."

I offered my hand in a friendly shake and felt another surge of relief when he said, "Mr. Drew left strict instructions that if you came while he was out, I was to take you directly to the family home. It's about a mile out of town. That is, if you don't mind traveling in this weather. My covered buggy offers protection against the rain," he added.

"I don't mind at all." I leaped at the offer, then finished on an apologetic note: "But I hate to take you out on a day like this, Mr. Winston. Maybe I could hire a carriage."

"No, no, I wouldn't hear of it. And Mr. Drew would be furious if I didn't personally escort you."

I couldn't even imagine Drew ill-tempered much less furious. Once he'd begun to recover from his wounds, he'd seemed to wear a perpetual smile.

Mr. Winston flipped a ledger shut. "My buggy is in the livery out back. If you'll give me a moment to close up the office . . ."

"Close up?" I blurted, watching him cross and lock the front door. "I don't wish to disrupt business, sir."

"Mr. Drew's orders," he assured me, putting on his hat. "He made it abundantly clear that you were not to be kept waiting."

As much as I appreciated Drew's thoughtfulness, I couldn't help wondering if his brother and their maiden aunt Patience, who held the purse strings, would approve of closing early. Three hours early, according to the sign posted at the entrance.

Mr. Winston brought the buggy to the back then helped me in. As he settled beside me on the leather seat, I saw that the wind had begun to drop. The rain, however, was still a resounding staccato. "If you wouldn't mind a brief stop," I ventured, "my bags are in one of the buildings on the wharf."

"Not at all." He snapped the reins and the dappled mare started forward. "If you're cool, there is a light lap robe."

Actually I was a little warm and had considered shedding my mantle. But it kept my clothes and my hair dry. "I'm fine, thank you," I said. "Is Mr. Drew at home, do you know?"

"Yes, he's home." A smile touched the corners of Mr. Winston's mouth. "And eagerly waiting to see you."

I could hardly wait to see him, too. I longed to feel his strong arms about me and the warmth of his tender mouth on mine. Drew Phillips seemed everything I ever wanted in a man, yet something deep within had kept me from accepting his proposal. He had pressed for me to return to Maui with him and begin wedding preparations. I hadn't understood his haste to marry. "It's because I love you so deeply, Rachel," he had insisted. But how could he even be certain that what he felt was love? We'd met under the worst circumstances and had only known each other ten days before he was put aboard a hospital train and sent north. Shortly afterward I was ordered home for ten days of long, overdue rest, and Drew had joined me there near the end of my leave. To me the sum total of two weeks wasn't enough time to truly understand one's heart, even under ideal conditions. There was always the chance that Drew might have mistaken gratitude, over my nursing him back to health, for love.

"It's good to see Mr. Drew happy again," the pleasant man beside me said as our carriage plowed the dirt streets turned to mud by the rain. "He's been through so much."

"The war was horrible," I murmured, pointing out the building where my bags were being held. Now that the wind had eased, I could hear the heavy surf breaking on the beach.

Mr. Winston pulled in and set the brake. "Yes, the war"—his voice had grown distant—"that, too."

That, too? I thought in surprise as he alighted. What else had Drew been through? Whatever it was, this man had made it sound as shattering as the four-year battle between the states. While I waited for my valises to be brought out, I went over the bits and pieces Drew had told me about himself. There was so little compared with all he'd managed to learn about me. Drew had talked primarily about Hawaii and his aunt Patience, who had settled on Maui in the twenties with her missionary parents. As for his brother Drew had simply commented that Jordan was a trifle older than his own thirty-one years and that they had come to live with their aunt after being orphaned in childhood.

A heavy wagon rumbled by and I glanced up, taking in the colorfully dressed, brown-skinned man at the reins. Beyond, low clouds shrouded the verdant mountains. If there had been another recent misery in Drew's life besides the war, I thought, he never mentioned it.

"Just these three bags, Miss Montgomery?" Mr. Winston's question brought my head around. Water dripped from the brim of his hat, though the rain had nearly stopped.

"Yes," I answered in a distracted tone. He stowed my luggage behind the seat, reboarded, and we continued on our way.

Lahaina's main thoroughfare was about a mile long, with several side streets joining from the east. Traffic had begun to pick up, and I noticed as we rolled along that there were almost as many churches as there were grogshops.

As Mr. Winston gestured to points of interest and named the varieties of several native trees, it suddenly struck me that I had seen Drew shaken from his usually lighthearted mood on one occasion. It was during our time together at my home in Ohio and had to do with the telegram he received. As he'd read, his mouth tightened and flaring anger erased the devilish gleam I'd come to know so well in his dark eyes. Without a word he flung the message into the parlor fire. "I'm sorry, Rachel," he said, drawing me close, "but I'll have to leave for New York in the morning."

We had planned on several more days together and I felt the corners of my mouth droop in disappointment. "I'm sorry, too. I hope it's nothing terribly serious, Drew."

He hesitated and I sensed he was trying to pull himself together. "It's nothing I can't take care of." He laughed, but there was a hollow ring to it. Drew never said who the telegram was from or why our visit was cut short, but I'd had the feeling the reason was far more important than he'd wanted me to know. Might it have been part of the "so much" that Mr. Winston mentioned Drew having been through?

My wandering mind had kept me from truly seeing the landscape, and in what seemed like a blink of the eye, we were heading up a long drive. On each side were trees and lush vegetation. Ahead, the beach and the churning Pacific Ocean. Following the drive, Mr. Winston urged the horse to a sharp left, and the immense, three-story Phillips home came into view. It sat upon a wide, immaculately landscaped plateau, surrounded by jungle that yielded to the beach on the west. Just looking at the house made me think of New England. White stucco, trimmed in blue and topped by a wood-shake roof, it was in the style favored there. It was a handsome place, with delicate fretwork at the gables and along the covered front porch, which wrapped gently about the waterfront side of the house. Above, and also overlooking the beach, were two immense bay windows. Left of the porch, and beyond a symmetrically laid-out flower garden, was a two-story wing and a covered walkway to the carriage house. For all its grace and splendor this house also held a foreboding look. But perhaps the mist and grayness of the day lent that impression.

As Mr. Winston pulled to a stop before the imposing structure, I glanced at the open balustraded captain's bridge above the porch. Then I returned my attention to the sea, and a shiver inched up my spine and sent a tingle along the nape of my neck. Home was so far away, and to me this island was in the middle of nowhere. Even if this was paradise, would I be happy living in such a remote place? I wondered for the dozenth time since Drew's proposal.

I lifted my chin and cast out negative thoughts as Mr. Winston helped me from the buggy. I was here to be with the man who had captured a part of my heart, perhaps a larger part than I realized. Now we could come to know each other better, and I looked forward to meeting Drew's family and to exploring this island. I was also here to carry out my duties as nurse-companion to his aunt, who suffered from a heart complaint.

In truth Drew was annoyed with me for insisting on being of service to the family during my stay. But I wouldn't have come otherwise. After all, he and I were not betrothed, and since the length of my visit was indefinite, it was against my principles to live off the family's generosity. "Good God, Rachel," Drew had written in his most recent letter, "the last thing I want is for you to be an employee, but if that's the only way I can get you here, then so be it. But I must warn you, my aunt is quite eccentric."

I appreciated the warning. Nevertheless, if Drew hoped it would sway me to his way of thinking to visit solely as a house-guest, the attempt fell flat. But then I hadn't mentioned I'd been raised in the world of eccentric professors—or at least my father and his colleagues had been unconventional. "I can help with the bags," I said as Mr. Winston tried to juggle all three.

He nodded appreciation and handed me the smallest. Moving ahead of him, I went up the stone walk and mounted the steps. On the porch, which was set with wicker furniture, I stopped left of the front door as Mr. Winston approached, set down one of the bags, and knocked.

A burst of excitement swept through me as my gaze went over the long, lace-curtained windows and the stained glass in the door. Drew was somewhere beyond, and within seconds we would be together again.

The door opened and an attractive Hawaiian woman, not much older than my own twenty-two years, appeared on the threshold. She was dressed in a gray servant's costume, and her luxuriant waist-length hair was captured at her nape with a simple ribbon. She smiled up at the man before her. "Mr. Winston," she said, "how nice to see you again, it's been a while."

He removed his hat. "Indeed it has been, Kalani."

I must have been caught in her peripheral vision because she looked around abruptly. Her eyes were liquid amber, and her features delicate, though they took on a sudden sharpness when she spotted the bag I held. Dismay tightened my throat. I assumed she knew who I was and was clearly displeased by my presence.

Gulping down the dismay, I greeted the housekeeper with a gracious nod as Mr. Winston introduced us. "Welcome, miss." She managed a cordial tone and invited us in.

In the vestibule Mr. Winston took the bag I carried and set it with the others on an Oriental rug. Ahead, in the stair hall, was another rug in the same muted colors. As he exchanged a few more pleasantries with Kalani, my gaze lifted to the closed door right of the stair hall, then I glanced into the library, visible through the wide entrance directly on my left. "Won't you stay and have refreshments with the family?" the housekeeper asked Mr. Winston.

He declined with a polite nod. "I must return to town. I hope to see you again soon, Miss Montgomery. Enjoy your stay."

"Thank you for your help," I said softly, "and for the ride out."

As he exited and closed the front door behind him, Kalani set aside my wet mantle, then gestured to the reception room opposite the library. "Please make yourself comfortable, miss, I'll tell Mr. Drew you're here. I believe he's upstairs with Miss Phillips."

Before I could even ask if I might freshen myself, she turned and headed for the beautifully curved stairs in the hallway beyond. Kalani moved with lithe grace, her feet gliding over the lustrous hardwood floors. Her waist was enviably slender, the narrowest I'd ever seen in a grown woman.

Lips compressed, I glanced down at my dress, limp with dampness. Worse yet, the curls I'd meticulously piled on top of my head felt the same, and I'd wanted so much to look my best for Drew. My heart fluttered at the thought of seeing him in a matter of moments, and I couldn't even begin to contain the renewal of excitement.

Just as I was about to step into the reception room, lavishly appointed in dark woods and elegant fabrics, I heard the door in the stair hall open. Instinctively I glanced in that direction and my breath suspended. Drew! He'd paused on the threshold, his attention wholly focused on the sheet of paper he was studying. I ached to call out to him, but feared his name would lodge in my suddenly dry throat. He stood straight and tall, with a confident squared set to his shoulders that I had never noticed before.

Swallowing, I boldly admired Drew's lean frame and the perfect fit of his well-tailored suit. It was as dark as his hair and eyes, and enhanced by a complementing white shirt. His expressive brows were knitted in a V over the bridge of his straight nose and the smiling full mouth I remembered was appealingly serious. As always, just gazing upon him gladdened my heart, and the impulsive side of me, which I had thought no longer existed, rushed forward. I was with Drew; I wasn't alone anymore.

On an overwhelming surge I lifted my skirts and whirled. "Drew," I called softly. He glanced up. His eyes swept over me, then widened. But I suppose I looked like a hurricane sailing toward him. In less than a breath my arms were about him, my head against his virile chest. His heart was beating as fast as my own, and his warmth and strength were giving me comfort and reassurance.

Without thought I rose up on my toes, and just as he was about to speak I put my mouth on his. Drew's lips did not yield beneath my pressure, and I feared that my boldness had shocked him. Heaven knew this was not like me, and try as I might, I could not stem the flood of emotion his warmth and strength had unleashed. For agonizing seconds I felt like a complete fool, that Drew wasn't responding because he'd had a change of heart, he didn't love me after all. Just as I was about to withdraw and try to salvage what was left of my dignity, a compelling current that was new to me arced between us. Caught in its power, I melted against Drew as his mouth began to move and his arms slid about me. His kiss grew deep and intoxicating. I could hardly breathe or even think beyond each delicious moment and the sweet torment of his lips on mine. Amid the heat and swirling sensations I heard a familiar masculine voice call sharply, "Rachel!"

As if shot through by a lightning bolt I jerked away and swung about. "Drew!" I gasped. He glared at me from near the stairs. No, this couldn't be. Certain my eyes were deceiving me, I shook my head. Then I looked from the well-defined planes of one handsome face to the other. The men were identical!

chapter 2

"WHAT IS THE meaning of this?" Drew demanded, crossing to stand before us.

"Meaning?" I cried in humiliation, and couldn't even bring myself to look up at the man whose kiss still smoldered on my senses. "I thought he was you. You never told me you're a twin."

"That's a little game my brother likes to play on new acquaintances," Jordan bit out scornfully. "But this time the joke turned on him."

"At my expense." Flaring anger jerked my gaze up and I impaled Jordan Phillips with an icy stare. "You knew I'd made a mistake, yet you kissed me back."

"You took advantage of an unfortunate situation," Drew hurled in my defense, and his brother's lips parted to comment.

But I cut him off. "Neither one of you is a gentleman."

Masculine eyebrows shot up, but Jordan was the first to respond and in a quiet tone said, "In this instance I agree. I'm sorry for embarrassing you, Miss Montgomery." Was he also sorry for the sizzling kiss that nearly buckled my legs? I wondered.

Drew reached for my hand, his expression apologetic. "Forgive me, Rachel, I hadn't meant any harm."

I lifted my chin. "I'll not be the brunt of jokes."

"It won't happen again," he promised, with a softness that made me wonder for a moment if I had overreacted. However, the look of amusement that came into his brother's eyes as we were formally presented to each other conveyed the fact that he was recalling our provocative introduction, and I bristled anew. Ordinarily I resisted the urge to make snap judgments. But in this

case I didn't even try to block out the insistent voice that told me
I was not going to like this man.

Drew gave my hand a gentle squeeze, and when he spoke
again, his voice held the same quality. "How wonderful to have
you here at last, Rachel." It was obvious from the yearning in his
eyes that if we were alone, he would take me in his embrace.
Despite his callous joke and the embarrassment I still ached for
that moment, though not with quite the same zeal. "Did Winston
bring you out to the house?" he asked.

For the first time I noticed that Drew also wore a dark suit,
though the cut was different from his brother's. "Yes, he insisted," I murmured. How in the world was I going to tell these
two men apart?

"Winston?" Jordan's brusque tone slashed through my web of
dismay. Even before he leveled a steady gaze on Drew, I knew
I was the unwitting cause of trouble. "You authorized him to
leave the office at this hour of the day?"

Drew flashed a lazy smile. "Relax, Jordan, closing two or
three hours early isn't going to throw us into financial ruin."

"That along with your other—" Jordan's attention flicked to
me and he broke off midsentence.

I shifted uncomfortably and thought to mention that I'd offered to hire a carriage for the ride out. But since that would
have been the reasonable option, it struck me the comment might
worsen the situation.

"We'll discuss this later," Jordan muttered to his brother, then
managed in a civil tone, "I'm sure Miss Montgomery would appreciate being shown to her room."

"Thank you, I would like to freshen up." Jordan's thoughtfulness gave me a measure of relief. In the hope that we might
forget our poor start and begin anew to be friends, I said, "Please
call me Rachel."

Jordan's short nod of acknowledgment was nothing more than
polite, and when he hesitated before inviting me to address him
by his given name, I knew that he had no interest in promoting
friendship between us. Surprisingly, I was overcome by an odd
sense of disappointment and couldn't imagine why I cared how
he felt about me. Of course if his brother and I should wed, it
was essential that I be in harmony with the family.

In view of Jordan's aloofness, I was also a little surprised when he offered to lend a hand with my bags. After all, Drew was here and there was household staff. For all I knew, Jordan looked upon me as a servant rather than a potential member of the family. His brother and I weren't betrothed and in essence I was an employee—although I refused to accept any compensation beyond my keep. Maybe Jordan was simply helping with my luggage out of ingrained politeness. Clearly he wasn't motivated by courtesy to his brother, for it was obvious from the firm set of Jordan's jaw that he was still irritated over the early closing of the office.

As Jordan started toward my bags he glanced down and stopped short. Lying on the Oriental rug was the sheet of paper he'd been studying before I'd swooped down on him.

Drew also saw the paper. "Yours?" he asked his brother.

"Yes, it slipped from my hand." Jordan caught up the white sheet filled with bold handwriting. As he straightened, our eyes met. For one heart-skipping instant, a heady current of remembrance surged between us and I knew, without a shadow of doubt, that he'd lost his grasp on that paper at the height of our kiss.

"Rachel," Drew said in alarm, "you're flushed." He put a supporting hand beneath my elbow. The unbidden memory had made me suffocatingly hot, not unsteady. Before I could even try to ease Drew's concern, he asked, "What is it? Are you all right?"

"It's nothing, really." I managed to speak past the troubling dryness that had come to my throat. "It's been a long day and I'm suddenly tired." I prayed Jordan hadn't guessed the truth, but one glance at the knowing look now in his dark eyes told me otherwise. Heat threatened again, but I forced it down. I'd never been so overwhelmed by a man before, so caught by a presence that it was a struggle to think clearly. Even Drew, who was the exact image of his brother, had not made my heart drum and my entire being turn to clay waiting to be molded.

"The bedrooms are on the third floor," Drew said. "Are you up to climbing two long flights, Rachel?"

"Yes, I'm fine."

Frowning, Jordan folded the paper and slipped it into his coat pocket.

The swish of cloth caused my gaze to return to the stairs.

Kalani was descending. Her delicate features were schooled in a friendly expression, though her eyes riveted on me for a long moment and were as cool as before. This time I also sensed a trace of resentment. Why would she feel that way about me, a perfect stranger?

"I'll have one of the maids bring up Miss Montgomery's bags," she said, exuding complete warmth as she shifted her attention to the men.

"Jordan and I will take care of the luggage," Drew told her. Kalani's gaze lingered on him and I felt my brows rise at the flash of awareness that brightened her eyes. Was she interested in Drew?

"Yes, sir. Would you like help with the unpacking?" she asked me.

Her polite but stiff tone set my teeth on edge and it was a struggle to keep from responding in the same fashion. But I summoned every ounce of the good manners my parents had instilled in me and replied with a gracious, "No, thank you, Kalani." In any event I was used to doing for myself and I preferred to keep it that way. My mother had said I was too independent, and that men weren't particularly fond of that quality in women. But Drew didn't seem to mind, although I still wondered what had first attracted him to me. It couldn't have been what he called my beauty. I'd looked a fright, all rumpled and exhausted and blood-spattered.

Kalani turned away, taking my wet mantle with her to dry somewhere at the rear of the house. From beneath my lashes I caught Jordan watching me, his eyes hooded. Something about his expression kindled another twist of excitement. "Your bags," he said abruptly, as if they'd been forgotten. With heavy steps that suggested irritation he continued to the vestibule. Was he annoyed with me now, as well as with his brother? For what, the kiss? Jordan could have ended it before— I broke off the thought, determined not to relive the intimacy again. "You travel light," he commented over his shoulder, noting there were only three pieces of luggage.

With his hand still at my elbow Drew replied as we also crossed to the valises, "I advised Rachel not to bring much. She can shop here for all her needs."

He made it sound as if I had ample money to shop. That had

never been the case and Drew knew it. All the clothing I owned was in those bags. Because there hadn't been uniforms for the military nurses, the balance of my once adequate wardrobe had been worn to threads or permanently stained crimson. My stomach flip-flopped in recollection, and I said in a distant voice, "I understand the weather in Hawaii is much different from back home and all I'll need is lightweight clothes."

"True. Today's downpour is deceiving." Jordan lifted two bags. "Back home is . . . Ohio?" His expression was casual, but his tone held an ambiguous quality. Was he testing me? Or perhaps what his brother had said about me?

An unsettled thought loomed and prickled my flesh. Might Jordan Phillips imagine I was a fortune hunter? All the poor-girl-meets-rich-man stories I'd ever heard swept forward. Surely Drew was confident that my interest lay solely in him. Still, when it came right down to it, how could he be certain when we really didn't know each other? The fact that I hadn't leaped at his proposal, and insisted upon earning my keep, should have indicated the depth of my integrity. But I supposed both could also be viewed as a ploy to make myself look good. "Yes, Ohio," I answered, and my spirits dropped even further on the grim possibility that I might be under a magnifying glass in this house. In light of the family's wealth I supposed I should have realized that could be the case.

Drew lifted the last bag, then said as we followed his brother up the stairs, "I believe I told you Rachel's father was a professor at Ohio University."

"You said she was raised in the world of academia."

Academia? The word alone made that life sound stuffy. In my family nothing could have been further from the truth. My parents had been full of life and ultra-social. And my brothers, Cameron and Eric, had included me in their daring adventures and misadventures. In truth I had never become proficient at needlework, like most of the girls I'd grown up with, but I had mastered climbing trees, riding horses at breakneck speed, and fishing. I knew that fun-loving Drew would appreciate the tomboyish ways of my youth, and even my occasional lapses. His serious-faced brother, on the other hand, was another matter. He had probably never even run barefoot in the grass with a female.

I stared at Jordan's back. The determined set of his broad

shoulders communicated that he knew exactly what he wanted from life, and I suspected he would accept nothing less.

"Since your ship was late arriving, Rachel," Drew was saying, "you must have encountered rough seas."

"Yes. But making my way down that treacherous ladder in the wind to the passenger boat was the worst part of the trip."

"Ladder?" Jordan said in surprise. "Why didn't you sail into Honolulu, then take an interisland ferry. It would have brought you ashore in Lahaina."

The surprise that shot through me was immediately followed by irritation. "If Drew had mentioned that option, I would have. Why didn't you mention it?" I halted and frowned up at him.

"I know I should have," Drew answered apologetically, "but docking in Honolulu would have put you here a day or two later. To me that seemed almost like forever. Besides, from what you told me about yourself I thought you would find landing at Maui an adventure."

"Adventure? I was petrified."

"I'm sorry, Rachel. Wanting you here as quickly as possible was selfish of me. Am I forgiven?"

This was the second time he'd asked that of me and we hadn't even been together fifteen minutes. Still, how could I be angry when he'd been motivated by love? "Forgiven," I agreed, though a part of my mind still stung with annoyance.

Drew caressed me with his eyes, then asked as we continued up the stairs, "Other than rough water were there any other discomforts during your crossing?"

"Seasickness."

"You?"

"No, most of the passengers, at one time or another."

"I hope you didn't let on you're a nurse and were pressed into service."

"Someone had to care for them, not that much can be done to relieve the distress."

"After we're married, no more nursing."

My mouth fell open. He'd never mentioned giving up my work before, nor had I agreed yet to marry him. "I love nursing," I reminded him firmly.

As Jordan stepped onto the second floor he glanced back with a glint of amusement in his eyes. Clearly he was enjoying this bit of a clash between his brother and me. That man had a perverse sense of humor and was probably chuckling under his breath over my so-called adventurous arrival in Maui. Trying to ignore him, I asked Drew as we came onto the landing, "How is your aunt?" In all the turmoil with the brothers she had temporarily slipped my mind.

"Aunt Patience has her good days and her bad. Of late she's been in fine spirits. I know that's because she's excited about meeting you." His hand at my elbow tightened affectionately. "I'll introduce you as soon as you're ready."

"All I need is a few minutes to freshen up a bit." I looked around before we began our ascent of the second flight. Apparently the first level was the entrance floor, for this was clearly the main floor. Through open doorways I could see a luxurious dining room and a drawing room, both overlooking the drive. On the ocean side of the house was an even more elaborate drawing room, with rich hangings and upholstered pieces that took my breath away. The door just south of the stairs was closed, so I couldn't see what lay beyond it, or the others down the long hallway to the rear.

"You'll be able to join us for refreshments, then?" I heard the smile in Drew's voice before I saw it in his dark eyes.

As always the expression was infectious and I automatically smiled back. "That would be nice."

Jordan hadn't paused on the landing, and he'd already disappeared into one of the front-facing rooms on the upper floor by the time Drew and I reached it. As we entered, Jordan was placing the two bags he'd carried on the four-poster bed. "How very lovely," I murmured, looking around. Upon the hardwood floor was a beautiful blue carpet; the swagged draperies and bed hangings were in matching velvet. The wood pieces were expertly crafted from fine mahogany, and gilt framed the dressing-table mirror and the landscapes on the floral wallpaper. This was the room of a valued guest, not a servant, as Jordan might prefer to think of me.

However, his tone and words, when he spoke again, made me feel as if I were indeed a member of the household staff. "Aunt Patience's quarters are readily accessible through that connecting door. You should have no trouble hearing her call." He hesitated for a second, his eyes lighting with challenge.

Was this more of the testing? Was he waiting to see if I lifted my nose, offended? Or if I would meekly whip out a nurse's uniform? I had never bowed to anyone, and even if I had brought along a uniform, I would not wear it now. I answered Jordan's challenge with a nod that seesawed precariously between polite and cool. I wasn't sure what response I had expected, but I was a trifle taken aback by the slight smile that touched the corners of his full lips. Was he secretly laughing at me, or was he applauding what my father used to call my "spunk"? "If you'll excuse me," he said, turning to leave, "I'll see you both at dinner."

Drew had placed the bag he held on the bed with the others. "I expected you to join us for tea, Jordan."

Pausing, Jordan shrugged. "Sorry, but Baldwin sent over some papers that require my immediate attention," he declined quickly, too quickly, I thought. The fact that he and I nettled each other made me wonder if he'd concocted an excuse to leave. Whatever his reason, I hardly cared. It was a relief to have him out of my sight. But of course the instant I turned back to Drew I came face-to-face with the dismal reminder that out of sight was not out of mind. Looking upon one man was to see the other. And when I met Drew's eyes as he pulled me into his embrace, my treacherous mind focused on the heat and strength of his twin's body and the searing kiss that had rocked my senses.

"I missed you terribly," Drew breathed. As his eager mouth came down on mine I told myself that his kiss would also shake me to the core, that the other times in his arms I'd been too numb from the war to be stirred deeply. Back then I'd savored the closeness and comfort of his touch. But now that I'd tasted tantalizing pleasure, my senses pleaded for more. The world faded around us as I matched the hungry pressure of Drew's lips on mine. His arms were a tender vise about me, his tongue insistent. I welcomed the darting, the exploration, and the feel of his strong hands pressing me close. For timeless seconds I was wanton. Then reality seeped back, leveling my expectation. There were no thrills, no surging or fevered blood. I prayed Drew didn't perceive my disappointment. I couldn't bear even the thought of hurting this kind man who had brightened my life at a time when I'd been desperately in need. For that alone I would do almost anything for him. What did scorching kisses matter anyway? I told myself as Drew lifted his head and smiled hap-

pily into my eyes. "I know you'll like it here, Rachel," he murmured. "You have me and my family. You need never be alone
again."

"I never feel that way when I'm with you." I laid my head
against his chest and listened to the steady rhythm of his heart.
Just from the few things he had told me about his brother and
their aunt, I knew they were as important to Drew as my family
had been to me. Sometimes I wondered if sympathy over my being alone in the world had first drawn him to me.

"Then you must stay with me forever," Drew whispered in my
hair, and I could tell from the underlying yearning in his tone
that he longed to verbalize the depth of his feelings. But for my
sake he was holding to his promise to give me more time to
know my heart. To hear his words of love, and not be able to return them, had made me uncomfortable. And that feeling had
placed a wedge between us. Now I feared Jordan's kiss might do
the same. Why, oh why had he kissed me back? But I couldn't
really blame him, for heaven sakes. I'd thrown myself at the
man. "That was a terrible trick you played on me." I frowned up
at Drew. "Older brother, indeed!"

He tipped back his head and laughed. "I didn't lie, Rachel,
Jordan is older."

"By what, five minutes?" My annoyance faded under the devilish lights that came into his eyes.

"Twenty, actually." Drew kissed me again and this time I kept
my mind on him and the joy of being together. "Now, hurry and
freshen up," he gently urged. "My aunt is eager to meet you. Oh,
before I forget, she's taken to rambling in flights of fancy." His
voice dropped to a warning. "Some of what she says these days
isn't based in reality."

I responded in a reassuring tone. "Unfortunately that's quite
common in older people. I'm used to dealing with it."

"I don't want you dealing with it, at least not on a steady basis."

"I hope you're not trying to talk me out of this post."

"I want you here as a guest, and as my soon-to-be wife. Nothing more."

"You promised not to pressure me."

"I know," he admitted grudgingly. "But just looking at you, so
beautiful and desirable, makes it difficult to hold my tongue."

His love was warm and persuasive and it was a struggle to keep from yielding to his will. "You're the dearest person in my life, Drew, and I'm happy just being here with you. Can't that be enough for now?"

He stared deeply into my eyes, then expelled a long breath of resignation. "I'll try to be more patient, Rachel."

"Thank you." I hugged him.

Drew cradled me near. "Another minute of this closeness and I'm liable to forget I'm a gentleman. Come to think of it, you told me I wasn't one."

"Oh dear," I gulped, then laughed. "I retract that statement."

"Somehow I had the feeling you would."

I stepped back. "Just give me twenty minutes and I'll be ready to meet your aunt."

Nodding, Drew glanced over my head to the bags on the bed. "Are you sure you don't want Kalani to help you with the unpacking?"

"I can manage." I hesitated. "Kalani seems displeased by my presence."

A muscle at the corner of Drew's mouth twitched. "She seemed friendly enough."

Yes, to him and his brother. "I sensed definite resentment."

"Oh, that." Drew waved a dismissing hand. "It's nothing personal. The natives look upon all outsiders with resentment, and with good reason," he added. "We came into their world, changed it, condemned their gods, and brought diseases that have wiped out over three quarters of their population."

"Three quarters? How devastating."

"Sometimes I wonder if the bitterness will ever fade."

I wondered the same about the North and the South. In any case, from the way the attractive housekeeper had looked at Drew, she did not resent him. And he was no more a native of this land than I was.

"I'll talk with Kalani," he said. "I don't want anyone making you feel unwelcome."

Then he would also have to talk with his brother, but I didn't want to get into that. "No, please, I shouldn't have said anything. I expect Kalani and I will work it out between us and I don't want to cause any trouble."

He raised a caressing hand to my cheek. "You are a woman of

gentle heart, my darling. Aunt Patience is going to be almost as taken by you as I."

I'd heard that same comment from Drew on two or three other occasions. Why was it so important to him that his aunt be taken by me? "What if she isn't?" I watched his face for a reaction.

A shadow crossed Drew's features, as if a pervasive chill had just crept through him. "I know you both," he said, "and that won't be the case."

He sounded so certain. Yet if that was true, why the brief, dark look? And why did I have the sudden feeling that our continued relationship hinged on his aunt's approval of me?

chapter 3

SURELY I HAD just misread Drew's expression, I told myself as he left the room. Yes, he was easygoing. That was even evident in his relaxed gait and the carefree tilt of his head. But there was also a strong side to him. I'd seen it during his ten-day stay in the hospital as he'd fought to regain his health, and in the encouragement and moral support he'd given to the men around him.

Like thousands of others Drew had volunteered for the army. He'd risked his life to preserve the Union, and the only complaint I'd ever heard from him was: "I wish I could have served longer." But for the first three years of the war he had been here in Maui, far from the battlefields and often even word of the numerous campaigns. It wasn't until urgent business had taken him to New York that he'd become caught up in the conflict and enlisted.

Drew Phillips impressed me as a principled man, a man of conviction, one who did not need others to shore up his decisions. Rightfully, out of love and respect for his aunt, he would want to please her. That would mean making concessions from time to time, not necessarily bending to her will. He seemed the perfect blend of gentle and strong, with the admirable ability to rise above the stubborn streak I'd noticed and strike a compromise.

I wasn't sure if I was quite as flexible, I thought as I unpacked my blue cambric. I was here on my terms, although I doubted anyone would fault me for adhering to my principles.

I lifted the scoop-necked dress and tried in vain to shake out the wrinkles. The other garments I'd brought would also be in this deplorable condition, which made the percale I wore the most presentable of the lot. Even so, the way it hung limp from the dampness made me feel like a rose struck by the first autumn frost. Actually, this lavish house had the same effect on me. The intricate detailing in the ceiling moldings and broken door pediments was superb. I'd seen this same expert craftsmanship in Southern mansions. Sadly, so many of them had been burned, ransacked, or despoiled by conversions to field hospitals. It was one of those transformed mansions where I'd met and cared for Drew. Just thinking about that once fine home brought a lump to my throat. Long before the last of the wounded were sent north, the place had reeked of death.

Swallowing, I laid the dress on the bed. Then I crossed to the marble-topped washstand near the gabled windows. The water in the pitcher was warm, so I assumed Kalani must have ordered it filled after she announced my arrival to Drew. The pitcher was china, the basin shaped like a seashell. I'd never seen one this large, or more beautiful.

As I rinsed my hands and face a twinge of nervousness tightened my stomach. I'd always managed well with people, and until my meeting with the less-than-friendly Jordan I hadn't even considered the possibility that Patience Phillips might not look upon me with favor. For all I knew, Jordan and his aunt were cut from the same mold and she, too, would regard me as a fortune hunter.

I shuddered at the distressing thoughts and clung to Drew's reassurance that his aunt would like me. *I know you both.* His words reran in my brain, but were instantly buried beneath the ever-present fact that he and I didn't truly know each other. But of course that's why I'm here, I reminded myself as I reached for a towel and dried my hands and face. Besides, as my practical father used to say, worry was a waste of time and energy. It could not influence the outcome of whatever would be.

On a surge of optimism I replaced the towel. Then I parted the lace curtains and glanced out. A few patches of blue had begun to show between the scudding dark clouds, though palm fronds still swayed in the brisk wind. This room overlooked the drive and the sprawling front lawn, bordered by lush foliage on one side and the ocean on the other. Directly below was the open balustraded captain's bridge on the second floor. What an idyllic spot for a moonlit rendezvous, I thought, envisioning myself standing there wrapped in Drew's embrace.

Dreamily, I lingered at the window. Just as I was about to swing back to the room, Drew stepped onto the bridge. He appeared so suddenly that it was almost as if I had willed him to the porch. No, lanai, I corrected myself on a flash of recollection. Drew had told me that in the islands a porch was called a lanai. Below, he crossed to the balustrade and stared out over the drive. Looking upon him brought back memories of our times together. Amid the sadness and tragedy of the war, there had been moments of laughter and gentle exchanges of words. Above all, I would never forget the brief touches of our hands and the warmth of his mouth on mine.

As I continued to watch him I felt my lips compress. Was that really Drew, or was I looking at his brother? Even if whoever he was turned and stared right up at me, I wouldn't be able to identify him, except maybe by the cut of his suit. With all the confusion and embarrassment of the kiss, I wasn't even certain if I remembered who wore which style.

I expelled a long, helpless breath. I'd always thrived on challenges, but something told me that living under the same roof with twins was going to be more an exercise in frustration than a challenge. Particularly when I had a romantic interest in one and feared I might stumble into another mortifying mistake with the other. Surely Jordan wouldn't allow such a thing to happen again. Just as important, Drew had learned his lesson about playing "twin tricks."

A knock sounded on the door. As I turned and called "Come in," the man below glanced up over his shoulder at my window. My heart lurched at the deep frown that hardened his features. The window curtain had fallen back into place and I knew he couldn't have seen me. Nevertheless there was no doubt that his ominous expression had been aimed at this room and at me, its sole occupant.

"I hope I'm not disturbing you, miss," Kalani said, entering.

"No," I answered as I dropped another look at the captain's bridge. The man was gone.

"Is everything to your satisfaction?"

"Yes . . . oh yes, this room is lovely." Compared with the comfortable but modest home I'd grown up in, this was a palace. I'd never had more elegant quarters. Not even in the converted Southern mansions, for the rooms had always been filled with the wounded. I'd slept wherever I could find a spot, which was generally on the floor or propped up in a corner.

"I brought some sachets." Kalani crossed to the bureau beside the closet, and for the first time I noticed she was carrying a small basket filled with ribbon-tied, floral bundles. "Mistress Patience likes lavender. But Miss Claudia insisted that scent was for older women. Her favorite was jasmine."

Was? That sounded like Claudia was dead. Who was she, anyway? Drew had never mentioned the name.

Kalani bit her lower lip, as if she'd said something she shouldn't have. "But if you don't care for jasmine," she added quickly, "we have ginger, hibiscus, rose, and several other fragrances."

"The jasmine is fine," I assured her.

The attractive housekeeper nodded, then began placing sachets in one bureau drawer after the other. "A maid will be in shortly to collect any laundry you might have," she commented over her shoulder.

"I'd appreciate that." I withdrew my comb and hairbrush from the smallest valise.

"Just set the laundry on the chair by the door." As Kalani straightened and turned back to the room, she spotted the wrinkled garment on the bed. "The maid will also collect any dresses that need pressing."

I flashed a grateful smile, then gestured to the cambric. "Would it be possible to have this one back in time for dinner?"

"Certainly. I'll take it down with me now. Is there anything else I can do for you, Miss Montgomery?"

"No, I don't think so, Kalani, thank you."

Without another word she picked up the dress and left the room. She'd been so nice that I wondered if Drew had disregarded my request and talked with her after all. As I set out the soiled garments and rumpled dresses to be picked up, I considered asking Drew if he was responsible for the positive change in Kalani. However, when he returned for me, I found myself yielding instead to the more prominent question in my mind. "Were you out on the captain's bridge a few minutes ago, Drew?"

"Why do you ask?" He offered me his arm and we stepped into the hall.

Couldn't he have just replied with a simple yes or no? "I thought I saw you from my window, but then I wondered if it was your brother." We started down the stairs.

"It wasn't me; I was in my study."

So the man was Jordan, but common sense should have told me that. Drew loved me and I had no reason to believe he would regard me in a bone-chilling manner.

On the second-floor landing Drew pointed to the nearby closed door I had wondered about earlier. "That's the kitchen; there's another one on the entrance floor. The servants' quarters are down the hall." Then he gestured ahead of us. "Aunt Patience is in the grand drawing room."

As we moved in that direction I asked in a quiet tone that would not carry to her, "Is your aunt on medication?"

Drew also kept his voice low. "Yes, laudanum and powders prescribed by Dr. Hawthorne. There's also an assortment of herbal concoctions from a local kahuna."

"Who . . . or what is that?"

Drew grinned. "A kahuna is a combination priest–medicine man. My aunt also has a Chinese practitioner come in on a regular basis. He performs what I call voodoo with needles."

"Needles? You mean acupuncture?"

"I believe that's what he calls it." Drew pulled up short before the drawing-room entrance. "Are you familiar with it?"

"No, I'd just heard it mentioned a time or two in San Francisco. There's a large Chinese community there."

"A very bizarre practice, if you ask me."

"I know it's an ancient one, and must have some benefit." I tried to ease the concern I saw come into his face.

Drew smiled appreciatively into my eyes. "I'm so glad you're here, Rachel. Just looking at you makes me feel good." He bent to kiss me, but a feminine voice intruded on the blissful moment.

"Drew, is that you?" the woman called from the drawing room.

A frown pulled down the corners of his mouth and he muttered impatiently under his breath, "Yes, Aunt Patience."

As we continued forward I wondered how Drew's aunt had been able to distinguish his voice from his twin's. Not only were the men identical, but they also sounded the same. Maybe she had just guessed. Actually, her voice was surprisingly vigorous for a fifty-three-year-old with a serious health problem.

As Drew ushered me into the elegant drawing room, with the huge bay window overlooking the ocean, I became increasingly aware of my less-than-crisp percale. And I felt like Cinderella, before the advent of her fairy godmother, when I saw his aunt seated on a crimson velvet sofa. The perfectly coiffed white-haired woman was attired in a superb olive-green foulard silk dress. Adorning its prim high collar was a cameo encircled with pearls. There were spots of color in her fair-complexioned face, which scarcely showed lines of age. She seemed the picture of health, but I knew looks could be deceiving.

Patience Phillips was a small woman, with fragile features that were in direct contrast to the strength reflected in her straight spine and the determined set of her shoulders. Both reminded me of Jordan. On the assumption that he and the family matriarch shared the same aloof and suspicious nature, my spirits slid to my toes. However, the instant she looked up from her cup of tea and smiled at me, the devilish twinkle in her pale blue eyes revealed the lightheartedness I'd come to know in the man at my side. "Rachel, aloha," she said. "Drew was right, you are indeed lovely."

Either she didn't notice my travel-worn appearance or she was understanding. In any case her warmth revived my spirits and I smiled back. "It's a pleasure to meet you, Miss Phillips. Drew has spoken affectionately of you."

"Just as he has spoken of you, my dear." She motioned me to the matching sofa across from her. "But please call me Patience. Perhaps"—her voice rose on a note of excitement and she gazed adoringly at her nephew—"Aunt Patience, one day soon."

Did this mean she had taken an immediate liking to me and hoped I would accept Drew's proposal? The pure delight coming into his dark eyes strengthened that impression. But surely I was jumping to another hasty conclusion. This woman only knew me from what he had told her, and he didn't really know all that much. "Forgive me for starting tea without you," she said, putting aside her sprigged china cup, "but I was in need of the lift I get from this blend created especially for me. I hope you'll find it as refreshing, Rachel." As Patience reached for the silver pot on the mahogany table before us, she asked Drew, "Will Jordan be joining us?"

Drew sat down beside me. "No, he excused himself to tend to some pressing business."

Business or just an excuse? I wondered again, picturing Jordan on the captain's bridge. Struggling against a frown, I scanned the room. Crimson velvet draperies, tied back with heavy gold cords, framed the windows, and the walls were papered with roses of the same color on a white ground. Suspended from the elaborate ceiling were bronze chandeliers dripping with crystal pendants and set with white tapers. On the polished floor was a Persian rug; its soft colors heightened the richness of the dark woods.

"Your home is beautiful." I admired the numerous gilt-framed paintings and the spinet near the rear-facing window.

"Why, thank you, dear." Rachel handed me a cup of steaming tea. "This house is a replica of my grandfather's home, right down to the furniture and hangings."

I knew the family hailed from Maine. Drew had told me a little about his childhood days there prior to the death of his parents in a blizzard. "The only difference between this house and the other is the absence of fireplaces," Patience explained. "We certainly don't need them in this climate. But what a shame it rained on the day of your arrival, Rachel."

"It rained almost the entire way over." I accepted the small plate of delicate pastries Drew had selected for me. As the three of us enjoyed the refreshments we talked briefly about my voyage across the Pacific.

Then Patience asked, "Do you like the tea, Rachel?"

"It's delicious and very revitalizing. Is it a mixture of raspberry and ginger?"

"Ah, you have a keen palate for herbs." She beamed and I could tell I'd just moved up another notch in winning her wholehearted approval. "Rose hips and hibiscus leaves are also blended in, along with two or three other leaves which the kahuna refuses to divulge. I suspect keeping some of the herbs a secret gives him a sense of power," she finished with a laugh.

"The man takes advantage of your good nature, Aunt Patience." Drew shook his head in disapproval.

The sparkle vanished from her eyes and she told him flatly, "No one takes advantage of me, Drew. You of all people should know that. If I didn't love you so—" she broke off. In the blink of an eye Patience swung her attention back to me, and just as quickly her tone became soft and grateful. "How can I ever thank you, Rachel, for the wonderful care you gave my nephew during that dreadful war?"

My lips had parted at her rapid mood swing and I hoped she hadn't noticed that I was a trifle taken aback. "His complete recovery was my thanks," I managed in an even voice.

If Drew had also been struck by her abrupt change, it didn't show in his face or his voice. "Without Rachel's expert nursing I surely would have died."

His praise brought the heat of embarrassment to my face. Although it was true that without the nurses thousands more of the wounded doubtless would have perished, for the doctors' time had been consumed in surgery from dawn to twilight.

Drew's voice grew distant with remembrance. "I'd never seen anyone more caring, and not just with me. It was as if all the wounded were a part of Rachel's family." He placed a gentle hand on mine.

Patience nodded as if she'd heard his words of appreciation before, which made me wonder anew if Drew hadn't mistaken gratitude for love. Over the rim of her cup Patience said, "I'd heard that you never missed a night of visiting with every one of the injured, Rachel."

"I did my best to comfort," I murmured as agonized faces flooded my mind, and my throat tightened. "The men were so brave." Most of all I would never forget the unfaltering courage of the hundreds of soldiers I'd seen pass on. Up to their last breath not one of them had shown even a trace of fear. After a deep swallow of the now tepid tea I complimented the man seated beside me. "Drew was wonderful with the other wounded. The moment he was mobile, he also visited with each one of them on a daily basis."

The older woman tilted her head and once more eyed her nephew adoringly. "Drew has always had a way with people. He takes after my side of the family," she boasted without modesty. "His mother and I were sisters, you know."

"Yes, he told me." I lifted a pineapple-filled pastry.

Patience sighed. "My sister never liked it here. As soon as our father would allow, she returned to Maine and lived with our grandparents until she married. But times were much different here back then." She set aside her cup and saucer. "Missionaries weren't welcomed by all, unfortunately."

I swallowed a bit of the delicious pastry. "The natives objected?"

"No, not them." Her voice fell to a whisper and the words just seemed to drift away.

"The sailors and traders objected," Drew explained. "There were many incidents of direct confrontation. American sea captains even cannonaded missionary homes."

"Good heavens," I said, "why would they do that?"

Sarcasm came into his voice. "Morality wasn't practiced in the islands by those outsiders and they didn't appreciate chastity being instilled in the natives, especially in the women."

"Drew," the older woman scolded, "you are offending our sensibilities." Before he could utter another word, she switched the subject, and so swiftly it took my mind a moment to catch up with her. "How lucky that you've come during the whale migration season, Rachel. Now that the business of whaling has dropped off substantially, some of the humpbacks and sperms make it in this far and we can see them from our windows. They're fascinating to watch."

"Oh?" I murmured, endeavoring to understand her enthusiasm for a pastime that didn't sound fascinating to me. Nevertheless, out of politeness, I showed interest. "I'd heard Lahaina is the whaling capital of the world."

"That's becoming a part of the past now," Drew said with regret. "And a major downswing in the island's economy."

"The growing and exporting of sugar is bound to revive it," Patience returned with optimism, though the vague expression darkening her eyes gave the impression her mind had taken flight. Without warning she stood up. "I have some magnificent sea and wildlife carvings in the solarium downstairs, Rachel. Come, I will show you."

Drew also rose. "The doctor warned you about unnecessary trips up and down the stairs, Aunt Patience. Remember?"

"Of course I remember," she retorted. "The man is overly cautious. I have never felt better."

Concern for the older woman prompted me to side with Drew. "I can see the carvings another time." I, too, came to my feet.

"There is no need to wait," Patience insisted. "We've finished with our repast and a stroll down to the solarium will give us a few minutes alone, Rachel." Drew's lips parted to speak again, but she cut him off with, "I'm sure you'd like for Rachel and me to become well acquainted." The words were simply put, yet I detected an underlying order. When Drew conceded with a mere nod, as if he'd been beaten down, I was sure his aunt exerted significant influence over him. Was it more than just the family wealth, which she controlled? What could the Phillips money have to do with me?

chapter 4

FROWNING, DREW EXCUSED himself. "I'll see you both at dinner. It's served at seven, Rachel, in the dining room on this floor."

I inclined my head in acknowledgment and tried to convey with my eyes that I was warmed by his regard for his aunt's well-being. Drew must have perceived my silent message, because his dark eyes brightened. In the instant before he turned away and exited, my mind returned to the converted Southern mansion and I saw him happily playing cards with a handful of the other men. Almost from the moment Drew was able to sit up, he'd gathered a group for daily games. "Cards is one way to keep minds off the war," he had told me. From what I'd seen that had been true.

Patience and I left the grand drawing room. On the main floor she said, "The solarium is at the rear." Then she added in a sympathetic tone, "Drew told me you lost your brothers in the war, Rachel."

Pain knifed my heart. "Yes. Eric died in the first Battle of Bull Run, and Cameron at Gettysburg."

"Your father succumbed to pneumonia, I'd heard. But what of your mother?"

"Her health had been severely strained by several miscarriages." My voice fell to a solemn whisper. "She just seemed to wither away."

"How sad. Claudia also suffered a number of miscarriages, the poor dear."

Claudia? I thought again. Before I could ask who she was, Patience once more changed the subject.

"Ah, here we are, my favorite room." She crossed the threshold and gestured with a possessive hand that indicated this was her personal domain. "What do you think, Rachel?"

"It's breathtaking," I complimented as I stepped in and surveyed the huge and airy sun room. There were floor-to-ceiling windows everywhere, and two pairs of French doors. One opened into a courtyard laid with what Drew had told me was lava stone, the other into a deep green jungle at the rear. On the west was the sweeping view of the ocean.

"I feel complete peace in here." Patience moved to a luxuriant fern and checked it for water. There were exotic plants all about, many with flowers in riotous colors. "That's a bird of paradise," she said. "Beside it a hibiscus, and the pot of tiny pink roses is called lokelani."

Among all the plants was brightly cushioned wicker furniture in cozy groupings. There were also tables and shelves, upon them superbly crafted wood carvings of whales and fish and birds.

Patience lifted what looked like a piece of ivory and held it up. "This is whalebone. The etching is called scrimshaw."

"How beautiful." I admired the delicate carving of birds in flight. "Is scrimshaw an art handed down through generations?"

She looked around as if someone had called out to her, and for a moment I wondered if she'd even heard me. "No, it only dates back to the early whaling days in the forties," she answered at last. "Woodcarving, weaving, and featherwork are old arts." She blinked, then added abruptly, "How thoughtless of me to take up so much of your time when you've only just arrived, Rachel. You must be exhausted and eager for a little rest before dinner." She pulled a bell rope. "A long soak in a hot tub will renew you."

"A hot bath sounds wonderful."

A young Oriental maid hurried in and Patience ordered that a tub be prepared in my room. "And be sure to add some of my special lavender to the water," the older woman instructed the girl as we moved back to the stairs. By the time we had ascended to the second floor, Patience Phillips was winded. "I think I'll rest for a while in my room, too," she said.

"Maybe you should catch your breath before going up the last flight," I suggested, and automatically cupped her elbow for support. "We could sit for few moments in the drawing room."

"No," she panted, pulling away from my touch. "I won't pamper myself and I don't want you to fuss over me, either."

I hadn't thought I was. Obviously her interpretation of pampering differed from my own. Patience put a hand to her chest, as if to ease pain, then continued up the stairs.

Helplessly I followed after her, praying the strain she was putting upon her heart would not be her undoing. At her door I ventured, "May I help make you comfortable, Patience?"

Her chest rose and fell with each labored breath. "No need, I'll take some medication and lie down. I'm not an invalid, Rachel."

It didn't appear she was going to be an easy patient, either. "I hadn't meant to imply that you are. But I am here to help care for you."

My gentle reassurance must have had a soothing effect, because her tone and expression softened. "I know dear, and it was sweet of you to offer your services. But tomorrow, or even the next day, is soon enough to start your duties." Patience opened her door and stepped in. "For now I want to come to know you solely as Drew's young lady." That wish was understandable, and her next words helped ease my concern. "If I require help, I'll ring for a maid." Quietly she closed her door.

Instinctively I listened for a moment, making certain there were no sounds of distress from her, then I went to my room. A porcelain tub had been brought in. As maids filled it with buckets of hot water, I finished unpacking my bags, my ears still attuned to Patience's quarters. It was quiet beyond the connecting door and I could only hope she was resting comfortably.

Clinging to that hope, I climbed into the tub. The hot water felt exquisite on my flesh and I breathed in the delicate scent of lavender that rose in the swirling steam. The heavenly fragrance reminded me of spring back home and I couldn't imagine why Claudia, whoever she was, associated lavender exclusively with older women.

I dozed for a while in the soothing water, and by the time I finally bathed and toweled dry, it was after six. Not wishing to be late for dinner, I quickly dressed in clean undergarments. Then I slipped on the freshly pressed blue cambric and fastened the pearl buttons that rose from the V waist to the scoop-necked bodice trimmed with Spanish lace.

Seated at the dressing table, I refashioned my thick blond hair with delicate side combs, put on my shoes, then stood before the full-length mirror in the corner. Compared with Patience, with her expensive gown and broach, I looked the poor cousin. Still, I gained a measure of comfort from the fact that the color of my dress was as vibrant as ever and the cut still stylish and flattering to my figure.

On that uplifting note I went down to the dining room on the second floor. The tall tapers in the chandeliers had been lit and the linen-draped table was laid with fine china, crystal, and gleaming silver. Beyond were French doors. Except for me the room was empty. As I was about to turn back to the hall, a familiar masculine voice said from somewhere behind, "You're a few minutes early, Rachel." My eyes narrowed in an immediate frown. Was the man Drew, or was he Jordan?

The moment I came around and saw the aloof expression, I knew I was looking at Jordan. Instantly my mind hauled forward his chilling glare from the captain's bridge, which I assumed lay beyond the French doors in this room. "I heard you on the stairs," he said from the threshold of the grand drawing room. "You're welcome to join me until the rest of the family comes down." I was surprised by his polite tone rather than the cool one I had expected. The surprise doubled when I saw his gaze go over me in quick appraisal and an appreciative sparkle come into his eyes.

In truth he looked exceptionally nice himself in the charcoal-gray vested suit and crisp shirt. And I felt a trace of heat at the realization that my eyes were probably as revealing as his. How annoying, and mystifying, it was to be physically drawn to a man who didn't like me any more than I liked him. My mind balked at his invitation to join him in the drawing room, but good manners pressed me to accept. As for my heart I struggled to ignore the quickening beat his presence alone generated.

In the drawing room we sat down opposite each other on the matching sofas and I glanced back expectantly through the wide doorway. Jordan noticed. "Aunt Patience and Drew should be right along," he said, as if he'd read my mind and knew I didn't relish being alone with him. Although maybe he was simply stating what he was thinking.

I was tempted to mention I'd seen him on the captain's bridge but quickly decided against broaching any subject that might exacerbate the strain between us. Instead I voiced the more dominent concern in my mind, "I fear your aunt overexerted herself climbing the stairs a while ago. I've been worried about her ever since."

"I'm sure she's fine," he said simply. "Kalani keeps a close watch over her. Unfortunately, Aunt Patience refuses to accept her limitations."

I hesitated. "Perhaps if her bedchamber was moved down to this floor," I ventured, hoping he would not regard me as pushy, "she wouldn't have so many stairs to contend with."

Jordan shook his head, clearly not offended. "She's vetoed that suggestion more times than I can remember. My aunt doesn't accept change, either. She's very stubborn," he criticized with obvious affection.

So Drew had inherited that bent from her. "I've heard." I lightened my tone. "But your brother also said she was generous and caring."

"To a fault," Jordan muttered grimly, and changed the subject by turning his attention to the moonlight beyond the windows.

From beneath my lashes I stared at his profile, strong and clean, and wondered if his comment was linked to what his brother had said earlier, that people took advantage of their aunt's good nature. A shiver of unease snaked down my spine at just the thought that this man had probably lumped me into that group.

I lifted my chin and was eyeing the doorway expectantly again when Jordan asked, "Were you in San Francisco long before sailing for Hawaii, Rachel?"

"A shade over two months." I sounded as distracted as I felt.

"You hadn't planned on returning to Ohio, then?"

"No, I haven't family there . . . anymore." Even though it was rude, I kept my gaze averted, for I didn't want him to see the surge of sadness that surely showed in my face. "And there are too many memories," I added, memories that had compelled me to move west and make a new start. If it weren't for Drew, I probably would have remained in exciting San Francisco. As I turned back to Jordan I caught him observing me through narrowed eyes. "Something wrong?" I asked, without thought.

"No." The word came slowly. "It's just hard for me to picture someone as small and delicate looking as you being caught in the middle of war. Were you an army nurse for the whole four years?"

Either Drew hadn't said much about me to his brother, or these questions were more of his testing. Whichever the case I had no qualms about answering, although the possibility of being interrogated did set my teeth a bit on edge. "No, just the last three years. Prior to that only enlisted men were permitted to be military nurses." Enlisted men and females of low repute, but it struck me as unseemly to mention ladies of pleasure.

Surprise touched Jordan's full lips, adding yet another appealing dimension to his aloof demeanor. "I'd heard there were women caring for the wounded all along."

I spoke past the annoying tingle of heightened awareness feathering my senses. "That's true," I agreed, and assumed he was referring to the mothers and sisters and sweethearts who stepped in and gave so freely of themselves. "But until the Sanitary Commission pushed to reorganize the hospital system, women were merely considered volunteers. A great many of them continued in that invaluable capacity."

"Rachel started out as a volunteer," Drew offered proudly as he entered, arm in arm with his aunt.

"Really?"

This time Jordan's note of surprise hardened my jaw. Clearly he had summed me up as a fortune hunter, for scheming women weren't prone to volunteering their time, especially to anything as unlucrative as war. Maybe now he would start reshaping his opinion of me.

"You never mentioned Rachel's volunteer work before, Drew," Patience remarked. Seeing her eyes bright and the tightness of strain gone from her face gave my spirits a boost. "What a lovely dress, dear." She smiled at me. "Blue suits you well."

How gracious she was. I acknowledged the compliment with an appreciative nod and openly admired her fawn-colored silk. As Jordan came politely to his feet my gaze automatically flicked back to him, and I noticed the men's suits were similar in hue and style. Apparently they shared the same taste in clothes. Too bad they didn't also share the same easygoing temperament, the infectious smile that Drew was lavishing upon me.

As the happy-looking pair crossed to stand before Jordan and me, Kalani announced dinner. Since Patience still had her arm in the curve of Drew's, his brother had no choice but to offer me his arm.

I braced against Jordan's touch and the heat I felt through the fine fabric of his coat, the heat I remembered only too well from our kiss. I forced out that memory as we crossed the hall to the dining room, but I couldn't force out the turmoil his nearness produced within me. And when a muscle in his arm twitched, I wondered if his senses were also awhirl, or if he could hardly wait to be free of my touch.

Patience was seated at one end of the long table, with Jordan opposite. From his chair across from me Drew said with a laugh, "As you can see, Rachel, the older nephew is honored with the head of the table."

"Twenty minutes' seniority does make a difference," Patience teased.

Jordan expelled a weary breath, as if he'd had it up to his eyebrows with older-brother jokes. That I could understand. Long ago I'd had my fill of little-sister teasing. What I wouldn't give now to have Eric and Cameron and all the playful taunting back. Warm memories dried my mouth and I sipped from my glass of water as the first course was brought in.

As a maid ladled steaming clam chowder into bowls, Patience told me a bit about the building of this big house. Then Drew offered, "My aunt and her family used to live in the small home nestled among the palms on the far edge of this property."

"How very long ago that was." Patience sighed, lifting her soup spoon.

"Does anyone live there now?" I tasted the creamy chowder, thick with clams.

"Our former housekeeper," she said. "We retired her to the place after thirty years of devoted service. She even helped me raise my nephews." Patience turned prideful eyes from one to the other, then added with a small smile, "She was able to cope with Drew's mischievous ways better than I."

"Now, Aunt Patience," Drew scolded playfully, "you mustn't tell tales on me or you might send Rachel packing."

"I doubt she discourages easily."

Jordan's frown conveyed that he hoped quite the opposite.

In a succinct tone I let him know his aunt was right. "I don't give up on anything easily."

The V of his brows deepened. Didn't that man know how to smile? Clearly his serious face was one way in which I could distinguish him from his twin. That along with the squared set of Jordan's shoulders. He said little during the first half of dinner and it wasn't until we were well into the main course of tender white fish in coconut milk and melt-in-the-mouth yams that he truly joined in the conversation. And that was after I'd once again glimpsed him watching me through narrowed eyes, as if I were some sort of mystery he was trying to puzzle out. "When did you start nursing, Rachel?" His question deepened that suspicion within me. At the same time just the thought of being an enigma to a handsome man gave me an unexpected thrill, one I hoped wasn't revealed in my face.

"I was eleven," I said in a quiet voice as my mind ran back through the years. "My mother had become gravely ill and in need of around-the-clock care. With my father and brothers working long hours, there really was no one but me to look after her."

"That's a big responsibility for one so young." His tone had grown thoughtful.

"Yes, I suppose. But I was fortunate in that our family doctor was also a good friend. He took me under his wing and taught me how to properly care for my mother."

"It must have been a very trying time for you, Rachel," Drew commented over the rim of his water glass.

"Yes, in one way, but in another the bond between us deepened. And through caring for her my capacity to help others was revealed."

Patience eyed me in wonder. "I admire your dedication and courage, Rachel."

"And your strong stomach," Drew teased, lightening the somber mood that had gained control.

Kalani came in to supervise the clearing of the main course in preparation for dessert. Her expression was pleasant, although it was clear from the tilt of her chin that she enjoyed her position of authority over the rest of the household staff. In her place I probably would have felt the same, except I liked to think in a more humble manner.

As I casually watched Kalani move about the table, I didn't once see her gaze rivet on Drew, as a woman romantically interested in a man might do. Nor did she linger at his side. If she hadn't any designs on him, then maybe Drew had correctly summed up her earlier resentment toward me. I was an outsider, like the members of this family. Only they paid Kalani's wages and had rewarded her with the superior position in this household. For that they were bound to have gained her respect and perhaps even affection.

As Kalani helped serve the rich mango custard I inclined my head in her direction. However, she didn't seem to notice the friendly gesture and a second later she turned and exited the dining room.

By the time we'd finished with dessert, the long but happy day had began to take its toll on me and it was a struggle to suppress threatening yawns. Shortly after the family and I left the dining room, I excused myself for bed. Drew saw me to my door. "Sleep well, my sweet," he murmured, caressing my cheek. "Tomorrow we'll spend the whole day together, maybe start with a long walk on the beach."

"That sounds wonderful," I murmured back, half-asleep. He kissed me tenderly, then I entered my room. A table lamp had been lit, the bed covers turned back, and my V-necked summer nightdress was laid out. I'd never been waited on quite like this before, and if I hadn't been so tired, I would have savored the luxury.

As I changed into the short-sleeved nightdress I groggily warned myself that I mustn't become too used to the Phillips' lavish life-style, just in case my relationship with Drew didn't work out as we both hoped.

On my way to the bed I paused at the window and moved aside the curtain. Moonlight dappled the lawn and shadows from the still trees fell here and there. Even at night this place was lovely.

I was about to drop the curtain back into place and turn away when a moving shadow caught the corner of my eye. Automatically my gaze shifted and fixed on a horse and male rider, heading down the drive. Squinting, I identified the man as one of the twins. But with his back to me and the distance between us I couldn't even begin to guess which one. Drew hadn't mentioned leaving the house. If that was he, where would he be going after nine at night? Where would anyone be going, for that matter?

Shrugging, I watched the rider disappear from view, then I climbed into bed and turned off the lamp. Moonlight flooded the room and I frowned, certain the brightness would keep me awake. But I'd hardly settled my head on the pillow and inhaled a long, weary breath when my eyelids became heavy. As I drifted into a deep sleep the contentment I felt at being with Drew convinced me that the haunting nightmares were over. My mind was at peace and my body free of tension. I hadn't known such complete relaxation since before the war. Then, without warning, my mind returned me to a dilapidated hospital tent. I was standing in a red sea as basket after basket of limbs were being hauled out for disposal.

A weird sensation shot through one of my limbs and I jerked awake, my body clammy with perspiration. Something was on my right leg. No, it's just the nightmares, too real, too real, I told myself. But the creepy sensation that felt like tiny cold fingers didn't go away. And when the fingers inched up a fraction, my blood froze.

Heart thumping, and without moving my limbs, I eased to a sitting position. In the glow of the moon I threw back the covers. My eyes widened. A lizard! A painful, choking scream stuck in my throat as the loathsome reptile's head came up with a start.

Shuddering, I swiped at the lizard, which couldn't have been more than three inches long, and leaped from the bed. When I looked back, the creature was gone. To where? Quickly I scanned the floor. As a girl I'd roamed the woods with my brothers, who had taught me not to be afraid of innocuous crawling things. Even so, I didn't want one on me, or scampering over my bare feet, either. Amid another shiver of repulsion I lifted my slippers, turned them upside down, and shook them. Assured neither one was a hiding place, I thrust my feet in. Then I carefully checked the bedding. Still no lizard.

I was about to ring for help in finding the elusive reptile when it skittered across the carpet and disappeared under a chair. I lunged and accidently sent it crashing to the floor. Wincing, I hoped the commotion hadn't awakened Patience in the next room. The lizard darted beneath the dressing table. Grabbing a hairbrush, I dropped to my knees and prodded.

A knock sounded on the door. With luck help was on the way. "Come in," I called, and the knob was twisted.

"I heard a noise. Are you all right?" one of the twins asked, and it suddenly struck me how ridiculous I must look in my nightdress and down on all fours. Nightdress? The word reared in my mind and embarrassment flooded into my face. As I moved to stand up the lizard raced for the bed.

"How did that gecko get in here?" the man rasped.

"That's what I'd like to know?" We both darted to the bed and nearly banged heads as we went down on our knees. I teetered a little at the near collision and he caught me by the arms with steadying hands. His fingers were hot irons on my flesh, and when I lifted my face to his, I saw that his attention had fixed on the hollow of my throat and he appeared to be struggling against dropping his gaze to the V of my nightdress. He moistened his lips and my insides flip-flopped.

Blood pounded in my ears, and when our eyes met, the compelling emotion I saw was like a magnet. I was mesmerized. My brain spun in crazy circles, yet somewhere in the whirl I'd managed to cling to a smidgen of reality. "Drew?"

A hesitant moment fell. "No." The word was a whisper, and an icy wave of disappointment washed through me. Why couldn't Drew have the same effect on me as his brother?

Swallowing, I pulled away from Jordan's grasp and the spell between us was broken. "Leave the gecko to me," he insisted, his voice a trifle hoarse.

Fearful my voice would be as revealing, I nodded and came to my feet. In less than a minute Jordan had cornered the reptile and I'd pulled on my wrapper and lit the bedside lamp. Then I went to the closet and emptied a hatbox. As Jordan put the squirming creature inside I asked, "What are you going to do with it?" Our fingers brushed as I handed him the lid. If Jordan's heart had also leaped in response, the reaction didn't show in his face.

"Take it outside and turn it loose. Where did you first notice it?"

"In my bed!"

"Good God, that must have given you quite a start."

I nodded. "That's the kind of prank my brothers used to play on me."

"No one here would have done such a thing to you. Well, Drew as a boy, but that was long ago. Anyway, geckos are abundant in the islands, they're everywhere."

"Inside houses, too?"

"Not inside this one."

"Then how do you suppose it got in here?"

Jordan shrugged. "Probably through an open window."

"None of these was open, at least not since my arrival."

"It could have come in a day or two ago." He turned away and righted the chair I'd knocked over.

"But how could it have gotten into my bed?"

"I know one that won't get back in," he muttered grimly.

His vague answer was hardly reassuring, and in a moment of awkward silence I said the first thought that came to mind. "I saw Drew ride out a while ago."

Jordan's lips compressed and his brows knitted. "He went into town." I hoped he would explain what prompted the sudden anger, but all he added was, "Good night."

As I watched him return to the door the scent of lavender on my wrapper brought a question forward in my mind. "Jordan," I called quietly after him.

"Yes?" He paused and looked back at me.

"If I may, who is Claudia?"

An instant of surprise crossed his features, then the muscles in his face tightened and the color drained away. "I think you'd better ask Drew." A second later Jordan was gone, and I was left staring at the closed door.

chapter 5

I FELL BACK to sleep that night trying to puzzle out Jordan's startling reaction to my question about Claudia, and when I awakened in the morning, he was the first one who came to mind. Why couldn't he have told me who Claudia was? And what did she have to do with Drew? I wondered.

As I sat up in bed and pushed back my tumbled hair, I instinctively listened for any sounds from Patience's room. The house was quiet and all I heard was the singing of birds beyond the windows. The warbling, along with the shafts of golden sunlight falling through the panes, reminded me of spring. But of course it was November. Back home the ground would be frozen and the songbirds long ago headed south for the winter.

Stretching, I crossed to one of the gabled windows and parted the curtains. The trees were still and vividly green against the flawless azure sky. Down by the ocean gentle waves lapped the pristine beach. For timeless moments the peace and beauty of this glorious morning occupied my thoughts. And it wasn't until I opened the window, and was breathing deeply of the salty sea air, that I remembered last night's incident with the gecko. As ridiculous as it seemed, I once again felt the prickling sensation of tiny cold feet on my leg and a shiver knifed through me. Had that lizard entered this room through an open window as Jordan suggested? On impulse I leaned out and scanned. Nothing but stucco and gingerbread, the captain's bridge, and a long drop to the ground. Evidently scaling three floors wasn't a deterrent for an adventurous reptile.

A light tap on the door brought my head back inside. "Yes, come in," I called, pulling on my wrapper.

The young Oriental maid entered and paused just this side of the threshold. She greeted me with a pleasant smile, then said, "Miss Patience is having tea in the morning room and would like to know if you can join her there for breakfast."

"I'd love to. I'll dress and be right along."

"Can I be of any service, miss?"

"No. Except, where is the morning room?"

"On the second floor, between the kitchen and the servants' quarters."

I thanked the maid and she turned away. Not wishing to keep Patience waiting any longer than absolutely necessary, I made fast work of changing into my brown checked skirt and matching puff-sleeved shirtwaist. The rest of my toilette was also accomplished in haste. During the war I'd mastered moving with quick efficiency, and in hardly more than a blink of the eye I was ready for the day.

As I moved into the hallway and pulled closed my door, I glanced at the other doors. There were at least a dozen. Which one opened into Drew's quarters? I wondered, continuing to the stairs. A few moments later I stepped through the entrance of the morning room. Instantly my gaze was caught by the huge corner windows, brightened by the sun, and draped with delicate English lace. Patience was seated near the windows on a floral settee that matched the blue-and-peach wallpaper. "Good morning, Rachel," she said cheerfully. Her white hair was swept up in the style similar to my own. And her dress was fashioned from select silk, with a wide band of delicate embroidery just below the high collar. "I'm delighted you could join me for breakfast."

"I am, too. I hope I didn't keep you waiting."

"Not at all." Patience set down her cup and saucer beside the silver pots on the table before her. In her lap lay some official-looking papers. "Come, sit by me." She motioned with a jeweled hand to the chair on her left. There was another cozy seating arrangement in this spacious room, along with the large mahogany table in its center, and the marble-topped sideboard adjacent to the swinging door I assumed opened into the kitchen.

On my way past the linen-draped table I noticed it was set for three and I immediately jumped to the conclusion that the extra place was for Drew. But Patience's next words made me wonder if I had guessed the wrong twin. "I've been looking over the claim Jordan hopes to submit to the Land Commission for some acreage he thinks we should acquire." She shook her head in exasperation. "He's pressing me for an immediate answer."

I hesitated before the chair. "Would you like a little more time alone?" I offered.

"No, no, dear, that's very thoughtful. Right now getting to know you is more important to me. Jordan will just have to wait. It will do him good," she insisted, thrusting aside the papers. "Lately he's been pushing me through one business transaction after the other. Why, I hardly have time to read the documents he hands over, and try to make sense of them, before he wants them back. He knows I hate being rushed to decisions."

"I feel the same," I confided. One twin was pressuring this woman over business, the other twin was doing the same with me and marriage. Obviously haste was a common trait in the brothers.

Patience inclined her head in appreciation of my support, then muttered to herself as she glanced out the window, "It's high time I took Jordan to task again." A vacant expression clouded her pale blue eyes, giving the impression her mind had drifted to a remote place. Her lips were pursed, though, as if to speak once more.

Quietly, I sat down. "Will he be joining us for breakfast?" I asked, after silent seconds.

"Who?" Patience's gaze remained transfixed on the sky and the billowy white clouds floating past.

"Jordan."

"Oh yes, we were talking about him." Without warning, she leaned forward and blurted, startling me, "Look, an iiwi. How beautiful. Did you see it, Rachel?"

I caught my breath. Would I ever get used to this woman's capricious manner? "You mean, the red bird that swooped by?"

"Red with black wings and tail," she pointed out with an authoritative air. "I think it's the loveliest of the honeycreepers. The natives used to collect the feathers to make capes for their kings."

"They don't do that anymore?"

"The iiwi is nearly extinct now," she said sadly. "Bird malaria and predators have taken a heavy toll." Patience paused as if a sudden thought had struck her. "I'm sorry, you asked a question. What was it? Oh yes, Jordan," she answered in the same breath. "He left for the office over an hour ago. Were you expecting to see him at breakfast?"

Good heavens, no, I thought with sarcasm. That man was a hurricane on my senses, and at the moment I didn't care to see him any more than I cared to have the gecko back in my bed. "No," I said, and mentioned the extra table setting.

"That's for Drew, he should be down shortly. Coffee or tea, dear?" Patience gestured to the silver service.

"Coffee, please."

"You made the right choice, Rachel." Drew chuckled from the doorway. "Just the color of Aunt Patience's prized morning tea closes my throat."

Drew's cheery voice brought an instant smile to my lips and I looked up into his happy face. His eyes were bright and intent on mine. But as he came forward I saw the faint smudges of fatigue beneath the pools of dark brown. How late had he been out last night? I wondered. But of course it was not my place to ask.

Patience regarded her nephew with a feigned scowl. "Don't you dare make fun of my tea, Drew Phillips. Green is a soothing color."

"Seaweed green?" he laughed.

"You are impossible," she scolded him mildly, and I could tell from the gleam in her eyes that she delighted in his teasing.

"True," he agreed, bending to kiss her on the cheek.

Their warmth and affection reminded me of the love and closeness that had thrived in my own family, and a pang of loneliness gripped the very depths of my soul. The engulfing emptiness must have shone in my face, for Drew reached out and gave my hand a comforting squeeze.

As Patience poured coffee into two fragile china cups, Drew pulled up a chair and sat down beside me. "You look as lovely as ever, Rachel," he complimented. "And bright-eyed. You must have slept well."

"Yes, though—" I broke off, reminding myself that now was not the time to mention the gecko, lest the incident distress his aunt. As for my curiosity about Claudia, Jordan's reaction convinced me to query his brother in private.

"Though what?" Drew's brow furrowed with concern.

"Nothing really."

Patience handed me a cup, filled to the brim with rich, dark liquid. "I hope your bed was comfortable, Rachel." Her tone matched Drew's.

"Very comfortable," I assured her, though that had not been true during my fright with the lizard. Casting out the unpleasant memory, I sipped the coffee. "Mmm, delicious."

"I'm glad you like it, dear. The strong, distinctive flavor doesn't appeal to everyone." She passed a cup of the beverage to her nephew.

"This is brewed from kona beans, grown on the island of Hawaii," Drew informed me, after he also took a sip.

"Coffee was always my favorite morning drink," Patience said, then added grudgingly, "The doctor insisted I give it up; something to do with heart palpitations. But thank goodness I have this wonderful, eye-opening herbal tea to take its place," she added on the wave of a grateful sigh. As she filled her cup I suppressed a grin. That tea *was* the color of seaweed. Even worse it smelled like limes picked before their peak. Involuntarily my lips puckered and *my* throat closed.

Drew met my eyes with a knowing look, the corners of his mouth lifting in a slight smile. I had the feeling he'd guessed my vow to avoid his aunt's morning tea at all costs. During those shared moments of silent amusement Kalani came in carrying a tray of sliced fresh fruit for the table. She regarded Drew and me with what appeared to be the featherings of a resentful frown. However, a second later I wondered if I had misread her expression, for she greeted us with a friendly, "Good morning."

"Good morning," I returned in the same manner. Drew tilted his dark head in Kalani's direction, though his gaze never left mine. Patience scarcely looked up from her cup of tea.

"Would you like anything before breakfast is served?" the Hawaiian housekeeper inquired.

"Rachel?" Drew asked, and I politely declined the offer.

"Nothing." Patience waved a brusque dismissing hand that teetered on rudeness. How unlike this gracious lady the gesture seemed, but then I hadn't even begun to know her yet. I hoped she wasn't the kind who looked down her nose at servants.

Kalani's attractive features tightened in a flash of hurt. But there was an even deeper emotion in her dark eyes. What was it? Worry? Desperation? Nodding, she turned on her heel and retraced her steps to the kitchen. Clearly there was discord between her and Patience. Had Kalani displeased her employer in some way?

I'd scarcely had time to consider that thought before it became lost in the first of the dozen or so questions Patience asked me about my family. For the most part I was pleased by what seemed her genuine interest, and talking about my loved ones helped ease the empty ache. However, a small part of me felt as if my personal life was being subtly but thoroughly inspected. In my capacity as a nurse I was used to such scrutiny and had never given it more than a passing thought. Being measured as a prospective bride, especially by a member of the lofty class, was altogether different, and I couldn't deny I was a trifle uncomfortable.

"Drew told me your father was a professor of literature," Patience said to me as we made ourselves comfortable around the breakfast table.

Before I could comment, Drew intervened, praising my father, "From what I'd heard during my visit with Rachel in Ohio, he was highly respected, both on campus and in the community."

Indignation brought his aunt's chin up. "You've already made that abundantly clear. Contrary to what you and your brother seem to think, Drew, I am not forgetful."

"Of course you aren't, Aunt Patience," he soothed, then turned affectionate eyes on me. "I fear my zeal for Rachel has led me to repeat myself."

"Hmmph," she sniffed. "It has also made her blush."

"Ah, but the color accentuates her beauty." His eyes danced with merriment, though his voice was a velvet caress.

My face had grown hot. Drew did know how to charm. And to persuade gently. Now, in view of his aunt's accusation about the repeated praise of my father, I wondered if Drew was using his magic to guide her to wholehearted acceptance of me. Going to such lengths hardly seemed necessary when she and I were off to a fine start. "My father loved teaching," I said quietly as the heat subsided. "And my brothers and I were fortunate to grow up in the world of books."

My comment erased the irritation Drew had kindled in his

aunt. "I grew up in the same world," she said brightly. "But maybe Drew told you." Patience laid a crisp napkin across her lap.

"I didn't say much about your mother." He slipped his napkin from its silver ring.

Or about the rest of his family, either. "Was she a teacher, also?" I asked the older woman as a maid entered, lifted the platter of tropical fruit, and stepped to Patience's side at the head of the table.

"Oh yes, indeed she was. Although my mother hadn't set out to that pursuit. In the late twenties, when the first mission schools were opened on the island, she and the other ministers' wives were the only ones available to teach. You must try the papaya, Rachel," she suggested absently, and the maid pointed out the fruit as I served myself from the platter. "It was a difficult job," Patience added, her voice fading in what sounded like remembrance.

"Difficult?" I echoed, and supposed she was still referring to the teaching. But Patience didn't seem to hear.

"Back then the natives didn't speak English," Drew explained as he helped himself to the fruit, "and it was necessary to talk through interpreters."

"What an impossible-sounding situation," I said. "My father never encountered such a formidable obstacle." I tasted the papaya. The fruit was deliciously sweet and of a texture that was pleasing yet unlike any I'd ever sampled before.

Patience blinked then continued in a faraway voice, "My mother also came to love teaching. I had hoped to follow in her footsteps. Instead"—regret altered her tone—"my father insisted upon grooming me to take his place in the family business."

"And he would be proud of you, Aunt Patience," Drew complimented her. "You've done an outstanding job."

Patience tilted her chin in the same confident attitude I had observed in Jordan yesterday. "Heaven knows I've given it my all. Nevertheless I'll always wonder if I would have made a good teacher. You're very fortunate, Rachel, to be able to make your own choices. My nephews don't have that option any more than I did, and in time one of them will take on an even heavier burden."

In the business, did she mean? With Patience's proclivity to subject jumping, I could hardly be sure if she was still on the same one. On top of that I was also a bit mystified by the triumphant look that suddenly crossed Drew's features. "Now, Aunt Patience," he said in cheerful reassurance, "you know Jordan and I regard the corporation as an exciting challenge. I can't imagine that will ever change."

"Eventually all things change," she pointed out bluntly, and her robust spirit continued to amaze me. It was hardly typical of one in failing health. Patience perked up as she told Drew about the rare, exotic bird she'd seen from the window. Over breakfast she kept the conversation primarily on the sea and the wildlife in the islands. I was impressed by her knowledge, and I gazed upon Drew with pride. He was almost as well versed in the varieties of birds and the winter migration habits of the whales from the frozen arctic to these warmer waters. As a nature enthusiast myself, I soaked up all they shared with me and looked forward to learning more. But most of all the insight I was gaining into this warm and accepting pair gave me the sense of home. If only Jordan was as welcoming, I thought as I lifted the last succulent sausage from my plate. Of course my main concern with him was the magnetism between us. Would it fade in time? Or, heaven help us, grow, no matter how hard we might fight against it? A shudder coursed through me. Did such physical attractions usually fall to a disastrous end, as I'd often heard? My throat dried and I nearly choked on the sausage.

After we'd finished with the morning meal, Patience said with a teasing smile, "I'm sure you two won't mind if I leave you alone. I'm going down and spend some time in the gardens. With luck I'll catch another glimpse of the iiwi. And don't worry, Drew," she assured him when his brows knitted in a frown, "I won't tax myself on the stairs."

"I'll take that as a promise," he returned firmly, and once again I was warmed by his concern for his aunt. Nodding, Patience stood, ending the brief reference to her health and my hope that she might mention exactly when I could commence my nursing duties. Considering that she seemed so fit, and certainly strong of voice, I was beginning to wonder if she truly needed a nurse.

Drew and I accompanied the older woman down to the entrance floor. She excused herself and moved slowly to the rear.

"Have you been shown around this level yet, Rachel?" Drew inquired.

I shook my head. "All I've really seen is the solarium."

"Then before we go for our stroll along the beach, allow me to take you on the grand tour," he volunteered with a flourish.

I was eager for the stroll and the opportune moment to bring up the subject of the mysterious Claudia. But a few more minutes scarcely mattered and seeing the rest of the house did interest me. The layout was unique. At least I'd never been in a home before where the main living area was on the second floor. But my practical mind intruded when I recalled that this was a workday. "I shouldn't be taking up so much of your time, Drew. You must be needed at the office."

He waved a hand in airy dismissal. "Not to worry, Rachel, this day is for you and me. Jordan and Winston can manage without me." The confident note in Drew's voice was reassuring. Although come to think of it, he had sounded the same yesterday over closing the office early so Mr. Winston could drive me out to the house. Jordan's anger over those lost hours of business was as vivid as ever in my mind, and for all I knew he was still irritated. "Come along, my love." As Drew took my arm in his I prayed that his wish to please me and to make me a part of the family wouldn't ignite war between him and his twin.

My insides shriveled at just the thought of battle, and as Drew showed me about the entrance floor I kept horrid memories from looming by immersing myself in the sheer elegance that also graced this level of the house. Besides the library and reception room to each side of the vestibule, there were the men's studies off the stair hall. Twin studies, actually, for the colors, hangings, and heavy furniture were identical. The only noticeable difference was the desktops. Jordan's was heaped with ledgers and a mountain of paperwork. It was all neatly stacked, yet cluttered looking. Drew's desk was spotless with nothing more on its shiny mahogany surface than a lamp and an embossed ink set. I favored an organized man. Better yet I delighted in the prospect of spending the entire day with this one. From the studies we went to the rear. There was a kitchen, a huge pantry, storage, the solarium, and a washroom. The house I'd grown up in would have fit three times into the entrance floor alone of this place.

With my hand in Drew's we returned to the vestibule. He opened the front door. Just as I was about to cross the threshold Jordan appeared on the other side as if he'd suddenly materialized. "Oh," I gasped, "you startled me."

He looked a little taken aback himself. "Sorry," he said, and my attention automatically swiveled from one man to the other. Would I ever get used to being around identical twins? At least they weren't dressed in the same style of clothes today. Jordan wore a lightweight business suit. His brother was more casually attired and had removed his coat and set it aside in his study.

As I stepped back, allowing Jordan to enter, I lowered my eyes to evade his mesmerizing power. His coat sleeve brushed my arm and my heart skipped a beat. Was I defenseless where this man was concerned?

"What brought you back to the house?" Drew asked his twin.

"I was on my way to a meeting with Marshall and remembered I'd forgotten some documents on my desk."

In view of the mess on Jordan's desk he'd never find anything, I thought, still annoyed by the unwanted response he had evoked in me. With a brisk nod he excused himself and hurried to his study. His back was straight, his strides long and purposeful. Everything about his carriage and gait smacked of determination and energy.

Swallowing, I forced my eyes from him by reminding myself of the unnerving glare he'd leveled at my room from the captain's bridge. A moment later Drew and I left the house and meandered across the front lawn. Lifting my face to the warm rays of the sun, I breathed in the fresh air scented with the fragrance of wildflowers blooming riotously among ferns and sturdy palms. The breeze was light and the melodic chirping of birds intermingled with the sound of waves breaking on the beach. "How wonderfully odd it seems," I said with a sigh, "to be out in late fall without a wrap."

"Hmm," Drew said softly, "that sounds like something you could get used to, Rachel. Before you know it, this idyllic island and I will have captured your heart completely." His face and his voice were alive with the promise that I, too, hoped would come true.

"This place does seem like paradise," I murmured, and for the first time in four years I felt absolute peace.

Drew stopped and stared longingly into my eyes. "With you here, my darling, this is truly paradise." He pulled me into his embrace and lowered his mouth to mine. As Drew's lips moved caressingly a heady thrill spiraled. At last, I thought, melting against him. Then disappointment once again settled in, for instinct told me the excitement stemmed from the secret side of me that yearned to be a little scandalous. And kissing in the open for all to see was a major breach of propriety. Although, as far as I knew, no one was watching us.

Drew lifted his head and playfully kissed the tip of my nose. Then with his arm about my shoulders he led me down to the beach. The smell of the sea was more pungent here, the breeze a trifle stronger. My skirts blew gently about my ankles and I could feel wisps of hair escaping the captivity of combs and pins. "Do you swim in the ocean?" I dreamily asked as we strolled the golden sand.

A wave of tension ripped through Drew. I felt it in his arm and heard it in the sharp intake of his breath. "Not anymore," he muttered, and glanced off into the distance, his jaw turning to stone.

His reaction took me by surprise and I could only assume that I had inadvertently kindled a painful memory. Had he suffered some terrible experience in the ocean? The lengthening silence that fell between us was a red warning flag and I curbed the impulse to press for an explanation. Instead I inquired, with a casualness that didn't even begin to cover the curiosity simmering deep within me, "Are those two islands inhabited, Drew?" I pointed across the water.

Another quiet moment passed then he exhaled slowly. "Yes, sparsely. That one is Lanai, the other Molokai. Neither island gets many visitors, especially *malihinis*."

"Mali-whats?" I laughed, trying to ease the tension I still sensed in him.

Drew blinked, then looked down at me with the trace of the appealing smile that always made me feel so alive. "A *malihini* is a newcomer to the islands," he explained, and I remembered he'd mentioned that during our days together in the war. "So if you hear any of the natives referring to you as one," he teased, "don't be offended."

"Oh, I'm not easily offended," I returned in the same light tone, and he hugged me to his side. As Drew and I continued up the beach he added more words to my growing knowledge of the Hawaiian language and the islands' customs. It wasn't until we were on our way back to the house that I cautiously voiced the question that had been nagging in my mind. "Drew, I've heard the name Claudia mentioned and I've been wondering who she is?"

He stopped short and stepped back from me. The same pain I'd seen in Jordan's face now tightened his twin's features. "Who brought up her name?" Drew demanded, his tone gruff.

An unexpected chill snaked through me. "Your aunt and Kalani," I murmured, and my heartbeat accelerated at the muscle that quirked in his jaw. I didn't know what to think and I prayed my inquiry wouldn't cause trouble for the other women. "Is there some secret about Claudia?" I asked, not knowing what else to say.

"How could there be? Everyone around here knows—" Drew broke off, raking a hand through his thick, wind-tousled hair. "Forgive me, Rachel, it's very hard for me to talk about her."

"She was someone dear to you?"

He hesitated, then said with the slowness of one trying to prepare another for a shock, "Claudia ... was my wife."

"Your wife?"

"She died two years ago."

Ordinarily I would have said, "I'm sorry." But I was too stunned to feel sympathetic. "Why didn't you tell me you'd been married? I have the right to know."

"Yes," he agreed, "And I apologize for my impropriety."

Dishonesty was the word I would have used. I stared up at Drew, feeling betrayed.

"Does it matter that I was married before?"

"No. But you should have told me at the beginning, certainly before you proposed."

"The memories are painful."

"You're still grieving?"

"In a way."

"Then how can you truly be in love with me?"

"I am in love with you," he insisted quickly. "What I feel now for Claudia has little to do with that emotion."

"Then what does it have to do with it?"

Seconds passed. "Guilt," he said grimly. "I should have been the one who died. Jordan and I," he amended, his lips twisting with a bitterness that turned my blood to ice.

chapter 6

"WHAT A HORRIBLE thing to say," I sputtered, hugging myself against the glacial chill in my veins.

"Horrible, yes," Drew agreed, his tone still grim, "but true. I'll never forgive myself for failing to save . . ." His voice trailed off and he stared glumly at the frothy surf lapping inches from our feet.

"How did she die?" I managed to bring my voice under control.

He exhaled a long agonizing breath. "In a canoeing accident. We were on our way to visit with friends just south of here when a fierce wind suddenly came up. The sea was wild, worse than I'd seen in a long time."

"Well, then, you can't blame yourself."

He shook his head in swift denial. "I'm a skilled oarsman, Rachel. I've been rowing since I was a boy and I could have gotten us safely ashore if—" His lips twisted once more. "If the outrigger on our canoe hadn't splintered and overturned the vessel. God knows I tried to save them," he choked, "but the undertow and the weight of their clothes pulled them down."

My heart twisted and I automatically reached out a comforting hand. "There was someone else besides you and Claudia in the canoe?"

"Ellen." The feminine name was barely a whisper.

For some reason I pictured a little girl and my voice sounded shrill when I echoed, "Ellen?"

"Jordan's fiancée."

An instant of relief swept through me. The loss of an adult life was bad enough, a child would even have been worse. "Two loved ones gone," I murmured. "I am sorry, Drew, for you and for Jordan."

He placed an appreciative hand over mine on his arm. "With those deaths and all of the others I saw later in the war, I'm sure you can understand why it's difficult for me to talk about this."

"Yes, but you could have at least mentioned you're a widower."

"I was going to during our visit together at your home, but then I was suddenly called away to New York."

"Then in one of your letters."

"That isn't something I'd put in a letter."

"When had you planned on telling me?"

"Soon. Before you found out from the locals."

"What about the household?"

"I asked them not to say anything until after I'd talked with you."

"You enlisted their aid in misleading me?"

Drew frowned at my sudden withdrawal from his touch. "Believe me, Rachel, they didn't like it any more than I. But informing you of the marriage was my responsibility."

The truth of that statement didn't ease the hurt. But at least now I understood why Kalani had tried to cover up after Claudia's name slipped out. And why Jordan wouldn't answer my question about her. However, that didn't explain his look of distress at the mere mention of her name, although I supposed it reminded him of Ellen. Was he still in love with her? And why had Drew insisted that both he and his brother should have perished instead of the ladies? A sea gull swooped and shrilled. The instant the strident sound faded, I put that question to Drew.

White lines of resentment formed around his mouth. "The canoe was Jordan's," he bit out. "He built it with his own hands, just as he's built others. Only that one was defective. It probably would have fallen apart no matter what the weather."

"Surely he hadn't known that."

"I suppose not."

Shock waves coursed through me. "He's your brother, I should think you would be certain."

"Certain?" Drew shook his head as if trying to sort out a puzzle. "If Jordan hadn't urged me to take that boat out and give it a try, the women might still be alive."

"Good heavens, you make it sound as if he intentionally sent the three of you to sea in a faulty craft."

A spark of emotion I couldn't define crossed the clear-cut masculine features. "That isn't what I meant. But since it was his boat, I do hold him partly responsible. That's all."

Was that really all? I wondered, considering the bitterness that still colored Drew's tone. Instinctively my lips compressed and I censured myself for letting my imagination run on. What would Jordan have to gain from sabotaging the vessel carrying his loved ones anyway? Moreover, a man capable of such a heinous act wouldn't be as distressed by the memory as he was. Would he? Unexpected chills prickled my scalp and slithered down my spine.

The unnerving sensation must have been evident in my face because Drew said, "I've upset you with all of this depressing talk, Rachel. I'm sorry."

"You've upset me by withholding important information," I told him bluntly, then warned, "Don't ever do that again."

"I won't," he promised, and before I knew it, he'd sealed the vow with a light kiss. Ordinarily I would have felt some warmth and comfort. But not even a flicker of either emotion penetrated the sense of betrayal that still weighted my heart. I had judged Drew a man of strength and principle. Now I didn't know what to think and I couldn't help wondering if I would ever feel close to him again.

As we continued to retrace our steps in the sun-bleached sand, Drew said, "Granted it may not sound like it, Rachel, but I have accepted what happened to Claudia and Ellen, and little by little I'm managing to leave the guilt and bitterness behind."

To me it still seemed so fresh in him. If that was true, then Drew wasn't currently a prime prospect for marriage. "You have to leave it behind," I said distractedly, "if you hope to get on with your life."

"I'm determined get on with it. With you at my side," he added in a gentle voice.

Up to an hour ago I had looked upon being with him forever as a real possibility. Now deepening doubts predominated. My obvious hesitation furrowed Drew's brow. "I'll do whatever I must to make amends for my thoughtlessness, Rachel. Is there anything more you'd like to know about my marriage?"

"Are there any children?" I promptly asked. I wasn't averse to being a stepmother. I just didn't want any more surprises from this man.

"No, unfortunately," he said, and I expelled a breath of relief. "But that seems an odd question when you haven't seen any around the house."

"Perhaps. But you could have tucked them away in boarding school or with friends."

"Yes, I suppose. That isn't the case, though." He caught up a small rock and threw it into an approaching wave.

My own attention had wandered to the lush vegetation that flowed down from the rolling mountains to meet the ragged shoreline. Somehow the landscape just didn't seem as lovely as before. With my gaze on the dock several yards ahead I questioned in a thoughtful tone, "How long were you and Claudia married, Drew?"

Once more his answer was immediate. "A little over six years. She was a fine woman, Rachel. She and I also met on the mainland."

So I was the second prospective bride he'd brought home from across the Pacific Ocean. Although, for all I knew, maybe before Claudia there had been others. It would be tactless to ask, and what did it matter anyway? Another curious thought surfaced, only this one tumbled unwittingly from my mouth. "Was Ellen from the mainland, also?"

"No, from the Big Island, born and reared there."

"Of Hawaiian ancestry, you mean?"

"Oh no," he said quickly as if there was something wrong with that race. "Her family hails from New York. Very upstanding people."

To me upstanding signified honorable. From the lift of Drew's chin I deduced the word meant aristocratic. Was Claudia's family also moneyed? But what did that really matter to me, either? If gaining a handsome dowry was important to Drew, I wouldn't be here. Right now whether I would even stay was an uncertainty.

As we left the beach and meandered beneath the tall palms on the immaculately landscaped grounds, whirling thoughts and mixed emotions rendered me silent. I was grateful that Drew didn't intrude on those moments I needed to myself. Now, here was an example of the considerate Drew I'd been attracted to, the man who had selflessly buoyed up the spirits of the other wounded soldiers in the field hospital. He'd never missed those evening visits with each and every one of them, I reminded myself. Nor had he failed to gather the interested able-bodied for the daily card games that kept minds mercifully preoccupied. Was I being too sensitive and critical over his failure to inform me of the marriage? After all, I couldn't even begin to imagine the horror of seeing loved ones die in such a tragic way. Nor could I know the guilt he carried over his futile rescue efforts. How would I have coped? I wondered.

A breath of confusion escaped my lips and I looked up at Drew as he tried in his special way to lighten my mood. "Watch out for the coconuts overhead," he warned teasingly. "They drop at the most unexpected times."

"Are they as heavy as they look?" I frowned at the clusters that hung threateningly in the palms towering above us.

"You wouldn't want one to come sailing down on you," he responded with a chuckle. "Did I ever tell you about the palm fronds I rigged to lob coconuts like cannonballs in my youth?"

From my tomboy days I could well imagine such a contraption, and a smile came to my lips. "No, but that sounds like something my brothers would have done. I hope you didn't lob coconuts at people or animals." I regarded him suspiciously.

"Only my brother."

"Drew, how unchristian of you."

The appealing devilish gleam brightened his eyes. "Aunt Patience used to scold me with those very words. Only coming from you, Rachel, they're delightful."

The part of me that still stung with hurt turned a deaf ear to the flattery, and I warned myself that I daren't let Drew's charm sway my judgment. "You didn't hurt Jordan with the coconuts, did you?"

"My aim wasn't very good," he confessed with a hint of playful regret. "But I made him furious. Not that it takes much, my brother has a short temper."

That didn't surprise me. However, curiosity did prompt me to inquire, "And how did Jordan vent his anger, by retaliating with coconuts?"

A fleeting shadow, which had nothing to do with the sun filtering through the trees, touched Drew's face. Then he shrugged. "He had his own way of getting even. Still does, actually." His tone was level. Nevertheless the ominous implication set my teeth on edge.

As we neared the rose arbor in a small clearing, a gecko skittering across the path startled me to a halt. "You needn't be alarmed," Drew said from beside me. "Those small lizards are harmless."

"So I discovered last night."

"Oh? You left the house after I saw you to your room?"

I shook my head. "There was one in my bed."

"What? You can't be serious?"

"Do I look like I'm joking?"

"Well, no. But how on earth did a gecko get in your bed?"

"I've been asking myself the same question. Jordan said it probably entered through an open window."

"Jordan? You told him about this even before mentioning it to me?"

"No . . . I didn't actually tell him."

"Then who did?"

"No one. He heard me trying to catch the little creature and he kindly gave me a helping hand."

"In your room? After dark?" Drew's eyes narrowed to slits and I wondered if he was reflecting on the heated kiss he'd witnessed between his brother and me.

That memory, along with the one of Jordan's provocative touch on my arms during those minutes we were alone in my room, threatened to turn my face red. But I firmly reminded myself that we hadn't committed any transgression and I willed away the heat. In a voice that was a bit more controlled than I felt I explained the situation to Drew. Then I concluded with, "Anyway, as you may recall, the windows in my quarters weren't open when I arrived here and you showed me up. Or at any later time yesterday, that I'm aware of. So if the gecko got in through one of them, it was earlier in the day, or during some other one. Do lizards get in the house very often?" I asked the same question I'd put to his twin.

I received the same reply. "Never." Only there was a smoldering look in Drew's eyes that made me wonder if he suspected someone had put the reptile in my bed. But who would do such a thing and why? Before I could press the issue, Drew said, "I'm sorry for last night's fright, Rachel. Nothing like that will ever happen again."

"I hope not, but how can you be sure?"

"Let's just say I'll be watching after you."

What an odd comment, I thought. Why, Drew made it sound as if I needed a protector. From what? Or who?

The word "protector" wove in and out of my brain as Drew continued to show me about the grounds. By the time we returned to the house and joined his aunt for lunch, I had convinced myself that the one I needed protection from was Drew and his persuasive ways. Naturally I didn't intend to dwell on his betrayal, but neither could I allow him blithely to dismiss it, either. Yes, he was sorry for deceiving me and I was trying to understand his predicament. Still, that was a long way from placing wholehearted trust in him again.

Patience was quiet throughout the meal, and when I inquired if she'd had any more sightings of the exotic red bird she'd gone out to look for in the garden, she answered with a simple no. And she slipped back to silence. At first I thought she was just preoccupied. Then I noticed she barely touched the melt-in-the-mouth smoked salmon, and fresh vegetables in herbed-butter sauce, and I wondered if she wasn't feeling well. Ordinarily I would have come right out and asked and once again offered my services. But since she'd put me off yesterday and insisted I not fuss over her, I refrained from voicing my concern.

During the dessert of rice pudding I only half listened to Drew's comments to his aunt regarding grogshop renovations he was overseeing. My mind had wandered back to his marriage and I wondered exactly how Patience felt about his failure to promptly mention it to me. Surely a woman of her strict moral upbringing would be appalled by his dishonesty. Perhaps she'd referred to Claudia yesterday in the hope the name might spark my curiosity, compelling me to inquire. In that way Patience wouldn't have actually brought up the subject and committed what Drew might look upon as an act of betrayal.

As he pulled back his aunt's chair and we moved from the table, Patience said to her nephew, "You must take Rachel out to see my father's church this afternoon."

"I had planned to do that," he returned.

"Perhaps you'd like company for a while longer, Patience," I offered.

"No, dear, that's sweet. But this day is for you and Drew." She flashed him an indulgent smile as we left the dining room. "I'm expecting the kahuna soon, anyway. Then I think I'll take a nap. "Oh yes," she grumbled under her breath as if a sudden and unpleasant thought had struck her, "I have those papers to finish reading. Jordan returned to the house this morning, Drew," she said in what I initially regarded as an abrupt change of subject. On second thought I wondered if the documents she referred to were the same ones he was pressing her for. Obviously he hadn't gone to his study alone after leaving Drew and me at the front door this morning. Jordan had also ventured out to the garden. To pay respects to his aunt? Or to try to retrieve the papers she evidently still had in her possession?

While Drew escorted his aunt to the informal drawing room overlooking the captain's bridge, and saw to it that she was comfortably seated, I went up and put on my sprigged straw bonnet. Then Drew and I descended the stairs and made our way to the rear and the carriage house. The smell of hay and horses kindled happy memories of the barn back home, where my brothers and I used to hide from one make-believe posse after another.

As I was introduced to the Hawaiian stable hand, his glint of curiosity reminded me of the expression I'd seen in the official at the dock in town where I'd asked directions to this family's office. Was there some speculation about me? That I might be the second Mrs. Drew Phillips? When it came right down to it, I supposed everything the wealthy and influential Phillipses did suffered the scrutiny of the community. On that stomach-tightening thought I returned my mind to a more important concern. "I'm a little worried about your aunt, Drew," I said as a buggy was being readied for us. "She was so quiet over lunch and scarcely touched her meal."

He lifted his broad shoulders in a shrug. "As I told you, Aunt

Patience has her good days and her bad. She'll rally, Rachel, she always does. She's stronger than she frequently appears to be."

"But does she have low spells often?"

"No, I wouldn't say so." He helped me into the open buggy. My mind lingered on Patience as Drew urged the mare down the drive and onto the road. As we turned toward town an ancient-looking man on horseback was approaching from the opposite direction. He raised his hand in a friendly greeting. Drew jerked his up in curt acknowledgment. "The kahuna," he muttered, "with his bag of pagan remedies."

"You don't think they do your aunt any good?" I glanced back at the rider garbed in dark trousers, bright tapa shirt, and a leis of colorful feathers.

"She claims otherwise, but I haven't noticed any difference. Whatever you do, Rachel, don't encourage her interest in the primitive, so-called medicine," he ordered firmly.

His view struck me as either narrow-minded or uninformed. "I know several people who owe their lives to remedies handed down through generations," I pointed out in the most tactful tone I could muster. "Most of the physicians I've worked with still rely on many of them."

"Precisely. And we have a fine family doctor, received his degree from Harvard. He even served in the war until he was nearly killed at Fredericksburg and sent home."

I hadn't been at that battle, which I'd heard was one of the most terrible. I didn't see how any could have been worse than the battle in the area called the Wilderness. The density of the woodland, with its swamps and steep-banked ravines, made the narrow tracks in that gloomy jungle all but literally impassable. And fires had repeatedly sprung up as blasts from muzzles hit dried leaves and, most horrifying of all, the paper cartridges at the waists of men trapped by flames and choking smoke. The ghastly visions of charred victims, and the overwhelming stench that had filled the air, haunted me nightly. Swallowing the bile that rose in my throat, I asked with an abruptness that reminded me of Patience, "What is that?" I gestured into a clearing surrounded by what Mr. Winston had called koa trees. Shadowed beneath their branches were the remains of a thatched structure built upon a large, rectangular stone wall.

Drew looked past me. "Oh, that's a *heiau*," he said, then went on to explain, "Before the missionaries, the natives in this locale used to worship there. Remnants of such temples are scattered throughout the Hawaiian chain. Some *heiaus* are bigger than that one, others considerably smaller."

How odd I hadn't noticed the remains of that *heiau* on the ride out to the Phillips home yesterday, and the occasional thatched-and tin-roof huts we were also rumbling by on this bright afternoon. But yesterday, of course, I'd been engrossed in trying to puzzle out what Mr. Winston had meant by the other tragedy in Drew's life. Now I knew it was the lost ladies.

Just this side of town Drew maneuvered the horse up a short drive, cloistered by thick tropical growth, and reined in before a charming steepled church built of plaster and stone. It was a small structure, yet it had an air of stately greatness. The narrow, covered porch sheltered the heavy arched door, inset with leaded glass. All about were long windows also arched and fitted with the same heavy panes.

Drew handed me down and we climbed the four steps. As we entered the house of worship I inhaled a fortifying breath and forced back memories of the converted churches I had served in as an army nurse. My mind obeyed my will, but for a chilling second my ears heard the rasping of surgeons' saws. I must have shivered, for Drew put a protective arm about me. "What is it, Rachel? Are you suddenly cool for some reason?"

The trade winds had picked up, but the air was still pleasant. I shook my head. "Just part of the last four years intruding," I admitted softly.

"Of course, I understand." His tone matched my own. "Would you rather wait and see this place another time?"

"No, I've been avoiding churches ever since—" I cleared my throat, then finished with resolve. "I mustn't let the past control my life."

"I guess we both have that to deal with."

"Yes," I murmured, though I didn't know which tragedy in his life he was alluding to. Probably both.

With his arm still about my shoulders Drew ushered me forward. Just inside the door was an inlaid table expertly fashioned from koa. Beyond, the pews and the altar were as well crafted of the same wood. For timeless moments my inner strength collapsed and my mind shut once more on the horror of the past. All

I saw was the beauty of this place and the only sound I heard was the chirping of birds. Then, as if by some miracle, the peace of this chapel whispered through my soul, and for the first time I relived the suffering of brave men without the burning torture that had plagued me. With my gaze fixed on the religious etchings in the stained glass behind the altar, I closed my eyes and issued a silent prayer.

"You all right?" Drew asked quietly, and I nodded. Then, with the minister nowhere in sight, Drew showed me pridefully about. He concluded the brief tour at a pair of marble headstones beneath the shade of a tree out back. "My great-aunt and uncle," he said in a solemn, almost reverent voice. "When Aunt Patience is called home, she will be laid to rest beside her parents."

"And you and Jordan?"

"No, the honor of being buried here is reserved exclusively for the founder of this church and his immediate family. My brother and I will have to settle for a cemetery in Lahaina."

The next thought that came to me was of Drew's wife, and when he said, "Claudia is buried in one of them," I had the uncanny feeling he'd read my mind. On our way back to the house I recalled Drew had said his brother's fiancée, Ellen, was from New York. The telegram that had upset Drew and sent him hastily packing from our visit together in Ohio had also come from there. Was that simply a coincidence? I was tempted to ask, to clear the air of that mystery. But what right did I have to delve so deeply into this man's past, especially when we weren't even engaged? And might never be.

The rest of the afternoon passed quietly. What a blessing after the shock of the morning. And it was a joy to see Patience looking bright-eyed again when Drew and I joined her for tea in the formal drawing room. Either the nap had done the older woman a world of good, or the kahuna had dispensed some miraculous potion. Maybe both, or maybe today was just an example of the ups and downs of her ailment. Although it had also crossed my mind that her low spell might have had something to do with Jordan and the pressuring his aunt had complained to me about. That alone could strain the heart.

Over dinner I studied Jordan from beneath my lashes, the determined set of his chin and the serious expression in his eyes. I had never been drawn by the aloof look before, although with

Jordan the dark pools also held stirring intrigue. Yes, I'd seen mystery in Drew, too, but it wasn't as profound and thought provoking. Had Ellen also be drawn by Jordan's enigmatic air? Was he still grieving for her? My throat tightened on the added anguish he must have suffered over the cause of her death and Claudia's. Did the distress I'd seen in his face indicate that he, too, blamed himself for the accident that had claimed them? And how was he coping with his twin's resentment?

I was so engrossed in those questions that I didn't hear what Jordan said to his aunt, but my ears perked up when she replied with exasperation, "Yes, I've finished reading them."

Dismay brought my lips tightly together. Was Jordan still pressing her about those papers? If he wasn't careful, he was going to put that dear woman in her grave.

"They're in my sitting room," Patience told him in continued exasperation. "You can pick them up after dinner."

Jordan thanked her politely, then tilted his chin in an inquiring attitude. "Does our offer on the land meet with your approval, Patience?"

She nodded.

Relief touched Jordan's full mouth. "I'll present the documents to the commission tomorrow."

"As you wish." Her spine stiffened. "But remember, no more rushing me to business decisions. Why, I only had those papers a day or two."

Drew spoke up, defending his brother. "I'm afraid it was an entire week, Aunt Patience. But the days do pass quickly," he soothed. "I often lose track of them myself."

Jordan met that last statement with a scowl. It heightened the question in my mind of Drew's diligence in regard to the family concern.

"The days don't slip away from me," the old woman retorted, and rang irritably for a maid.

Moments later, as Kalani supervised the clearing of the main course, I sat back and stared through the open French doors behind Drew. The play of moonlight on the captain's bridge was mesmerizing, the air mild and fragrantly scented. My thoughts swirled around the unbidden memory of Jordan glaring up at my room from out there. And I was only vaguely aware of Drew now teasing Patience over some change she wished to make in

the solarium. Clearly he was trying to soften her mood. Judging
from her chuckle, he had succeeded.

It was the silence from Jordan that turned my gaze back to
him. He was sipping from his cup of coffee, his attention on the
chatting pair. However, the remote look in his eyes conveyed that
his mind was elsewhere. On what? Personal interests, whatever
they might be? Or the family corporation, which he seemed to
live and breathe? Maybe, I thought on an involuntary sigh of relief, he hadn't really pressed his aunt about the documents for the
Land Commission. After all, having those papers for a week
should have provided ample time for her to study them.

To my embarrassment Jordan's attention swiveled to me and
he caught me watching him. Surprise showed in his lean face,
then his eyes narrowed as if he was trying to read my expression,
or maybe my mind. At the moment it was dumbly blank, and all
I felt was the flush inspired by his hooded eyes searching mine.
Had he made this same mishmash of Ellen's senses with just a
look? I wondered on a twinge of unexpected jealousy, and resisted the urge to shift uncomfortably in my chair. What was *he*
thinking? Jordan moistened his full lips, then his gaze lifted for
a second. "Your dessert," he said, after clearing his throat.

I blinked, but reality still eluded me. "What?" I murmured
inanely.

"Dessert, miss," Kalani responded, and I looked up, startled.
How long had she been standing beside me?

"Daydreaming, Rachel?" Drew grinned at me from across the
table.

"Yes, I guess so." I managed, meeting his eyes briefly. Then
I lowered my head and focused on the wedge of coconut cream
pie Kalani had set before me.

The next time I glanced up, the pretty Hawaiian housekeeper
was serving Drew pie. As she reached past him to put his dessert
plate on the table, I once again watched for the look of interest
I'd seen her cast his way upon my arrival at this house. Kalani's
exotic features remained set and her dark eyes were solely fixed
on the task at hand. However, the tightness about her mouth reminded me of the strain I'd sensed between her and Patience this
morning before breakfast. Did this tension have anything to do
with that?

Drew and his aunt had resumed their conversation about the

solarium and neither one of them appeared even to notice Kalani. Later, though, as the family and I were preparing to adjourn to the drawing room, I glimpsed the exchange of glances between Jordan and the housekeeper. There was no mistaking the flash of appreciation that brightened her eyes. Appreciation for what? I wondered, looking from her to Jordan.

chapter 7

I SAW MYSELF running, falling, and repeatedly stumbling to my feet in what I knew was the swampy Wilderness. Heavy rains poured down, plastering my clothes to my body. My hair was a stringy, sodden mass and my mouth twisted with hysterical sobs, yet I heard no sound. All about me the deluge from the dark, hovering sky unearthed the remains of soldiers from their shallow graves. Eyeless, slack-jawed skeletons stared up at me. And a bony, disembodied hand tugged ruthlessly on my mud-caked skirt, dragging me helplessly down into the mire. It filled my throat, gagging me. The more I struggled, the more I inhaled. I was suffocating. My chest heaved with spasms that threatened to burst my lungs.

An agonizing constriction jerked me awake and I coughed as I sucked in blessed fresh air. I could still feel the bog in my throat and taste the putrid muck. My heart hammered and my flesh was wet with cold perspiration. Trembling, I rose up on one elbow and gazed around the moon-washed room. Overwhelming relief swept through me. I was in Hawaii, safe and sound with Drew and his family. The war was over. No more horror, no more gruesome, wrenching sights.

I hugged myself, reassured, and lay back down, drawing the lightweight bedclothes to my chin. I knew the evening air was warm, yet I still felt a penetrating chill. Would the nightmares ever end? I had been hopeful that might be so after the pure peace I'd felt in the church this afternoon. If only Drew hadn't mentioned Fredericksburg and jogged the grisly stories I'd heard, stories that had led me to remember the Wilderness and what I'd seen during my service there. Clearly those rekindled memories had lingered at the front of my brain and lay waiting like a loathsome viper to strike tonight with full force in my sleep. Bodies had resurfaced when the rains came in that region. Men had— I flew bolt upright, shaking my head in an effort to cast out the unwanted visions. Somehow I must come to grips with the past four years. And I certainly could not blame Drew and his brief reference to one battle for this night's bad dreams. Where was the inner strength I'd always taken pride in? The pluck my father had encouraged and admired in me?

Pushing back my unbound hair, I moistened my dry lips and breathed deeply of the flower-scented air that drifted in through an open window. The tension was easing from my body. Unfortunately my eyes were wide and falling back to sleep wasn't imminent. I frowned at the prospect of tossing and turning for heaven only knew how long and wished I'd had a good book to read. I'd brought several with me on the crossing, but I'd devoured every word in them at least twice. There was the family library on the entrance floor. Surely the Phillipses wouldn't mind if I went down and borrowed a volume or two.

In the glow of the moonlight I left the bed and thrust my feet into slippers. As I pulled on the pink wrapper that matched my cotton nightdress and was securing the sash, the crash of glass from the adjoining room brought my head up with a start. In an instant I was at the connecting door. "Patience," I called, and my hand automatically went to the china knob, "are you all right?"

"Yes, yes, just a little cut," she muttered, sounding annoyed.

"May I be of help?" I waited expectantly.

At the word, "Please," I swung open the door and entered the older woman's domain. Clad in a voluminous nightdress and with her white hair in a long braid down her back, she stood in the radiance of the night-table lamp, staring at her hand. Shards of glass lay on the table in a puddle of water, which was trickling onto the carpet to join more glass. It was all about her bare feet and the lower portion of her gown was damp. "The pitcher slipped from my grasp," she said, looking around at me.

"Don't move," I warned, then carefully crossed and examined the hand she held out. A spot of blood had surfaced from a superficial cut. "Soap and water will take care of this," I assured her, dabbing at the spot with a fresh handkerchief from my pocket. "But let me clean up the glass first."

"That won't be necessary," she insisted. "I'll ring for a maid." Before I could say another word, she pulled the bell rope beside the four-poster. After I checked the bed for shards and slivers, I helped Patience back onto it, and away from the possibility of further cuts. "I'm sorry for waking you, Rachel. How clumsy of me to drop the pitcher." She wrinkled her nose at the mess on the Aubusson carpet.

I was about to explain that she hadn't roused me, but a glance at the clock on the opposite night table convinced me to remain silent. The fact that I was awake at 11:45 might raise questions and I didn't want to go into the nightmares or try to fabricate some other reason. So I simply replied with what was indeed a truth· "I'm used to being awakened in the middle of the night. But what about you, Patience, were you having trouble sleeping?"

She nodded. "I suffer from insomnia from time to time. I have powders the doctor gave me, but they leave me feeling a little light-headed in the morning."

"Did you advise him of that?"

"Oh yes, and he told me it was nothing to be concerned about. Easy for him to say," she grumbled, "it's not his head! So I took matters into my own hands and turned to the kahuna for a sleep remedy. Have you met him yet, dear? No, of course not," she quickly answered her own question. "You and Drew were out when he came this afternoon. I'll introduce you on his next visit, Rachel. He's most interesting and wise."

I'd never come face-to-face with a medicine man before and the prospect piqued my inquisitive nature. "I'd like to," I said, and wondered if Drew might view my response to his aunt as encouraging her to what he called pagan remedies. Why, he'd almost made it sound as if the kahuna offered up live animals and human beings to the Hawaiian gods. Hadn't those heathenish sacrifices ended a long time ago?

A tap sounded on the door. "Enter," Patience called, and a sleepy-eyed maid came in. Her employer merely gestured to the mess and the young girl crossed to the closet. She secured a broom and a dustpan, lighted another lamp, and went straight to work. As I excused myself to fill the washbasin with fresh water to bathe Patience's hand, I scanned her spacious quarters. The wood pieces were dark and accented in rose and pale green on a cream ground in the hangings, wallpaper, and rich upholstered chairs. To the rear was her private sitting room, visible through a wide arch that could be closed off by sliding doors. The room was in shadows, so I couldn't really see more than the luxurious settee and a Bible stand, complete with the Good Book.

At the washbasin my eyes widened as my attention was caught by the vast array of medicine bottles and decanters on the bureau across the way. Either this woman's health was more precarious than it appeared to be, or she suffered from imaginary illnesses.

After the carpet was free of glass and the maid had begun mopping up the water with a thick towel, I urged the older woman to the basin and cleansed her minor wound. By the time I was finished and had blotted the area dry, she and I were alone again. "A light dressing over this would be wise," I said, and she directed me to the top drawer of the bureau with all the bottles. I recognized the sleeping powder, laudanum, and two or three other common medications; the rest were labeled with names I'd never seen or heard of before. Casually I mentioned that fact as I applied the dressing to Patience's hand.

Her delight in telling me what was in each container plainly indicated she enjoyed catering to her health. "The majority of these are herbal remedies from the kahuna," she summed up the explanation.

"Do they work well for you?" I asked, more from my own interest than from Drew's dim view of the medicine man's remedies.

She nodded emphatically. "I've yet to use one that didn't alleviate my discomfort and without any residual effects. I was about to try this elixir the kahuna brought today when I accidently broke the pitcher." She lifted a small bottle and held it up for me to view.

I eyed its dark green liquid. "What malady is that for?"

"It's to help me sleep. I'm to add a spoonful to a glass of water. Except I see my supply hasn't been replenished. I'll have to ring for the maid again."

It was so late that I hated even to think of another interruption of the girl's sleep. "I have water in my room," I hurriedly offered before Patience could yank once more on the bell rope. "If I may, allow me to help you into a dry nightdress and make you comfortable in bed. Then I'll prepare the sedative for you." That

I knew was in direct conflict with Drew's orders about the kahuna's concoctions. But I was just as aware, from this woman's determined look, that if I didn't mix the elixir, she'd do it herself.

"I'd appreciate that, dear. I am growing a bit weary."

"Then maybe the sedative isn't necessary."

"From past experience I know it is." She waved a hand at my subtle attempt to talk her out of the elixir and I had no choice but to follow through on every step of my offer. The first two were accomplished in a matter of minutes and then I was on my way back through the connecting door for water. As I lifted the pitcher from my night table, the whinny of a horse floated up from the drive. Who could be out after midnight? I wondered, and my mind returned to the previous evening and Drew's trip to town after dark. Curious, I crossed to the window and looked down. All I glimpsed was the tail end of a horse as the animal was swallowed up in the shadows of palms forming a canopy to the rear carriage house. Had Drew gone out on this night, too? Or was the rider someone else?

After Patience had finished with the sedative and I was arranging the bedclothes about her, my own wakefulness prompted me to ask if I might use the family library. "Of course, dear," she said. "Please make yourself completely at home."

I thanked Patience, then left instructions for her to call me if she needed anything further. "I will," she promised, and I exited, hopeful that I had indeed begun my nursing duties in this house. I'd never been one to idle away the hours, not even in my youth. And while touring some of this enchanting island today with Drew had been enjoyable, I needed my work to feel truly complete. I couldn't deny either that now more than ever I didn't want to be indebted to him. Of course that wish stemmed from the sense of betrayal that still pained me and I wondered if I would ever again be able to view him in a romantic light. Once more the thought circled that maybe I was judging him unfairly, but the dictates of my heart continued to convey quite the opposite. Would time and coming to know Drew better bring my mind and my heart into accord?

That question lingered in my brain as I tiptoed to the connecting door. With no sounds coming from Patience's quarters, I felt at liberty to venture from my room for a few minutes. Noise-

lessly I moved to my door and stepped out. The mounted oil
sconces lit my way down the stairs to the vestibule and the library on the east. Just inside its doorway, I lighted a table lamp
and surveyed the large room. The lace-curtained windows on the
front wall overlooked the covered lanai, the rest of the walls held
shelf upon shelf of fine leather-bound books. Upon the plush carpet centering the floor were cozy armchairs and more tables and
lamps. For a moment I felt as if I'd been transported back to the
South and the extensive libraries I'd seen in the mansions there.
Only in the South I hadn't had time to read.

My father would have reveled in this room, I thought as I
lighted another lamp and moved to stand before a wall of books.
"Someday we'll have a library of our own," he'd often commented, and we'd had plenty of volumes to fill one. But, sadly,
in our modest home we'd never had the space to convert a room,
or the funds for an addition to the structure, and Father's dream
had gone unfulfilled.

Sighing, I scanned the books. There was a complete set of
Shakespeare, Byron, all of the other classics, volumes on history,
art, wildlife, theology, and just about every other conceivable
subject. Jane Austen was among my favorite authors and tonight
I needed to lose myself in the merry world of one of her mag-
nificently crafted social comedies. What appeared to be the full
set of the English author's work was on an upper shelf. Quietly
I rolled the library ladder into place and climbed halfway up. I
ran my fingers lightly over the gold-embossed lettering of *Pride
and Prejudice*, *Emma*, *Sense and Sensibility*, and had just lifted
Mansfield Park from its place on the shelf when one of the twins
said from directly below, "Rachel, what are you doing up at this
late hour?"

I'd been so engrossed that I hadn't heard anyone enter and I
looked around, startled. The book flew from my hand. As I automatically tried to recapture the volume I lost my balance and
tumbled backward. The plummeting book struck the floor with a
resounding thud. I was certain that I was destined for the same
fate, and a muted scream escaped my lips. The next thing I
knew, strong arms had caught me on my ungainly descent, as if
I were a mere feather floating down from the heavens. Breath-
less, I laid my head against the warm, masculine chest and murmured words of gratitude that were laced with embarrassment.

"I didn't mean to catch you unawares," he apologized with the same softness that had been in Drew's tone this morning, and held me comfortingly close as he had done many times before. "I saw the light on my way to the stairs and couldn't imagine who was in here." For an instant his betrayal reared within me and I resisted even the thought of being in Drew's arms. Then memories of his compassion and caring during our mainland days together flooded forward. On the firm reminder that Drew had been there when I'd been in desperate need of a bright spot in my life, my heart softened. Without thought I snuggled near, savoring his heat and clean manly scent through the soft fabric of his casual shirt, opened at the throat, just as it had been on our outing today. The quickening beat of his heart communicated his heightened awareness and my blood surged when I remembered I was in nightclothes. Light-headedness overcame me and my brain whirled with the wanton longing inspired by the very essence of this man. I could feel the cords flexing in his strong arms, one beneath my thighs, the other about my back. His touch seared my flesh right through the cotton nightdress and wrapper. There were so many sensations that I lost sight of where we were, and if anyone had asked my name during those moments of delirium, I would have babbled like an infant. The warm breath in my hair sent shivers of delight down my spine. As Drew set me on my feet my breast brushed his virile chest and I thrilled at the sharp intake of his breath.

"Your hair is beautiful down," he murmured huskily, lifting his hand to caress the golden mass that curtained my shoulders. I ached for the feel of his lips in my hair and at the sensitive hollow of my throat. But more than anything, I yearned to have his mouth on mine. The smoldering within me was unlike any other I'd ever known and I was overcome by the strange feeling that I had been possessed by the spirit of another woman. A female who boldly encouraged and sampled all of life's pure pleasures. The hot fingers on my arms pressed me closer and I eagerly lifted my face to the handsome one intent upon mine. The dark pools were veiled with thick lashes, the full lips moist and inviting. As my lips parted in anticipation a muscle near the clear-cut masculine jaw tensed and somewhere in the heavy fog of desire a warning light flashed in my brain. Sanity rolled back like a wave of arctic water on my senses. I was about to jerk away from the touch I'd helplessly encouraged when I was released with startling abruptness. Had he, too, been shocked back to reality?

"Jordan," I rasped, glaring at him.

He frowned as if he were furious with himself, or maybe just with me. I had practically thrown myself at him again and I could well imagine his already low opinion of me was dropping even further, by monumental degrees. "Sorry," he muttered, regarding my face that surely looked as beet red as it felt.

"If I'd known it was you . . ." I stammered in self-defense.

The heavy veil of lashes fell back over his eyes, making it impossible for me to read his expression and even wildly guess what he might be thinking. When Jordan spoke again, neither his words nor his tone held a clue. "My fault, I caught you off guard."

He literally caught me, I thought sarcastically.

"I was just a little surprised to see you up at this hour." He hesitated, his chin tilting in a wary angle. "Are you a night person?"

Would he object if I were? "No," I replied brusquely, but then I was struggling to salvage what was left of my dignity. It had suffered more in just over a day under the same roof with this man than in the entire twenty-two years of my life. "I was restless and came down for a book." I bent to pick it up, anything to tear my eyes away from the penetrating gaze.

But Jordan said, "Allow me." A second later he was handing over Jane Austen's *Mansfield Park*.

In accordance with good manners I thanked him. But propriety didn't also dictate that I must be sweet and warm and I made no effort in that regard.

The frown returned to Jordan's brow. "Being around twins is difficult, I know." His continued attempt to make amends only perpetuated the memory of our heat. Every second of our intimacy was alive in my mind, and it was obvious from the glow deepening in his eyes that he was also envisioning provocative pictures. "Perhaps from now on I should identify myself," he suggested, "at least in the face of any potentially compromising situations."

"There won't be any more of them," I retorted, then felt like a complete fool. If I couldn't consistently tell the twins apart, how in heaven's name could I have replied with such certainty? That must have also occurred to Jordan because a flicker of amusement changed the expression in his eyes. With a haughty lift of my chin I bade him a curt good night and swung about. All the way from the library I felt his eyes boring into my back. My cheeks flamed anew and I wished I'd thrown a figure-concealing cloak over my nightclothes.

Back in my room I sank down on the bed and roundly chastised myself for failing to recognize immediately that I had been in Jordan's arms. How could I have been so mindless? I fumed. The instantaneous current of awareness should have signaled a warning. But his concerned tone and the casual clothes, almost identical to those Drew had on earlier today, had misled me. Until our meeting in the library I'd only seen Jordan in conservative suits, like the dark brown one he'd worn at dinner. Why had he changed afterward? And what was *he* doing up so late? Might Jordan have been the rider I'd heard on the drive a short time ago? First Drew was out last evening, and now maybe his brother on this one. Such nocturnal wanderings struck me as a bit odd, and I was doubly grateful now that I'd had the good sense not to rush into marriage with a man I hardly knew.

With so many thoughts running rampant in my brain, I was too preoccupied to read, but I did shore up my resolve to guard against Drew's persuasive ways. Even more important I must shield myself from the overpowering magnetism of his brother.

chapter 8

THE NEXT FEW days passed quietly and thank goodness without further intimate moments with Jordan. But then I'd made it a point not to roam the house alone at night and chance another encounter. During the day he was in Lahaina embroiled in business, and about the only time I saw him was over evening meals. On those occasions we were polite to each other, and he appeared to go just as much out of his way to avoid eye contact as I did.

Drew, on the other hand, was more attentive than ever and the hurt he'd kindled in me over his deceit was gradually fading. But the closeness I'd felt for him hadn't even begun to rally.

He and I had breakfast together every morning with his aunt. Then he left for the office. Considering Jordan was on his way practically at the crack of drawn, I was concerned that maybe Drew was delaying his departure because of me and his wish to please. So one afternoon I casually asked Patience if that was a possibility, then I finished with, "I wouldn't want to upset Drew's work schedule in any way."

"You're not, dear," she assured me as we tended to the tropical flowers in the solarium. "Drew isn't an early riser, hasn't been in years. Fortunately that has not affected his part in the corporation. Somehow he always manages to keep up with his share. Primarily he oversees the grogshops, but he's probably already told you that."

He hadn't and I might have commented, but Patience didn't give me the chance. "Did I tell you about the feathered capes and helmets I've displayed on that wall?" she inquired with her usual abruptness. By now I had become used to this quirk in the older woman and had even come to look upon it as an endearing aspect of her nature.

I shook my head and turned my attention from the hibiscus I'd been watering. "Were they worn for Hawaiian ceremonials?" I eyed the handful of resplendent garments woven from the brilliant plumage of birds.

"The red feathers are from the iiwi I pointed out to you the other day," she commented before answering my question. "Not ceremonials. Finery like this was worn only by men of rank, especially during battle, and became great trophies of war. The noblewomen decorated themselves with prized featherwork leis. I have one in my sitting room, maybe you saw it."

"No," I said. I'd been in Patience's suite several times since the incident with the water pitcher. But I had been too engrossed in learning the uses of the unfamiliar elixirs and cures, which treated just about every malady from dyspepsia to sore throats and female disorders, to really notice her sitting room.

"Remind me to show you the lei tonight, dear, before you prepare my sedative."

"I will," I promised softly, then ventured, "Maybe you should try to fall asleep this evening without a sedative, Patience. It's really best not to rely upon them, if at all possible."

She frowned at my suggestion, then grudgingly admitted, "Dr. Hawthorne said the same, and heaven knows my nephews have repeatedly lectured me on the subject. No one seems to really understand my needs. No, I take that back," she amended. "Jordan is a bit more tolerant of what his brother calls my 'weird concoctions.' " A distant expression narrowed her gaze. "We'll see about tonight," she said vaguely, and her words drifted away on the breeze flowing in through the open doors. As Patience went back to removing spent blooms from the lush potted plants, I regarded her appreciatively from beneath my lashes. Despite her capricious bent she was keen of mind. And if she suffered flights of fancy as Drew suggested, she hadn't done so in my presence. So far everything I'd heard this woman say was based in reality—a little out of sequence in many instances, but nevertheless real. Along with her sharp wit Patience was indeed a fine-looking woman, of regal bearing. Just as noticeable was the strength and pride reflected in her straight spine and in the tilt of her chin. Were it not for the occasional drop in her color and the accompanying dullness in the eyes, one would never suspect her heart was less than robust. She did, of course, become easily winded on the stairs, but that was normal in those past their prime. Thank heaven her condition was far from critical, and while she didn't really need an around-the-clock nurse, anything I could do for this dear woman was gratifying.

She and I were just finishing with the plants when Kalani came in carrying the tray of afternoon refreshments. The delicate salmon-filled tea sandwiches whetted my appetite. A glance at the pulp-laden beverage in the tall crystal pitcher produced the opposite reaction. Patience eyed the pinkish liquid with delight. "Ah, my favorite fruit punch."

Favorite? My mouth involuntarily puckered. Wasn't that the word Drew had used to describe his aunt's cherished morning tea? The sea-green brew that smelled of unripened limes? There was no aroma wafting up from this drink. Still, I viewed it warily.

Kalani set the tray down on the table before the wicker settee. As she straightened she asked politely, "Shall I pour, Miss Phillips?"

Once again Patience dismissed the Hawaiian housekeeper with a brusque wave of the hand and a tone that matched. "Rachel will do the honors."

Kalani's lips thinned, and when she turned and left the solarium without even looking in my direction, I had the sinking feeling she somehow blamed me for the older woman's coolness. As far as I recalled, I hadn't said or done anything that might have given such an impression. And I certainly could not usurp the housekeeper's position in this house, if that was of concern to her, especially when I wasn't truly an employee. Nor was I Drew's intended, which might afford me at least a small say in the running of this household.

Thoughtful, I lifted the pitcher and filled two etched glasses. Patience sipped from hers the minute I handed it over. "Have a taste, dear," she urged, noting my hesitation.

My throat closed in automatic protest, and I sternly chided myself for prejudging as I took a small sip. Relief swept through me and I said in surprise, "This is delicious."

Patience beamed. "I knew you'd like it," she said with confidence. "This is one of the kahuna's special recipes. The main ingredient is guava. My nephews are partial to the fruit, but not in punches. Actually, they don't like fruit drinks of any kind. Their loss." She laughed, and I inclined my head in agreement.

As we enjoyed the refreshments, and Patience talked at length about the kahuna and his skill with herbs and extracts, my mind wandered back to the pretty Hawaiian housekeeper. I hadn't noticed any dissension between her and Patience on my first day in this house. But then I'd been exhausted from the long voyage and so caught up in settling in with Drew and the family that any friction between the women might have escaped me. What had been evident, though, and remained clear in my mind was Kalani's look of displeasure upon my arrival here and the smugness she had displayed on that day. Was she typically complacent? If so, what had dashed that characteristic and caused it to be replaced by the sudden but much-welcomed warming toward me?

Later that afternoon, as I wandered the beach alone, I once again pondered the change in Kalani and wondered if Patience had always been curt with her. The older woman wasn't that way with the other servants, though she was a trifle condescending. Drew was much the same with them. For all I knew this was the way of the wealthy, a means by which to keep the help in their place. As for his aloof twin, I didn't see enough of Jordan, fortunately, to form an opinion in regard to him and the servants. The only incident that stood out in my mind was the glance I'd caught him exchanging with Kalani and her returned gleam of appreciation. For what? I pondered for at least the tenth time. Then irritation loomed and I firmly reminded myself that the interactions between Jordan and the housekeeper were none of my business.

Lips compressed, I stopped dead. As I whirled to retrace my steps in the windswept sand, a cottage well back in a sheltered cove captured the corner of my eye. I turned and focused on the charming dwelling, constructed of wood and stone. There were windows in abundance to admit the tropical sun, and in the yard neat flower beds yielded to lawns that ringed palms and other native trees. Beyond was the encroaching jungle, from which came the faint lilting sound of birds that intermingled with the gentle trade wind blowing in from the sea. There wasn't a soul about the premises. Still, it was obvious from the well-kept appearance that someone lived there.

Odd I hadn't seen this place on one of my other afternoon strolls along the water's edge, I thought. But a glance down the beach confirmed I'd walked well past my usual turning-back point, which was just beyond the family dock that jutted a good two hundred feet into the Pacific Ocean. Actually, from the lay of the land in the bend of the cove, the cottage wasn't all that far from the Phillips home. Might this be where the family first settled back in the twenties? The house Patience and Drew had told me about?

Over dinner I mentioned the cottage. "Oh yes," Patience said, "that's where my family and I lived for many years. Very happily," she added on a wistful sigh. "Sometimes I almost wish my father hadn't come into his inheritance and built this bigger place."

"Now, Aunt Patience," Drew said with a teasing laugh, "you know you love it here."

"Ah, yes," she agreed, her tone still wistful. "But from time to time I miss the coziness of the cottage."

In truth it was a little difficult for me to imagine this grand lady of luxury living in a home that wasn't any larger than the one I'd grown up in. But the fact that she hadn't always had the best of everything made me feel even closer to her.

"I doubt you would find it cozy anymore. And without the inheritance there would be no family business," Drew reminded her.

Patience nodded and offered a reminder of her own. "Without it I could have fulfilled my dream to teach."

"In many respects we might have been better off without the corporation," Jordan said with a touch of bitterness.

His twin viewed him sharply, as if the negative comment had been targeted solely at him. When Drew responded, his tone was defensive. "You more than I would miss it."

"I'd miss the day-to-day business dealings," Jordan admitted. "But the other—" He broke off at the rustle of gray silk as his aunt shifted in her chair.

Why did she suddenly look so uncomfortable? And what had Jordan meant by "the other"?

"We've strayed from the subject," Patience said flatly. "Now, what were we talking about, dear?" she asked me.

"The cottage in the cove," I replied absently, my thoughts still on the brief crackle of tension among the Phillipses. Clearly it had something to do with the business and, further back yet, the inheritance. But what? "I believe you said your former house-keeper now lives in the cottage." I glanced at the older woman.

She lifted a bite of succulent roasted pork. "Yes, Mrs. Malo."

"I take it you haven't met her yet, Rachel." Jordan regarded me over the rim of his water glass.

"No," I told him. I hadn't intended for my attention to linger, any more than he probably had. But his eyes had darkened in a way that quickened my pulse. In less than a breath the heady current once again flowed between us and our gazes fused. Try as I might, I could not stem the evocative flutterings, the feeling that a whisper of warm breath was strumming every sensitive nerve ending within me. Little flames ignited in Jordan's eyes. I wasn't the only one with fire in the veins. On that realization my heart leaped out of rhythm and my brain refused to focus on anything but the profound ache he kindled for some mysterious satisfaction. I prayed he couldn't read my thoughts, couldn't perceive the need I didn't fully understand. And I almost slumped in my chair in pure relief when Jordan blinked, forcing himself and me back to reality. I was free of his encompassing power, yet strangely a deep inner part of me felt empty. Most of all, though, I was grateful those mesmerizing moments had gone unnoticed by Drew and his aunt, who had turned their full attention to the meal.

Jordan cleared his throat, then said in an amazingly level voice, "You must get my brother to introduce you to Mrs. Malo, Rachel. You'd like her, everyone does."

An instant of surprise coursed through me. Regardless of the heat we inspired in each other, I hadn't expected Jordan to suggest anything that might make me feel welcome in this home. I swallowed then somehow I, too, managed an even tone. "I'd like to meet her."

Drew hesitated, as if we had just thrown him an unpalatable challenge. "Of course," he said slowly. "I'll take you around to the cottage one day soon, Rachel."

After dinner, as he and I strolled the lava-stone walk in the moonlit rear garden, I said, "You didn't seem eager to introduce me to Mrs. Malo. Is there a problem, Drew?"

He lifted his shoulders in a noncommittal shrug. "Certainly not, she's a fine woman, served our family well for many years."

"I understood she helped raise you and Jordan."

"Yes, that's true, and I have great respect for her. But there are so many people I want you to meet, Rachel. I hardly know where to start. I think the best way would be through small dinner parties here. Frankly, I prefer luaus and barbecues. But Aunt Patience leans to the more formal and intimate gatherings. Nowadays I suppose they're less tiring for her."

"Does she get away from the house much?" I looked down at the freshly cultivated rose bed on my right. Moonglow glistened on the riot of delicate blooms that perfumed the mild evening air.

"Lately just to Sunday church services. My aunt retired from her charitable work a few months ago. More recently she's taken to overseeing the corporation from here, as best she can."

"What about her friends? I haven't seen any come to visit."

Drew inhaled a long breath. "I'm afraid most of them have passed on. The others don't get out any more than she does. But now, my darling, you've come into her life." He ran a caressing hand over my cheek. "She delights in you, as I knew she would. And it's easy to see you're fond of her."

"Yes, very," I admitted, taking comfort in the warmth of his touch. In the past, when Drew had stood this close, I'd leaned near, savoring his strength. Now that urge seemed but a sweet memory.

Drew lifted my chin and gazed tenderly into my eyes. "I know Aunt Patience wants you in the family almost as much as I do, Rachel. Marry me," he implored, after a long kiss, "and make us all happy."

The side of me that longed for home and family begged me to accept, but my practical side stubbornly insisted I must not wed for those reasons alone. I moved apologetically in his embrace. "I'm sorry, Drew," I murmured the words he'd heard before, "but I still need more time."

I felt his chest tighten with disappointment. A second later that emotion colored his tone. "Say you'll have an answer for me soon, Rachel."

In all fairness to Drew I knew I must reach a decision in the near future. "I promise," I told him, then thanked him for his understanding with a gentle hug. In one respect Drew let the subject of marriage rest, in another he pressed it from the angle of introducing me to his social circle. He was confident I would fit into his aristocratic world, and I was flattered that he wanted me at his side. But I wasn't so sure that I, the former tomboy of modest means, would truly blend in. Maybe the affluent lifestyle wouldn't even be attractive to me. Yes, I enjoyed being in this lavish home, complete with servants, but this was also a novelty, and I'd learned long ago that the appeal of novelties eventually faded. In the end I agreed to Drew's plans for dinner parties. After all, I'd journeyed thousands of miles to come to know him in his element. Maybe in the process my fondness for him would deepen.

As we continued to wander the symmetrically laid-out garden, I listened with rapt interest as Drew talked at length about the social climate on this enchanted isle. Then I excused myself to help ready his aunt for bed. Drew saw me up to the third floor. On the landing he once again took me in his arms. He bade me good night with another long kiss, then murmured, "I'll see you at breakfast, my sweet Rachel. Sleep well."

I wished him the same and turned away. At Patience's door I glanced over my shoulder. Drew had moved up the long hall and was crossing the threshold of the third room on the right, which afforded him an ocean view. Was that the room he'd shared with Claudia? I wondered, returning my attention to his aunt's door. At my tap she called for me to enter. I twisted the china knob and stepped in. The bedside lamps were aglow and more illumination fell through the arch of the adjoining sitting room. By now I knew that at this hour Patience was finishing with her nightly reading of the Bible. As I moved to the arch she was replacing the Good Book on its stand. "Did I tell you this was my father's Bible, Rachel?" She looked around at me.

I shook my head. "It must hold many memories."

"Indeed it does." She sighed. "So often lately I find myself wishing I could return to my youth. Wishing I could sit beside my mother in the front pew of Father's church and listen to his sermons again. He was a dynamic speaker, truly inspiring. I don't think I ever missed one of his sermons. Oh, he had his faults, we all do. But in the overall my father was a good, God-

fearing man. I hope you'll join my nephews and me for Sunday
services, Rachel," she said with a quickness that suggested the
thought had suddenly struck her and she feared it might slip
away just as rapidly. "We didn't go last Sunday because you'd
just arrived and needed to get your bearings."

"I'd like to attend," I said softly. Before we left the sitting
room, Patience showed me the beautiful featherwork lei she'd
told me about earlier in the day. A few moments later, as I
helped her into a fine lawn nightdress that buttoned to the throat,
I mentioned the dinner parties Drew had suggested.

She smiled and responded in wholehearted approval. "Splendid idea. He and I can work out the arrangements." It wasn't until she was in bed that Patience brought up the sedative. "I'm
afraid I'm just too restless to sleep without it, dear."

I offered an alternative. "When I'm restless, I curl up with a
good novel."

"Ah, yes, I used to do the same. It was very relaxing," she admitted. "But nowadays reading in bed is uncomfortable for me."

"I'd be happy to read to you."

"How sweet of you, dear. But . . ." Her words trailed off.

"I'm about to begin Jane Austen's *Northanger Abbey*," I went
on enthusiastically. "But of course you can choose one of your
favorite authors."

Patience brightened. "My, but we do think alike, Rachel.
Austen is also one of my favorites, as is Catherine, her heroine
in that novel. It's been years since I last enjoyed that story."

"We can enjoy it together, if you'd like. It'll only take me a
moment to fetch the book from my room."

"That is a tempting offer." She hesitated. "You truly don't
mind indulging an old woman?"

I laid a gentle hand over hers. "Indulging you would be a
pleasure, Patience." The delight that shone in her pale blue eyes
warmed my heart. I propped her comfortably in the bed, then
told her I'd be right back with the novel.

Before I left her quarters, I closed the windows against the
breeze that had picked up. In my room I crossed to the billowing
curtains at my windows. As I pulled down one after the other I
glimpsed a horse and rider moving toward the head of the drive.
The silvery moonlight clearly identified the man as one of the
twins, garbed in casual clothes and his hat pulled low. I'd seen

Drew enter his room. However, that didn't mean he was still there. As for Jordan I had no idea where he'd disappeared to after dinner.

Brows knitted, I turned slowly, went to the night table, and picked up the leather-bound volume. As I stepped back into Patience's suite something at my hemline caught her attention. "Is that a stain on your skirt, Rachel?" she asked from the bed.

I stopped and looked at the flounce on my blue cambric. "Oh dear, I'm afraid so. I must have brushed against something in the garden." I bent and flicked a hand at the egg-shaped spot, but not even a speck of the smudge dislodged. "I hope the stain hasn't permanently set." A shiver slithered down my spine and I forced out the visions of the blood-spattered clothes I'd lost to the war.

"Ring for a maid," Patience graciously suggested. "Have her take the dress directly down to the laundry and tend to it."

Again I hated to trouble anyone at bedtime. So I said, "Thank you, but I'll take care of it myself after we finish with the reading. A few more minutes probably won't matter."

"Maybe not. There's a bottle of cleaning compound in one of the washroom cabinets. Give it a try, dear, it works wonders."

I nodded appreciation, then pulled up a chair to the bedside and turned to page one of *Northanger Abbey*. By the time I reached the end of the first chapter, Patience's eyes were drooping and her breathing had deepened. Halfway into the next chapter she was asleep. I remained at her side until I was certain she'd drifted into sound slumber. Then I extinguished the flames in the lamps, tiptoed back through the connecting door, and put aside the book.

For a long moment I stared at the nightdress and wrapper that had been laid out, then rejected the notion of changing into them before heading down to the laundry. If Jordan was home, it wasn't likely he would come upon me there. Nevertheless, I wasn't going to take even the speck of a chance on being caught in nightclothes again. On that resolve I descended the two flights to the washroom at the rear of the entrance floor and searched out the bottle of cleaning compound. As I sponged the obstinate stain on my skirt with the corner of a small cloth, my thoughts strayed to the rider on the drive. Which one of the twins had I seen? And where had he gone?

My throat constricted as fumes from the strong cleaning solution assaulted my nostrils and I sneezed. Above the sound was another, which floated in through the open window. I listened. Muted pounding. From where? I wondered, and glanced out at the yard. The breeze had dropped and the clouds that now over-shadowed the moon hid the trees and shrubbery from my view. I was about to turn away when a trace of light from the room ad-joining the carriage house caught my attention. Someone was in there. Who? And doing what at this late hour?

Those questions prowled in my mind as I returned to sponging my skirt. To my relief the cleaning compound lived up to Pa-tience's praise and my dress wasn't ruined as I'd feared. With so few garments left in my wardrobe, I couldn't afford to lose an-other. And I certainly did not have the funds to "shop," as Drew suggested. Oh, maybe one or two new dresses, especially some-thing appropriate for formal dinners.

The pounding from beyond the washroom window gave way to a fainter, unidentifiable noise. Again I listened, intently. Grat-ing. No, it was the sound of a saw being drawn through wood. This time curiosity got the best of me, as it often did. And after I straightened my skirt, I went outside. Instantly I was swallowed up in the blackness of night. The air was close and thick with the smell of imminent rain. Good sense told me to mind my own business and go straight up to bed. But the continued sawing drew me like a magnet. Carefully I made my way over the lava-stone walk to the light spilling through the panes.

At the window I pulled up short. The sawing stopped. Was that a coincidence, or had someone heard me approaching? The latter wasn't likely, I reassured myself, for my steps had been quiet. In the distance a crack of lightning rent the sky, and a horse in the adjacent carriage house whinnied nervously at the roll of thunder that shook the ground.

Inhaling a deep breath, I leaned forward and peered in the window. Lantern glow beyond revealed a shop, with tools and workbenches all about. In the center of the wooden floor was a pair of sawhorses, upon them the hull of a canoe in the initial stage of construction. A breath caught in my throat as a tall, broad-shouldered man stepped from a darkened corner. The other twin! He, too, was casually dressed. As my gaze swept over him I noted the collar of his linen shirt was open at the throat and his sleeves were rolled up, exposing strong, suntanned arms. His slim waist was accentuated by a belt with a silver buckle and his form-fitting trousers tapered to leather boots. But what really caught and held my gaze was the intent expression on his handsome face and the lock of dark hair that had fallen over his brow, emphasizing the inky lashes that shadowed his clear eyes and well-sculpted features. Even before I remembered Jordan was the twin who built canoes, the accelerated beat of my heart had identified him in my mind. What was it about Jordan Phillips that triggered the instant recognition, the unseen magnetism that melted my insides?

Briefly Jordan moved back into the dark corner, then stepped forward again, carrying a long, smoothly planed board. He fitted it to the hull of the canoe, and I watched with keen interest as he made critical measurements. For as long as I could remember, I'd admired those skilled with their hands, people blessed with the ability to fashion something of worth from nothing. Maybe that was because I hadn't even one scintilla of such creativity, at least none that had as yet revealed itself to me.

As I continued to observe Jordan I became increasingly aware of how precise he was and of the pride he radiated in this endeavor. If he even partially blamed himself for the death of the two women, as his brother did, would Jordan continue to make canoes? Or would he have bitterly turned his back on them?

Thunder rumbled again, loud and low. I started, and stepped back in dismay as reality reclaimed my senses. What on earth was I doing standing in the dark, secretly staring in the window at this man? Admittedly I had more than my share of faults, but one of them was not snooping. Squaring my shoulders, I straightened and retreated to the house. By the time I reached my room, rain was pounding down. Concerned it might have awakened Patience, I looked in on her and was relieved to see she was still asleep.

Unfortunately sleep did not come easily to me and all because of the mystifying attraction for Jordan. Why, he and I weren't even friends. Yet everything about him was vivid in my mind, his gestures, the tilt of his head, and the inflections in his tone. There were many moods to him, who was so different from easygoing Drew.

I tossed onto my back and stared into the darkness. Obviously Drew had been the twin on the drive tonight, just as he'd been on my first evening in this house when Jordan muttered that his brother had gone into town. Drew might even have been the rider I'd spotted returning home on the night Jordan came upon me in the library. Had Drew once again gone to town? If so, for what reason? And why had he been so defensive over his twin's comment that the family might have been better off without the corporation? Which also meant without the inheritance?

I fell asleep with those questions circling my brain, and for the first time since before the war bad dreams did not loom and shake me awake. Instead there were visions of Jordan, romantic and provocative. In their own way they were as disturbing as the nightmares. Maybe, I thought as I listened to the rain still pelting the roof, my fondness for Drew wasn't deepening because of my unwanted attraction for his brother. It had nothing whatsoever to do with Drew's failure to promptly inform me of his marriage.

When I awakened in the morning, the only really bright spot that lifted my spirits above the dreary weather was the fact that Patience had slept soundly all night. "The reading relaxed me more than I had thought possible," she confessed cheerfully. "I haven't felt this rested in years." The next three nights were just as peaceful for the older woman. However, on one occasion she did awaken in the early hours of morning and asked me to fix her a headache powder. I obliged without hesitation, for the powder was mild compared with the sedative. And in less than an hour she was back to sleep.

It was a pleasure to care for Patience and we both delighted in the comfortable pattern we had fallen into. Each morning after breakfast we spent a little time together, generally in the solarium. Then there was our late-afternoon tea and last of all the treasured bedtime reading. "My aunt's spirits seem much higher these days," Drew said happily to me one evening. "Your friendship and expert care have done wonders for her, Rachel. And thank you, my darling, for turning her away from the sedatives."

"I hope I truly have," I said, appreciative of his compliments. "It may be too soon to know for certain."

Even Jordan, who continued to keep his comments to me at a minimum, had offhandedly remarked that Patience appeared more relaxed. I'd acknowledged his statement with a nod of agreement. But the change in her I'd noticed the most was the gradual softening toward Kalani. Oh, there was still a bit of a strain between the women, and whatever lay at its base still eluded me. Heaven knew the pretty housekeeper went out of her way to please her employer and was clearly competent. Did Patience's more agreeable attitude toward Kalani stem from the restful nights of late, or from something else? I wondered.

Several days of torrential rain came and went, and on one mild evening Drew said to me over dinner, "I plan to come home early tomorrow, Rachel. Can you meet me on the beach in the late afternoon, and we'll spend a little time alone?"

The narrowing of Jordan's eyes grimly reminded me of his anger over Drew's early closing of the office on the day of my arrival. "I can meet you," I said hesitantly. "But you know how I hate to intrude on your business hours. Maybe—"

Drew held up a silencing hand and tried to reassure me with the words I'd heard from him before: "Not to worry, my sweet."

Jordan cleared his throat and looked as if he were about to level a retort. But a glance at his aunt's happy face apparently held him in check.

"Now, if Aunt Patience can spare you from tea tomorrow, Rachel," Drew went on, seemingly oblivious to his brother's annoyance, "you and I could have refreshments together, sort of a picnic." The bright smile he flashed at the older woman ignited an indulgent gleam in her pale blue eyes.

"For you, Drew," she said, "I can spare Rachel from tea."

I couldn't deny that the prospect of being out of doors again and on the beach sounded wonderful. Still, in the face of Jordan's anger, it was impossible for me to accept Drew's invitation with bubbling enthusiasm. But then he had enough for both of us.

Drew turned his smile on me. "I'll stop by the kitchen first thing in the morning, Rachel, and instruct the cook to prepare a special hamper for our afternoon outing. Would four o'clock tomorrow be convenient for you?"

"Yes."

"Wonderful. I'll meet you at our favorite spot."

Actually, it was Drew's favorite spot. But it was nice and I voiced agreement.

Shortly after 3:30 on the following afternoon I selected a book from the library and picked up the hamper waiting in the kitchen and a blanket to sit upon. Then I wandered down to the beach.

The place I favored was near the dock, where I could enjoy the clear view of Molokai and Lanai across the channel. But Drew preferred the shelter of the jutting, ragged plateau nearer the house. "The sea sweeps in closer here," he had told me the first time we'd sat there together, "and that gives me such a peaceful feeling."

This day itself was peaceful and gloriously sunny, with puffy white clouds sailing the azure sky. The breeze was light and the frothy surf gently lapping. I spread the blanket at the base of the plateau, rising several feet above my head, then sat down. Tendrils of blond hair blew about my face, and I pushed them beneath my wide-brimmed straw bonnet.

For several minutes I stared dreamily at the waves, one after the other rolling closer before breaking on the sand. This place was indeed serene and particularly warm against the backdrop of the plateau. Between the sun and the salty air my mouth quickly dried, and I reached for the hamper. Packed within were tea sandwiches, delicate pastries, a bottle of wine for Drew, and a container of punch for me. Lifting it, I poured a glass of the cool fruit drink. The taste was decidedly different, a little tart. Still, delicious and refreshing. Another one of the kahuna's special blends, I guessed, smiling to myself. As I sipped more of the exotic beverage I glanced up the beach. No Drew, yet. But my pendant watch told me it wasn't quite four o'clock.

My skirts billowed, and I tucked them under my legs, then I opened the book by Tennyson and lost myself in a succession of familiar poems as I slowly finished the glass of punch. The sound of the surf was lulling and the sun a soothing balm on my body. I couldn't remember when I'd last been this relaxed. It was a wonderful feeling after last night and the sleep I'd lost when the horrid nightmares once more shook me awake. As I read lyric after lyric my eyelids grew heavy and it became a struggle to keep them from closing. As yawns overcame me I stretched and put aside the book. Then drowsily I removed my bonnet and covered my face with it as I lay back on the blanket. If I dozed off, no harm, I told myself. Drew would be along soon. The soft breeze was caressing and the sound of the sea seemed distant and yet strangely louder as all thoughts eased from my mind and I was drawn into the dark and silent vacuum of dreamless slumber.

I don't know how long I'd been asleep when something cool

slapped against my flesh. Startled, my eyelids fluttered open. My clothes were sodden weights and there was a strange pulling sensation beneath me. Whatever I was lying upon was being sucked away and I felt as if I were floating with it. Floating peacefully. Bobbing. To where? My mind was mired in fog. I couldn't gather thoughts, or even move my limbs. My teeth chattered. Cold, cold. Freezing. Groggily I forced open my eyes. Involuntarily they reclosed. But not against the sun, for all I'd glimpsed was a speck of gray. Dusk? Again I opened my eyes. Through wet lashes I glimpsed more gray, only in the water undulating all about me. The sea! Tide in! Panic soared. Heavy spray splashed over face. Choking. Salty. Terror jerked the words up in my brain, but my body remained paralyzed. And a painful scream stuck in my throat at the huge wave that loomed, then crushed down on me.

chapter 9

I WAS SUFFOCATING beneath the heavy weight of the water, choking, gagging. My senses spun and every fiber within me was jolted by the panic and terror that shot life back into my limbs. My hands went up, flailing, and I kicked my legs against the suction of the receding wave. I was tumbling as it dragged me along, my skirts a plastered vise about my body, my shoes bricks. The water wasn't dangerously deep . . . yet. But inevitably more waves were building. Another sharp burst of terror doubled my strength and I kicked and clawed, painfully regaining a spot on the beach. As I fell exhausted in the sand, gasping, a roller thundered at my feet and another rush of horror propelled me to struggle even further forward. My lungs felt as if they were about to burst from exertion and my throat burned as I coughed up salty water.

For an instant blackness encompassed my brain and I shook my head. I had to stay conscious, had to get away from this place before the rising tide claimed me. Trembling uncontrollably, I pushed myself up and stumbled to my feet. The foamy sea lapped just inches from my dripping skirts and the plateau rose sharply behind me. Dizzy, I glanced around in the rapidly falling dusk, trying to orient myself. As I turned to head up the beach and back onto the path to the house, another boiling wave sailed toward me. Before I could move, it slammed against my legs, almost buckling my knees, and struck the plateau. The water shot up its rugged face, looped, then came down in a solid wall over me. If I hadn't braced against the blinding onslaught, I would have been knocked flat. Instinctively I dug in my heels and summoned every ounce of strength I possessed to maintain balance against the treacherous pull that threatened to drag me out to sea.

As the breaker ebbed I shoved back my hair, which had been jarred loose from its pins and now fell over my face like a limp rag mop. Ahead of me on the water my straw bonnet bobbed and the items I'd carried from the house were nowhere in sight. I gulped, then threw another look up the beach. My lips parted and I nearly cried in relief. Drew! He was coming my way. Was that shock in his face? What he saw in mine was pure panic. He paused. My heart lurched on a burst of hysteria. Wasn't he going to lend me a hand? Instinctively a shout for help rose in my throat, but I swallowed the words, grateful, when Drew called, "Rachel," and ran forward.

Shakily, I tugged up my sodden skirts and slogged toward him. As the distance between us closed, his expression changed to one I could not read. A sharp blast of wind set my teeth chattering anew and all the horror sped back with spine-tingling clarity. Anger flared. Why hadn't Drew appeared on the beach at four o'clock, the hour he'd chosen? The sun but an orange crescent on the horizon clearly conveyed that it was well past that time. "Where have you been?" I snapped as Drew stopped and bundled me in his coat. "Or was leaving me to the rising tide another one of your jokes, like my landing at Maui? And not telling me you're a twin?" The minute those words were out I knew the gripping terror had made me momentarily unreasonable. Yes, Drew was late for our outing. But it wasn't his fault I'd fallen asleep on the sand.

My eyes widened, for the hardening masculine jaw told me this was not the twin I had expected to see on the beach. "I don't play jokes," Jordan retaliated with anger of his own, and hurried me to safer ground. "How in the devil did you get yourself into this ridiculous situation, Rachel?" He pulled up short and eyed me as if I weren't particularly bright.

"Ridiculous?" I blurted past the soreness in my throat. "I almost drowned." But what did he really care? If all he'd seen was the wall of water that drenched me, then I had been a laughable sight. For that matter I still was, dripping before him. The flush of embarrassment came to my face and my sense of dignity thudded to my toes. Why did it always suffer with this man? Chin high, I stepped past Jordan. The clinging shreds of my self-esteem were sucked into the sand when my soggy shoes made horrid squishing sounds and his coat flapped about my knees. I winced and did not look back. If he was chuckling to himself, I didn't wish to know. All I wanted was for him to disappear.

But Jordan caught up with me and placed a supporting hand beneath my elbow. "You're still unsteady on your feet," he said, and the thoughtful gesture eased my misery. "What did you mean, you almost drowned?" he questioned gravely as we moved along the beach.

Did he care about me after all? I wondered. But a glance at the grim set of his mouth gave rise to the probability that my harrowing experience had reminded him of Ellen and Claudia and their tragic deaths in the ocean. "I was caught by the waves." My quiet tone softened his expression.

"I'm sorry," he said. "Couldn't you tell the tide was coming in?"

"Yes, but I didn't know it came up that high."

Jordan hesitated, then remarked with the caution of one trying not to belittle. "If you were watching the tide, then the danger must have been evident."

"It would have been, except . . ."

"Except what?" He paused and stared searchingly into my face.

My mouth dried and my cheeks felt flushed again, from the renewal of embarrassment, I supposed. "I fell asleep," I admitted, sheepish.

"Well, you certainly picked the wrong time and place to nap," he censured mildly. From his trouser pocket Jordan withdrew a handkerchief and dabbed at the water on my face. How could I be chilled to the bone from the wet clothes and yet at the same time be uncomfortably hot?

I swallowed then said in swift defense as we continued forward, "I was expecting Drew to come right along. But as you can see, he didn't show up. Thank God you did. I'm not sure I would have made it to safety on my own."

"Yes, thank God."

The hint of resentment that filtered into Jordan's voice set my teeth on edge. Was he sorry he'd come along just in time to help me? "Do you know where Drew is?" I asked, blotting out the distressing thought.

The hand at my elbow tensed briefly. "I assumed he was with you."

"He left the office early, then?" I pressed as I was assisted up the slight incline to the path.

"Yes," he said, then muttered more to himself than to me, "as he often does."

Often? I had meant to voice the word, but the dulling fog swirled back into my brain and all thoughts vanished. Light-headed, I stopped and pressed fingers to my temple.

Jordan halted beside me on the path. "Are you going to be all right, Rachel?"

"I'm a little dizzy."

"Probably from the scare."

"And all the water I swallowed." My throat still burned and my mouth tasted of salt. "But I'll be fine." My attempt at reassurance failed as I swayed and clutched his shirt sleeve. Through all the whirling that flung bright colors before my eyes I felt myself being scooped up in strong arms. The next thing I knew my head was against Jordan's chest. "What are you doing?" I protested in a voice that equaled the weakness in my body.

"Taking you back to the house." He swung about and continued up the tree-lined path.

"I can walk."

"That's not how it looked to me."

"But I'm getting you all wet." How inane that sounded, yet at the moment I couldn't seem to grasp even one intelligent thought. I'd never felt so distanced from myself or so lethargic.

"I'll dry out," Jordan said simply, and there was something soothing about his warm breath in my sodden hair. "First we have to get you out of these clothes and into a hot tub."

We? My senses spun crazily. Surely Jordan hadn't meant that he was going to help me from my clothes. No, of course not, of course not. Those words zigzagged in my mind, and I felt a shocking tug of disappointment. Had all good reason left my head? If so, then I didn't want to know if it was from the fright in the ocean, or from the pure heat of this virile man. With scarcely a pause in his stride Jordan carried me up the front steps, then the two long flights to my room, and he wasn't even winded.

As he set me down on the bed, though, I felt his pulse quicken and heard the catch in his breath. His handsome face was breath-suspendingly near, his masculine scent tantalizing. The world tilted as our eyes met and held. The moment was fleeting, little more than a second, yet the undercurrents of desire surmounting my lethargy seemed timeless. Jordan's gaze dropped to my mouth and lingered. Then he moistened his full lips and spoke, but the surging in my ears deafened me to all other sounds. What was he saying? I strained for the words, but all I caught as he slowly straightened was the name Kalani. Then Jordan pulled the bell rope and I knew he was summoning the housekeeper to help me undress. That's probably what he'd been trying to tell me, I thought vaguely as I struggled against the impulse to lie back and close my eyes. How could I still be sleepy? The cool ocean should have snapped me wide-awake. The water and the horror, actually. A shiver lightning-bolted down my spine.

Jordan tilted his dark head and regarded me with doubt. "Are you sure you're going to be all right, Rachel?"

"Yes," I murmured, though how could I really be certain? I'd never felt this way before.

"There's something about your eyes."

"Oh?" I gulped. "Red from the water, you mean?"

"No." He hesitated. "More like someone who has had too much drink."

"I don't imbibe," I told him stiffly.

"I hadn't meant to imply you do. Disoriented," he said abruptly as the word struck him. "That's how you look."

"Well, of course, I almost drowned." The moment that grim reminder was out I was sorry, for once again what appeared the pain of remembrance tightened his features. I inhaled a deep breath, then softened my tone. "If you don't mind, I'd like to be alone."

"Certainly, though Kalani should be right along."

"That's fine," I returned, then thanked Jordan for his concern and for seeing me safely back to the house. The minute he exited, I inched off the bed before I soaked through the expensive coverlet. The room swam before my eyes and I gripped the bedpost until my vision cleared. My legs were still wobbly and my energy drained. Even Jordan's coat seemed heavier. The brown cashmere had sopped up moisture from my drenched clothes, but not enough to weight my shoulders.

As I shrugged out of the coat and draped it over a chair to dry, I distractedly wondered what had brought him to the beach. Jordan instead of Drew? That question floated aimlessly away as Kalani entered and her dark eyes widened at the sight of me. And I was a sight. A glance in the mirror confirmed that truth. My blond hair was a twisted, stringy mass. Frayed hemp looked better, I told myself, and blushed when I saw how my dress clung to every curve of my body, every curve Jordan had now seen. Just the thought of facing him again deepened the crimson stains in my cheeks. "Mr. Jordan told me what happened." Regret touched Kalani's delicate features. "You must have been terribly frightened, miss. Here, let me help you out of those wet clothes. Hot water is on the way for a bath."

I expressed appreciation, and in what seemed no time at all I was in my wrapper and Kalani was adding fragrant ginger to the tub that had been readied. Every move I'd made was an effort and I could hardly remember going through the motions of undressing. As the housekeeper helped me into the porcelain tub, she said, "Mr. Drew came home around three."

My lips parted. "That's before I went down to the beach."

Kalani nodded. "He was in his study for a while. Then just as he was about to go down and meet you, a message came for him and he was unexpectedly called away to one of the grogshops."

I splashed warm water over my face, then frowned up at the other woman. "He could have at least let me know," I grumbled.

She inclined her head in silent agreement. "I assumed he was going to find you and explain before leaving. Maybe he just didn't have the time."

"He could have sent someone."

"True," she murmured. "And we can all we grateful you weren't harmed."

I looked up at her in surprise. Did Kalani's concern mean her resentment toward me, an outsider, was truly fading? She placed a fresh towel beside the tub, then left me to soak while she took my clothes down to the laundry. Tipping back my head, I tried to relax, but the memory of Drew's lack of consideration for me intensified the strain on my nerves. Heaven knew his list of thoughtless acts was growing. This was not the Drew I'd known on the mainland. And just how much time did he give to the grogshops, the unsavory places that catered to men's vices? In truth it was hard to understand how the family of missionaries, bent on saving souls, was now offering them up to the devil.

By the time I left the tub, dressed, and allowed a maid to dry and refashion my hair, my brain was fairly clear. The lethargy, however, was still upon me. Stretching, I gazed longingly at the bed. It was too early to turn in. More to the point there was no reason I could think of for this sluggishness. Yes, I hadn't slept well on the previous evening, but one restless night had never affected me this way before. In an effort to regain the strength in my legs, I moved about the room. Beyond the windows thick clouds obliterated the moon and the blackness gobbled up the trees. I couldn't see the palm fronds and branches threshing in the stiff trade wind that howled beneath the eaves. Nor could I hear the pounding surf I all too clearly pictured in my mind. Prickling chills crept up my arms and collided at the nape of my neck.

Hugging myself, I swung about and my gaze fell on the masculine coat Kalani had forgotten to take out with my wet garments. For long moments I stared at the coat, my mind reliving the warmth it had offered and the enticing scent of its tall and enigmatic owner. As if drawn by a mystical force, I crossed and ran my hand lightly over the superb cashmere. The texture was soft and warm to the touch. The silk lining, however, was still damp. Strangely the sensitive pads of my fingers felt heat, which radiated to the very heart of me. Startled, I jerked back my hand. Would I ever understand the stirrings that just the thought of Jordan evoked?

A helpless sigh escaped my lips and I slowly went down to the second floor for dinner. The family had already gathered in the dining room. The men rose as I entered, and I bit my lower lip in annoyance as my eyes involuntarily sought out Jordan. The unease I had felt over the thought of facing him again, after the revealing wet garments, dissolved at his look of relief, which I assumed stemmed from seeing me up and about. I acknowledged his continued concern with a tilt of my head. "I'm sorry to be late," I said, and noticed the other twin's brows had knitted at the knowing look that passed between his brother and me. At the moment I didn't care what Drew made of the brief exchange or that the expression I leveled on him was cool.

"We've just come in ourselves," Patience assured me from the head of the table.

"I'm the one who is sorry," Drew said apologetically as he hurried forward to seat me. "I hope you'll forgive me for missing our outing this afternoon, Rachel. My absence was unavoidable."

He sounded sincere. Nevertheless, his lack of consideration still rankled. "I would have appreciated word that you couldn't join me," I told him in a firm yet polite tone and lowered myself into the chair he'd pulled out.

"Drew," Patience scolded, "how rude of you not to have let Rachel know. You were taught better manners."

"Yes," he admitted, then added in self-defense. "An urgent business matter came up and I'm afraid I left in a whirlwind. The thoughtless oversight won't happen again," he promised, and touched my shoulder in gentle assurance. "Am I forgiven, Rachel?"

How many times had he already asked that of me since my arrival? I bit back the question and nodded, though my heart was not in it.

Jordan cleared his throat as if to comment, but no words came from him. What was there for him to say anyway? His brother's breach of etiquette didn't merit a family discussion. And I was the only one to blame for letting myself fall asleep on the beach and placing my life in jeopardy. I was a little surprised, though, that Jordan hadn't mentioned the hair-raising incident. Clearly neither Drew nor Patience gave any indication that they were aware of it. Was Jordan leaving it to me to bring up the subject? If so, then the others would never know, for the more I thought about it, the deeper was my embarrassment. Now that the fright of those moments had subsided and my strength had begun to return, I couldn't deny that Jordan was right. I had gotten myself into a ridiculous situation. But why had that made him angry?

Throughout dinner that question circled in my mind. Later, in the quiet of my room, I focused on Jordan's anger and on the resentment I'd heard come into his voice. I'd assumed both negative emotions had been generated by me. However, if that was true, would he have shown such concern for my well-being?

Frowning, I eyed the chair where I'd draped Jordan's coat. The garment was gone now. One of the maids must have removed it while I was at dinner. Listless, I wandered the room. If I hadn't caused the anger and resentment, then who or what lay behind it? Drew's name had come up several times, and Jordan's mutterings about his brother's frequent early departures from the office had conveyed unmistakable displeasure. How often did Drew really leave early? I wondered. And where did he go? Did Jordan know? What about Patience?

I expelled a long breath and glanced at the bedside clock. It was almost time for my nightly reading with the older woman. I didn't feel up to it this evening, any more than I'd felt up to eating dinner. But I'd forced myself to taste a little of every course lest Drew or his aunt raise questions about my loss of appetite and the whole embarrassing beach incident come to light.

A dull ache throbbed at the back of my head and I seriously considered begging off from the reading. Patience would understand. But might she, I wondered worriedly, revert to the sedatives to help her sleep? As far as I knew, she hadn't touched them since I'd begun reading to her. Not wanting to risk a relapse, I started for the connecting door. With each step the ache in my head intensified. What was the matter with me? Gritting my teeth, I forced down the pain and reminded myself it was minor compared with what could have happened to me in the ocean. On that heart-numbing thought I issued a small prayer of thanks that Jordan had come to my aid. How could I have suspected even for an instant that his hesitation at the water's edge suggested he meant to turn his back on me?

I tapped on the older woman's door. A second later, as I entered, I remembered what Jordan had said about my eyes. I knew they were fine now and that the disorientation he'd seen in them had no doubt stemmed from my fright. On the other hand that look of confusion along with my lingering symptoms were similar to those in many of the patients I'd tended. Only those people had been under treatment with pain-quelling drugs. That certainly was not the case with me. So what was the cause? I hadn't eaten anything that hadn't tasted quite right or might have disagreed with me. I hadn't drunk anything out of the ordinary, either, except— A tremor coursed through my body as my mind fixed on the glass of distinctively different fruit punch I'd had on the beach. I'd hardly finished off the beverage than I'd fallen sound asleep.

chapter 10

THE POSSIBILITY THAT I might have been drugged rocked my
senses and it was difficult for me to concentrate on the reading
with Patience. Throughout the hour I spent with her my eyes
kept lifting to the store of sedatives and potions atop her bureau.
Anyone could come in and help themselves. Anyone could have
doctored the fruit punch I had taken from the kitchen to the
beach, the exotic drink meant for me alone. But who in this
house would have done such a malicious thing? The almost fatal
deed, as it turned out. Although no one could have known it
might come to that. After all, Drew was to have been at my side
and he wouldn't have allowed any harm to befall me. It wasn't
until the last minute that he was called away. By then I'd finished the glass of punch and had doubtless already dozed off.

What would anyone have to gain by drugging me? That question pressed forward and refused to budge as I retired to my
room and climbed into bed. Just to make me ill or simply uncomfortable? I wondered. But who? Jordan? I frowned at the
way his name loomed and shook my head in rapid denial. However, there was no dismissing the fact that he still regarded me
with some distrust. Even so, I couldn't imagine that he would go
to such an extreme. And for what reason, just to discourage me
from marrying his brother?

The scent of jasmine on my lawn nightdress reminded me of
Kalani and the fragrant sachets she'd placed in my bureau draw-
ers on the day of my arrival. I wasn't apt to forget the thoughtful
gesture, especially after her initial coolness toward me. Her
change to friendliness had been so sudden I still wondered if
Drew had talked to her. If he had, then she could be masking the

resentment I'd seen in her face and heard in her voice, resentment that might have seeped out in a spiteful act.

I tossed in bed and emphatically rebelled against the suspicions that were too thin to dwell upon. Believing anyone in this house wished me ill was tantamount to believing Drew had played another of his jokes on me, one that had truly gone astray. Now that he knew my distaste for pranks, I didn't want to think he would dare single me out again as an unsuspecting victim.

I fell asleep considering the more realistic probability that the warm tropic sun and the exotic juices, both still new to me, had conspired with my inadequate rest of the previous night. And it was the combination of all three that had lulled me into the deep slumber, which had left me headachy and sluggish. Thank goodness those symptoms were gone when I awakened in the morning and I felt amazingly revitalized. Even the recurring nightmares of the war hadn't shaken me awake.

The day dawned bright and I moved through it with high energy and spirit. No more exotic drinks beneath the full sun, I silently vowed as Patience and I admired the ocean view from the grand-drawing-room window late that afternoon. "Oh look, a whale." She gestured excitedly. "Watch, it might jump again. There! Isn't that a magnificent sight?"

"Yes, indeed." I stared in fascination. Who would have ever thought I would gape at a whale in pure wonder. It leaped again, and my eyes widened as it spouted water. Even from the distance its grace was evident, and breathtaking.

Patience released a sigh of pure pleasure. "Now that whaling has dropped off and we should be seeing more of them, I must ask one of my nephews to bring my father's telescope down from the attic."

"Nephews?" A protesting masculine voice came to us from the doorway and the mischievous lilt identified the speaker as Drew. "Are you going to put one of us to work, Aunt Patience?"

She glanced around, smiling. "Are you volunteering, dear?"

"Volunteer?" He chuckled. "Sounds like I came in at the wrong time."

Patience pursed her lips to respond. Instead she swung back to the window, as if she'd had a sudden thought or had heard someone call out to her. This was the second time I'd seen this same reaction in her and it was more than a trifle mystifying. Patience's eyes now held a remote look, and when she commented again about the beauty of the whale, her voice had grown strangely distant.

Drew's mouth tightened in a manner that indicated he did not understand his aunt's vagary. But at least, as far as I knew, he'd never made an issue of it, which could upset or embarrass her. He expelled a long breath, then his handsome countenance brightened. Drew turned the familiar devilish gleam on me, the expression that had first drawn me to him. Warm memories swept forward, thoughts and pictures that dissolved the trace of lingering irritation over his lack of consideration for me. And I didn't resist when he crossed and slipped an affectionate arm about my waist. His aunt's attention remained transfixed on the playful antics of the mammal in the ocean beyond the window and she didn't seem to hear her nephew when he spoke: "Is this your first whale sighting, Rachel?"

I nodded, and for the first time in days I felt a resurgence of the contentment and comfort Drew and I had shared on the mainland. Then his brother came in, and just the sweep of his intense eyes triggered deeper emotions.

Over dinner Patience once more brought up the subject of the telescope, then regarded Drew expectantly. "It would be nice to have it set up," he agreed. "I'll have someone take care of it right away."

"No need, I'll do it." Jordan lifted his fork.

The appreciative smile Patience flashed him brought a frown to his twin's face.

"I would have offered, Aunt Patience," Drew said apologetically, as if he and his brother were in competition for her favor, "but you know how unskilled I am at putting things together."

"Yes, I remember." The old woman's jaw set and she viewed Drew with the same accusatory expression I'd seen in my mother whenever I'd tried to wheedle out of a household task. "There is nothing to setting up the telescope. The hardest part will be hauling it down from the attic."

"Really?" He shrugged. "I didn't realize."

He didn't offer to help his brother bring it down, either, I noted. Instead Drew switched the subject to the dinner parties he had suggested in my honor. The mere mention of the social events erased his aunt's touch of annoyance with him over the telescope and I marveled at her animation as the two of them discussed guest lists and family friends Patience hadn't seen in several weeks. From time to time Jordan commented briefly over a name that came up, but for the most part his distant expression conveyed disinterest and he listened in silence. "I do hope the Walkers will be able to attend one of our gatherings," Patience said as we finished the main course of tender roasted turkey and melt-in-the-mouth yams. "The last I'd heard Lawrence was under the weather with gout."

"Just be certain your health doesn't suffer through all of the planning and socializing," Jordan warned her gently.

His concern was heartwarming and Patience regarded him with maternal affection. "No need to worry, dear, Rachel watches over me like the proverbial mother hen. In a subtle, nonsuffocating way," she added gratefully. "I'm beginning to wonder how I ever managed without her."

"I've been wondering the same about myself." Drew turned shining eyes to mine, and my face grew hot beneath the praise. Or was it from the feeling of Jordan's penetrating gaze on me?

"Speaking of health," Patience said as the table was cleared for dessert, "the kahuna will be by tomorrow, Rachel. I hope you'll be home to meet him."

"I'll make it a point to be here," I promised, and Drew shot me the silent reminder not to encourage the "voodoo medicine." How could I encourage what I knew nothing about? The fact that Patience swore by the remedies had piqued my interest. I liked to think I was open-minded enough to accept anything proven beneficial. The thought of her cache of cures brought instant recollection of the beach incident and I inhaled another breath of relief that Jordan apparently still hadn't mentioned it. From the continued silence on the subject I could only assume Kalani hadn't said a word, either. Was that upon Jordan's orders? I wondered. Or was it simply inappropriate for servants to discuss personal happenings in the household? In any case Kalani was unusually quiet this day and I noticed as she brought in the sprigged china tea service edged in gold that her brow was furrowed in obvious worry. Over what I couldn't even begin to hazard a guess. However, I doubted it had anything to do with the strain I'd observed between her and Patience. That tension appeared to have lessened in the past few days.

As the sumptuous three-tiered pineapple cake, lavished with fluffy white icing, was being served, I saw Jordan raise concerned eyes to the attractive housekeeper. Did he know what was troubling her? I bit my inner lip in immediate annoyance. What transpired between them, if anything was, had nothing to do with me. On that stern reminder I turned my attention to the slice of cake that was placed before me. I savored every delectable morsel. What a difference from yesterday and the loss of appetite I'd suffered from the fright.

Shortly after the meal was over, Drew excused himself and descended the stairs to his study to prepare the guest lists for the forthcoming dinner parties. "I'll go up for the telescope," Jordan said as he escorted his aunt and me back to the grand drawing room.

"You needn't do that tonight," Patience told him. "There's no hurry."

He shrugged. "I'm free and this time is as good as any."

"It's so dark in the attic now."

"I'll take a lamp up with me. In which room would you like the telescope, Aunt Patience?"

"Hmm, I hadn't thought that far ahead." She glanced around. "This one offers the best view. But a telescope wouldn't fit in with the formal elegance. As you may recall, my father had it before the window in his study, but now of course it's your study."

"You're welcome to have it in there," Jordan generously offered. "If you can bear my clutter," he added with a teasing smile, one I'd never seen from him before. The lighthearted expression was more characteristic of Drew, and if I hadn't known better, I would have thought I was standing before him. But Drew was downstairs, wasn't he? A thread of suspicion looped, then quickly faded when I remembered Jordan also abhorred twin jokes and wasn't apt to be a willing participant.

Patience waved a jeweled hand. "Thank you, dear, but the study is too confining for me."

"If I may," I ventured, "the solarium also provides an excellent ocean view, and since you spend much of each day in there, Patience . . ."

"Why, yes, what a wonderful suggestion."

Her nephew inclined his dark head in agreement, and as our eyes met, my spiraling senses left no doubt this twin was indeed Jordan. He left us then for the attic, and Patience and I went down and waited for him to join us in the solarium. Within the hour the viewing device was mounted on its wooden tripod before the window Patience and I had selected. Setting it up was an easy task, just as she had flatly told Drew. Why, I could have done it myself. Lugging it down three flights would have been an altogether different matter, however.

Patience ran her fingers lightly over the telescope. "This brings back so many memories of my father and of childhood days." Her eyes had darkened with remembrance and she reminisced for several minutes. Then she thanked her nephew with a heartwarming hug and kiss. This was the first open display of affection I'd seen between them, and their quiet, comfortable-looking closeness turned my mind back to Ohio and my family. Unexpected tears stung behind my eyes, but I did not yield to the rekindled loneliness until I was alone my room. Then the tears spilled over and I indulged in self-pity before I pulled myself together and joined Patience in her quarters. "Would you read to me from the Bible tonight, Rachel," she asked as I helped settle her in the bed.

"I'd be glad to." On my way to lift the Good Book from its stand in the adjoining sitting room I said, "I'll need a new dress or two for the dinner parties, Patience. Can you recommend a local seamstress?"

"Indeed I can. There are several good ones in Lahaina, but the woman who has been doing my gowns for many years is exceptionally clever with her hands."

"That's obvious from your exquisite wardrobe. But my funds are limited." I sat down in the bedside chair and opened the Bible.

"Not to worry," she said, sounding just like Drew each time he'd tried to reassure me about the hours he took from the office to be with me. "Madeleine is as well known and appreciated for accommodating every budget as she is for her skill with the needle. I'll take you in to town and introduce you. We should make the trip soon, though; the first dinner party is only two weeks off. Is tomorrow convenient for you, Rachel?"

"Yes, but I don't wish to trouble you."

"No trouble. It would be a treat to get away from the house for a few hours."

"As long as the outing wouldn't tire you."

"I shouldn't think it would. Having you here has given me new energy, dear." She reached out a grateful hand to mine. "I love my nephews as if they were my sons. But there's nothing like having another woman around to talk with."

How well I knew that from my four years in the war and the dismal fact of often being the only woman in the field hospitals. Not that there had been much time for socializing and in many cases no time at all. Still, just to look up and see another female, a kindred spirit, so to speak, was comforting.

Patience pushed back wisps of white hair that had escaped from the single plait fashioned by her personal maid. "Besides, a trip to town will give me the opportunity to visit the office and assure myself that the business is prospering as well as I've been told."

Did she have some doubt? I wondered, regarding her suddenly thoughtful expression.

"Shall we plan on tomorrow, then?" she asked.

"Yes. Oh, what about the kahuna?"

The old woman clucked her tongue in exasperation. "How forgetful I've become. Of course I must be here, the man travels some distance just to see me. The day after for our outing, is that convenient?"

"Yes, Friday is fine." We exchanged a few more words on the subject, then I turned to the marker in the Bible and began to read. The next forty minutes passed quickly and I gained a tremendous sense of peace from the passages I'd come to know as a small girl.

The serenity stayed with me long after I'd returned to my room and changed into my lawn nightdress. Maybe tonight I'd be free of the haunting war dreams, I prayed, slipping into bed. As I snuggled down I buried all negative thoughts beneath pleasant childhood memories of Eric and Cameron. My brothers had been so bright and handsome and full of life. Despite all their teasing, they had diligently watched over me, and to this day they remained my heroes. In my mind's eye I saw the three of us fishing in the pond behind our house. But what I'd enjoyed even more was riding in the countryside. Cameron had sat a saddle as if he'd been born to it and had never missed an opportunity to goad Eric and me to heated races. We'd seldom won. Even so, the challenge had been exhilarating.

As a yawn overcame me I heard the faint clip-clop of hooves. With horses on my mind, was I just imagining the sound? Or was it real and floating up from the drive? I was too drowsy to lift my head and listen. Real or not, what did it matter, anyway?

As I tugged the lightweight covers to my chin, I determined to ask Drew or Patience if I might borrow a horse from the stables and ride from time to time. What fun it would be to canter along the beach and the sugarcane fields. Drew had told me how the trade winds rattled the towering stalks, then emphasized that they grew so thick it was unwise to venture from the road. "For within seconds," I recalled his words as I drifted off, "one can easily become lost among the canes and never find their way out."

chapter 11

AFTER BREAKFAST ON the following morning the kahuna came to call. He was a short, sturdy man with a thick mane of snow-white hair that made him look older than the forty-some years I suspected he was. He was dressed as he had been on that day I'd glimpsed him on the road, in a colorful tapa shirt over dark trousers. About his neck was a delicate red-and-yellow featherwork lei, which was identical to the one in Patience's sitting room. As she introduced us a wide smile lit his rich brown face and he accepted the hand I held out.

"Welcome to the land of the ancient gods," he said, and my lips parted at his perfect English. I didn't know why I was surprised. Kalani and the other Hawaiians employed by the Phillipses also had a good grasp of the language and the Orientals in the household spoke it fairly well. Still, something set him apart from the others, an underlying quality that bespoke the old ways. It wasn't until we were comfortably seated in the solarium that I realized what the quality was. Wisdom! I saw it in his dark eyes, the essence of one who had lived for a long time and had gained infinite down-to-earth knowledge. True, this man wasn't ancient, but clearly he lived and breathed the teachings of the old culture.

"I've looked forward to meeting you, sir," I said. "Miss Phillips speaks highly of you and your cures."

The kahuna beamed at the praise. "Ah, yes, they have made her better."

"Oh, indeed." Patience quickly supported his comment, then elaborated on the shoulder pain one of his remedies had recently alleviated. As I listened in rapt silence Kalani came in carrying a silver tray, upon which was the tea service, fresh-baked scones, and tropical-fruit jam. This was the first I'd seen of her this morning and I was taken aback by the shadows beneath her eyes and the drawn look in her face. If anyone needed a potion or elixir, I thought, it was this woman. My lips parted to inquire about her health and offer my services, if she was in need. But from the way Kalani avoided turning her eyes to any of us, I inferred that she did not wish questions or help. So I switched my attention back to the pair seated nearby. They were so engrossed in talk of aches and pains and remedies I doubted they even noticed that the pretty Hawaiian looked as if she should be lying down. Kalani placed the tea tray on the table before us and exited the solarium as quietly as she had entered.

Over the refreshments I continued to soak up all I could about the herbs the kahuna mentioned and managed to ask a few questions. He was a fascinating man and I envied him his knowledge of the old and his determination to preserve the Hawaiian culture. He in turn was delighted by my interest and respect. "Not many young people cherish the ways handed down through the generations anymore," he said sadly, then added on a brighter note. "You seem well acquainted with herbs and their healing value, Miss Montgomery."

"Oh yes. Although I haven't the slightest idea of how to dry and blend them, or earnestly wish to do so myself."

"Ah, then"—he laughed—"I can be assured you won't be asking me to reveal age-old secrets."

"As I've tried to pry out of him on occasion," Patience confessed lightly.

He nodded, his eyes shining. "To what purpose I do not know."

She tilted her white head. "Simply my inquisitive nature."

Was it my own inquisitive nature, or perhaps a trace of lingering doubt over the punch I'd drunk on the beach, that raised the next inquiry I put to him? "Are there any fruits or berries, sir, that could tend to make one sleepy?"

His gaze narrowed and he viewed me as if that were an odd question to ask. Maybe it was, but something deep within me pressed to know if I might have somehow been given such a drink. "None that I'm aware of. However, there are herbs I use in sleeping elixirs. Are you having trouble sleeping?"

Certainly not on the beach, I thought wryly. "No, I was just curious." As the kahuna continued to relate more about the herbs, my stubborn brain conjured a picture of Patience's sleeping potion. But again I asked myself what would anyone have to gain by drugging me? And I put the incident from my mind. For the most part the medicine man was indeed guarded about his cures, but from the information he did share, I was intrigued.

The two hours Patience and I spent with the wise old healer was a treasured learning experience for me and not just in regard to the remedies. The kahuna had also touched on the subjects of the Hawaiian religion, which involved nature worship, legends, belief in ghosts, and a multitude of strict rules called *kapus* by his people. "The list of them is long," he said.

Patience frowned. "The kapus that women could not eat with the men or partake of some foods has always annoyed me."

"That wouldn't sit well with me, either," I admitted.

The kahuna responded with a simple shrug and wisely returned the conversation to the inoffensive topic of herbs. By the time he left us, I had gained a better understanding of his people and my respect for the Hawaiians and their culture had deepened.

The morning passed quickly, and when Patience and I entered the dining room for lunch, I was pleased to see color back in Kalani's face and that the shadows beneath her eyes had faded. Perhaps she just hadn't slept well last night, I thought. On one or two occasions I'd seen the same shadows under Drew's eyes, smudges I attributed to his after-dark trips to town. Had he gone there last night? I wondered, remembering the clip-clop of hooves I'd heard. Had the sound been real or simply a figment of my imagination?

After lunch Patience and I wandered the flower gardens. Then, with her approval, I borrowed a horse from the stables and went for a long ride along the main road. The late-afternoon sun warmed my spirit as well as my body, clad in a green habit, and the air was perfumed with the heady scent of tropical blossoms. This island was paradise, I told myself again, and listened to the warbling of birds in the abundant trees. Even the geckos skittering here and there didn't wrinkle my nose at the memory of the reptile that had somehow gotten into my room and my bed.

I lifted my face to the sunlight slanting through palm fronds and spreading branches. It was heaven to be enjoying springlike weather in the late fall and pure joy to be in the saddle again.

Later, on the way home, I urged the sleek chestnut mare along the beach. The foamy surf licked at his hooves and he nickered in a playful way. As I savored the sounds and the tangy smell of the silver-gray sea, I refused to let my mind wander back to my near drowning. In the bend of the deep sheltered cove I dreamily glanced at the house that sat well back from the beach. I hadn't come this way since I'd learned the Phillipses' former house-keeper lived there. Nor had I really given her or the place more than a thought. Apparently Drew hadn't either, because he hadn't said another word about introducing me to Mrs. Malo.

Oddly, I was just wondering if any of the family ever visited the woman who helped raise the twins when I spotted one of the them approaching the cottage. Which one, though? Curious, I reined in and scrutinized the dark-suited figure closely. Clearly learning to tell the brothers apart had become a gripping challenge. The man in the distance walked with purposeful strides and it only took me seconds to identify Jordan from the confident set of his broad shoulders. If he'd looked around, he would have seen me silhouetted against the orange sunset. But his attention remained intent upon the immaculate cottage, which was just as well. I didn't want him to think I was being nosy or spying on him. As I urged the mare forward Jordan stepped onto the small covered porch and paused before tapping on the door. A moment later the panel was opened and he disappeared inside.

I didn't see Jordan again until the family and I met in the dining room for dinner. He was still wearing the same handsome dark suit and there was a pensive look in his eyes. He greeted me and the others with a quiet "good evening," and was pleasant enough whenever he joined the conversation. However, even then the deeply serious expression remained in his eyes and I wondered if something was troubling him.

Shortly after the meal Jordan excused himself and crossed the hall to the kitchen. I couldn't imagine what business he might have in there. To speak with one of the servants, perhaps? Or discuss something to do with the running of the kitchen? Although the latter probably fell under his aunt's supervision.

Patience also excused herself early and went up to her sitting room to read from the Bible. The night air was still and mild and Drew suggested we wander out on the captain's bridge.

"That would be nice," I agreed, and he took me by the arm and we moved to the French doors.

Outside at the railing we stood in peaceful silence, both of us lost in our own thoughts. As I gazed over the moon-washed landscape I was tempted to ask Drew about his after-dark trips to town. But in the end I rejected the idea. We weren't engaged and such an inquiry might be viewed as presumptuous.

Drew slid an arm about my shoulders and hugged me close. "You've been particularly quiet tonight, Rachel."

"It's been a full day and I'm a little tired."

"Did the kahuna come by, as expected?"

"Yes."

"What did you think of him?"

"I was impressed," I said simply, and wasn't surprised when Drew's lips thinned. Just because he disapproved of the kahuna didn't mean I had to share that opinion. And I wasn't going to lie. Instead, I explained my view. "He projects confidence and the feeling of inner peace. Not many of the physicians I've met fare as well in that respect."

"How can you compare him with a doctor, Rachel?" Drew demanded as if I had betrayed him. "The man's so-called cures are old and verge on witchery."

"Good heavens, he's a priest, not a sorcerer. If his remedies work—"

"But do they work?"

"According to your aunt they do."

"It's probably all in her head."

"Perhaps," I conceded, "but as long as she feels better—"

"I just worry he might do her more harm than good. Why, even the majority of Hawaiians have turned away from the kahunas and rely upon modern medicine."

"New isn't always better," I reminded him. "And the man's not completely old world. Patience told me he was one of the first students at the Lahainaluna Mission Academy and later completed his education on the mainland."

"True," Drew muttered.

"And it's my understanding she consults a licensed physician on a regular basis. I do wonder, though, about the way her mind drifts."

"That's just Aunt Patience. She's been that way for as long as I can remember."

"Then it has nothing to do with any of her medications or the herbal cures?"

"No, I don't think so. It's her flights of fancy that concern me, Rachel."

"I've yet to see her that way."

"I don't think Jordan has, either."

"You're the only one?"

"I spend more time with her than my brother." The reply was matter-of-fact. "Although, as I recall, Kalani said something about Aunt Patience's flights once."

"What are they like?"

Drew tipped back his head and stared up at the moon. It was breathtakingly bright and the twinkling stars seemed so close, as if I could reach out and lift one from the black sky. "Well," he said after a long moment, "it's just a matter of getting her facts twisted. Then Patience rambles on in the wrong vein."

"Some people past their prime begin to gradually develop that tendency."

"So I've heard. Still it's sometimes hard to accept such changes."

"Yes," I murmured, wishing I'd had the opportunity to see my loved ones through the various changes in life. "Your aunt is so lovely in every respect I can't imagine why she never married."

"Oh, she had two or three opportunities, but she never felt strongly drawn to any of the men. It might have been different if she hadn't inherited the business at an early age and immersed herself in it. Then Jordan and I came to live with her and Aunt Patience told us that from then on her life was rich and full. I don't think she has any regrets."

"Except about fulfilling her dream to become a teacher."

"Yes, I'd forgotten that." Drew's arm about my shoulders tightened and he planted a light kiss in my hair. "Tell me, my darling, how did you spend the rest of this day?"

For some inexplicable reason the endearment and heightened affection shot a twinge of discomfort through me and the urge to slip from his touch. "I went riding this afternoon for the first time in years." I managed an even tone. "Do you like to ride for pleasure, Drew?"

"When the mood strikes me."

"Your voice suggests that isn't often."

Gently Drew turned me in his embrace. He tipped up my chin. "If riding is your love, Rachel, then it will be mine, too."

A lump of emotion rose in my throat. "How sweet and thoughtful. But I wouldn't expect that."

"I know. But I want you to be happy, my precious Rachel . . . and to be with me forever." Drew's breath on my face was warm and his expression soft. Yet there was a hint of desperation in his eyes, as if his entire life was in my hands.

chapter 12

ON FRIDAY MORNING Drew delayed his departure for the office so he could escort his aunt and me to town. "That isn't necessary," I told him. "I can manage a horse and carriage."

"There's no need, dear," Patience said, "one of our stable hands also serves as a driver. But having Drew accompany us would be pleasant." She viewed him with the adoring smile I was coming to know so well.

As always her glow of pleasure brought delight to his dark eyes, and their affection for each other shown brighter than ever. "Then it's settled," he said. Before I knew it, Drew was ushering his aunt and me to the covered family carriage that had been brought around. "You sit up front with Drew, Rachel," she insisted, and I helped make her comfortable in the backseat. Patience was particularly attractive this day in a braided walking suit as deep blue as the sky, and with spots of color in her cheeks that revealed high excitement. "My, oh my"—she sighed as Drew handed me aboard—"I haven't been to Lahaina for longer than I care to admit even to myself."

I hadn't been back since the day of my arrival, nearly two weeks ago. That stormy afternoon when I'd almost been blown off the ship's ladder. What a sight I must have been, I thought with amusement, and was glad I could now reflect on that perilous episode with laughter. When I added that hair-raising incident to my unplanned soaking in the ocean, the gecko in my bed, and the heated but embarrassing kiss with Jordan, I could hardly sum up my days on Maui as uneventful.

To my gratitude the ride to Lahaina was peaceful, and those memories along with the more painful ones of the past four years slipped a little further back in my mind. As Drew maneuvered the pair of bays through the moderate traffic on Front Street, I marveled over how much more appealing this place was under the sun. It wasn't as bustling and up to date as San Francisco. But that city wasn't blessed with luxuriant tropical growth and verdant mountains lightly draped with clouds resembling giant puffs of cotton. Nor did the people in San Francisco wear such lively colors and dare dress with little concern for formality. Why, even many of the American, European, and Oriental immigrants to this island donned the native tapa garments, from men's bold-patterned shirts to women's high-necked shifts, which I'd heard were called muumuus.

"That's part of our family's corporation, Rachel." Drew lifted a hand to the impressive two-story hotel fronting the sparkling Pacific Ocean. Further down, he gestured to the Phillips Mercantile and the lumberyard they also owned. I waited for him to do the same with the two grogshops that appeared to require a substantial amount of his time. But Drew didn't mention them and neither did his aunt. As we passed tavern after tavern I entertained the notion of asking which ones belonged to the family. But the places were all so seedy looking and noisy, with hooting and yelling and raucous music pouring through open doors, that it struck me as unseemly for a woman even to speak of the wild establishments. Was that why Patience didn't bring up the subject? What of Drew, though? He was the one who had first told me about them. Although telling was altogether different from pointing them out, and I could only assume his silence was born of respect for feminine sensibilities. What I didn't understand, however, was why his straitlaced aunt would even consider owning such places.

Drew reined in before a small shop that boasted an attractive display of stylish dresses and bolts of shimmering silks and satins. The sign in the window read MADELEINE, DRESSMAKER & TAILOR. Three doors down was the Phillips Land Development Corporation. As Drew helped me alight a young Hawaiian woman passing on the boardwalk greeted my companions by name and with a cheerful, "Good morning." Then her gaze swept over me, appraising, and there was something about the glint in her eyes that touched a familiar chord. Only I couldn't recollect in what regard.

Drew helped his aunt from the carriage. "Remember," she said, "I'll be by the office to consult with you and Jordan as soon as I'm finished here."

"I haven't forgotten, Aunt Patience. If you'd like, I'll wait and drive you there."

"That's very thoughtful, dear, but the short walk will do me good." He nodded, turned a disarming smile on me, then reboarded the vehicle.

As Patience and I stepped into the shop the bell over the door jangled, announcing our entrance. No one was about, though the steady hum of sewing machines beyond the curtained archway at the rear indicated we were not alone. On shelves all around were fabrics of every kind and color and more notions than I'd ever seen before. The only garments in sight were those in the window for show.

The curtain at the rear was parted, and the hum rose a degree as a diminutive, Caucasian woman in her early thirties stepped out. She beamed when she saw Patience and sailed forward amid the rustle of superbly crafted beige taffeta. Next to the well-dressed ladies my percale suddenly lost the last of its luster. The smiling pair exchanged pleasantries, then I was introduced to the auburn-haired Madeleine. "How very nice to meet you, Miss Montgomery," she said, and I returned the warm acknowledgment.

As the dressmaker showed me around the shop and introduced me to her two assistants in the back room, Patience made herself comfortable in an overstuffed armchair. On the table beside her were several fashion magazines and a pattern catalog. She reached out to the latter. "My favorite creations are in here," Patience said. "You must look these designs over first, Rachel."

Hoping "these" weren't expensive garments, I crossed and opened the cover on the Alexandra Chandler-Steele collection. "In there you'll find apparel for every age," Madeleine explained, "from toddlers to the mature woman."

"What she means is women well past their prime, like me." Patience chuckled and once again her easygoing nature reminded me of Drew.

Madeleine met the light remark with accomplished tact and genuine-sounding flattery. "Ah, but you are a joy to sew for, Miss Phillips. Just as these patterns are a joy to work from. Alexandra's fashions are in such demand among my clientele," Madeleine said to me, "that I have most of her patterns on hand and I seldom suggest doing my own creations anymore. Are you familiar with the American couturière's collection?"

"I've heard of it, but it's been a long time since I've purchased new clothes."

"The war, you know," Patience offered.

"Oh yes," the dressmaker murmured. "Thank God it's finally over and Mr. Drew returned safely. I understand you nursed him back to health, Miss Montgomery."

Now it was my turn to murmur yes, only with a touch of surprise. How many others on the island knew I'd seen Drew through those critical days after he'd been wounded? How many knew I was a nurse who earned her own keep and had reasoned I wasn't apt to be moneyed? How many were questioning my motives in regard to Drew, as his brother was? The mere thought of being regarded as a scheming fortune hunter once again set my teeth on edge.

As I studied the pattern book it suddenly occurred to me why the glint in the Hawaiian woman's eyes had strummed a familiar chord. Her expression was identical to the one I'd seen on the face of the dock official and a stable hand back at the house. Initially I had interpreted that look as curiosity, and it was only natural to regard a stranger in such a light. It would be just as natural to speculate on why the handsome and wealthy Drew Phillips, who could doubtless have the pick of women in his own class, would choose one of modest means. Hadn't I asked myself that same question a dozen times?

Patience broke in on my thoughts. "That gown would be perfect for our dinner parties, Rachel." She gestured to an attractive, square-necked dress with simple lines and I quickly noted it probably wouldn't cost a fortune to make.

Madeleine glanced at the design. "It would look lovely on you, Miss Montgomery, and the style should remain in vogue for some time."

In view of my limited funds that last comment made the gown even more appealing, and I kept it in mind as I continued through the catalog. As I moved on to the fashion periodicals, scanning styles Madeleine said she could duplicate, she remarked, "Next year Butterick and Company will be adding women's clothing patterns to their line of men's and boys' wear. Then at long last we'll have a larger selection to choose from." In the end I settled on the initial gown Patience had pointed out. Then with the continued help of the other ladies I made one more selection. It, too, was from the Alexandra Chandler-Steele collection.

As I rose from my chair at the table to look over fabrics with the dressmaker, Patience also came to her feet. "I must be on my way to the meeting with my nephews," she said, and I agreed to meet her at the office at one o'clock. If I'd had a choice I would have preferred sitting through a business meeting to sorting through colors and textures. Yes, I enjoyed nice clothes and being as well turned out as my budget allowed. On the other hand I loathe the process of reaching that point. To my relief Madeleine made it fairly painless and went out of her way to suggest quality fabrics within my financial reach. But even modestly priced garments wouldn't have been possible if it had not been for the funds from the sale of my family home in Ohio.

In what seemed like no time at all the details of the gowns were settled, a fitting arranged for the following week, and I was thanking Madeleine. What a pleasant and accommodating woman she truly was.

Back outside I consulted my pendant watch. With an hour left before I was to meet Patience, I strolled the boardwalk, browsed around a handful of shops, and made a few small purchases in the Phillips Mercantile. It was a spacious, well-arranged store that carried every conceivable item from hardware, pots and pans, and furniture on the first floor, to apparel and lacy undergarments on the second level. From the mercantile I continued down the walk. I was about to cross the street at the corner of Front and Dickenson when a striking home I hadn't noticed before caught and held my attention. The walls of the two-story house were constructed of lava stone and the mortar was of crushed coral, which I'd seen in other structures on the island. I moved closer, admiring, and my gaze fell on the placard near the front door on the lower-level lanai. This was the home and office of Dr./Reverend Dwight Baldwin. As I read the fees posted below the name on the sign, amusement burned in my throat. Of all things, the doctor charged by the "size" of a sickness; very big was fifty dollars, diagnosis three dollars, refusal to pay ten dollars. Did Dr. Hawthorne, Patience's physician, also charge in this usual manner? I wondered as I crossed the street.

By now it was almost one o'clock and I quickened my pace. As I neared the office of the Phillips Land Development Corporation, Jordan stepped through the doorway. He moved straight to the hitching post and the tethered gelding. This time I identified the twin in an instant and not just because the cut and color of his suit was different from his brother's. Jordan's stride was longer, his step determined, and there was no mistaking that same quality in the attitude of his chin. He released the reins, secured the leather portfolio case he was carrying to the back of the saddle, and swung up into it. Jordan sat straight and tall, his shoulders square beneath his coat and his hands in firm control of the powerful animal beneath him. As he turned the gelding toward the street the intense dark pools that consistently heated my blood with just a look caught sight of me. My heart fluttered on an irrepressible surge, and I knew I was now being drawn toward Jordan by the magnetism in his eyes. A golden glow flowed between us and I sensed he was as powerless to avert his gaze from me as I was to avert mine from him. Jordan was near, and yet too far away to touch. Even so, every sensitive nerve within me leaped to life as if I were being caressed by those strong hands holding the reins. I'd never heard of a mental caress, but such a thing existed. My drumming pulse drowned the city noises and I was only vaguely aware of Jordan's horse pawing the ground, impatient. My mouth became dry. Jordan's must have done the same, because he moistened his lips. The piercing shrill of a ship's whistle penetrated the rush in my ears. I winced at the strident sound and the unbidden spell was broken. Jordan met the return to reality with a deep frown. Was he annoyed with himself over those moments that had seemed suspended forever in time? Wordless, he nodded in my direction and touched the brim of his Stetson in a polite but impersonal gesture. Then he swung his horse about and headed up the street. He didn't look back, and I chastised myself for staring after him.

My mouth was still dry when I entered the office and Mr. Winston stood and flashed me a bright smile. "Good afternoon, Miss Montgomery. Are you enjoying your stay on our fair island?"

I swallowed; it was a painful effort. "Yes," I replied, and for the most part that was true. "It's nice to see you again, sir."

The conservatively dressed, gray-haired man nodded, pleased. "I'll inform Mr. Drew you're here." He stepped to a closed door at the rear, tapped, then poked his head into the room. Seconds later Patience came out, followed by Drew, moving in his familiar leisurely gait. Their happy faces told me the family meeting was a success and Patience was reassured that the business was prospering as well as she'd been told.

"Did all continue to go well with Madeleine?" Patience asked me.

"Oh yes. With her help I selected pale violet silk for the dress you suggested and patterned blue organdy for the other."

"Both colors should be lovely on you, dear."

"All colors are lovely on Rachel," Drew said, and his aunt beamed at us.

"Not all of them," I admitted, "but I thank you for the compliment."

He took my arm in his. "Are you ready for lunch?"

"Absolutely."

"Jordan won't be joining us," Patience told me. "He just left on a business trip to Hana. It's a long ride and he won't be home until tomorrow evening."

Tomorrow evening? A sudden emptiness settled in my stomach and Drew tilted his head at the frown that knitted my brows. Did he perceive the source of my disappointment? I wondered as the three of us left the office. As we climbed back into the carriage I told myself it was a blessing Jordan wasn't able to join us for lunch. Now I was spared from viewing any friction that might have arisen between the brothers over Drew's late arrival at the office this morning, tardiness that revolved primarily around me and my need to visit the dressmaker.

Drew drove us to the hotel and we'd hardly entered the lobby, tastefully decorated in the vivid colors of the island, when a distinguished-looking older man came forward. A moment later I learned he was the manager and we were introduced. With all the pomp of royalty he personally showed us into the airy, well-appointed dining room. Patrons at the pristine, linen-draped tables glanced up, nodded at the Phillipses, then regarded me with arched brows. We were seated at a choice table before a huge window overlooking the ocean. I'd never dined in such a splendid establishment before and it was a struggle to keep from gaping in wonder.

Over delectable smoked salmon, fluffy rice, and tropical fruit I admired the spectacular view. Clouds now played hide-and-seek with the sun, and small boats went to and from the tall ships tied to one another in a sinuous line out in the bay. "How odd to see ships in a row, especially so far offshore," I said.

Drew sipped from his cup of strong kona coffee. "The water closer in isn't deep enough for the big boats. So they anchor out there, in what has become known as the 'Lahaina roads.' "

"Roads? In water?"

He met my laugh with a grin. "Figuratively speaking, of course."

Patience glanced at the ships, thoughtful, and I remembered how I'd looked back on the vessel that had brought me to this island. The desperation I'd felt then at being so far from the mainland had faded and now there were just twinges of homesickness.

By the time we'd finished with lunch, the busy morning had taken its toll on Patience and she was eager to return to the house. "I have business to attend to," Drew remarked as we left the hotel. "I'll arrange for Mr. Winston to drive you home."

For the sake of brotherly harmony I was relieved that Drew hadn't insisted upon driving us himself. But there wasn't any need to impose on Mr. Winston, either, and I said again, "Really, Drew, I can manage a carriage."

He gave my hand a gentle squeeze as he helped me back aboard. "Oh, I'm sure you can, my love, but it gives me pleasure to look after you. Indulge me," he entreated, smiling into my eyes.

His attentiveness was flattering and I nodded. But when the moment passed, the occasional hints of dismay I'd seen in him over my independent streak rushed back on a wave of unease. Self-reliance was an integral part of my nature and now more than ever I was grateful for the inner strength to stand on my own feet. I only hoped Drew wasn't nurturing the notion of shaping me into a docile female. Such an effort would be futile and strain our friendship to the limit. Heaven knew it had nearly ended with his failure to inform me early on of his tragic marriage.

Back at the office Drew pulled up out front, and his aunt and I waited in the carriage while he went in to look for Mr. Winston. Several passersby paused to pay their respects to Patience and she introduced me. The one who really brightened her eyes, though, was a tall, dark-haired man who walked with a marked limp. "Why, Dr. Hawthorne," she said. "How nice you happened along. I've been eager for you to meet Rachel." Patience presented me to her personal physician, who I'd heard also hailed from the mainland.

"Ah, yes," he said with a knowing smile, "Drew's young lady. I'd heard you'd arrived."

Apparently so had everyone else in town. But then from experience I knew how fast word spread in small communities. As I returned the warm expression and held out my hand to the nice-looking man of middle years, I wondered again with suppressed amusement if he also charged by the "size" of an illness.

"You must come by the house for a visit soon," Patience told him. "Although you and your wife will be receiving an invitation shortly to a dinner in honor of Rachel. I do hope you'll be able to attend."

"We'll look forward to it. In the meantime I believe I'm scheduled to come by on a professional call next week. I hope I'll see you then, too, Miss Montgomery. I'd enjoy hearing about your nursing."

So he also knew of my profession. "And I'd enjoy talking with you, sir." Mr. Winston and Drew emerged from the office. They shook hands with the physician, and a few minutes later the carriage was back on the road to home. "Dr. Hawthorne seems very nice," I said to Patience, who was seated beside me in the backseat.

"And most competent. He was also in the war, almost died. By the grace of God he survived and came home with nothing worse than a bad leg."

"He was fortunate." My voice fell to a whisper as my mind returned to the field hospitals. Patience and I fell silent. She tipped back her head against the carriage and within seconds dozed off. I blinked, casting out the painful memories, and said a silent prayer for the brave soldiers who had passed on. Then I gave my full attention to the incomparable scenery. In the distance ominous smoke swirled up, smutting the sky. Alarmed, I leaned forward and pointed. "Something's on fire, Mr. Winston."

He lifted his eyes to the sky. "Oh, that's nothing to be concerned about, miss. It's just a sugarcane fire. The dry leaves are burned off the crop just before harvest."

Air escaped my lungs in a rush of relief. "What keeps it from going up in the flames."

"The high moisture in the cane stalks and their tough covering."

"It must be tough to withstand such a hot blaze." I settled back, still staring at the billows of smoke.

Patience dozed all the way home and then finished her nap in the comfort of her room. By dinner she was revitalized and chatting gaily about our pleasant trip to town. She slept soundly that night, and in the morning she and I spent our usual time together in the solarium. Since it was Saturday, Drew was home by midafternoon and I invited him to ride with me, but he begged off with a look of regret. "I'm sorry, Rachel," he said, "Aunt Patience challenged me to a game of chess. I wouldn't want to disappoint her." I didn't want that either, and I nodded in understanding. "Keep us company," he urged, taking my hand in his.

"It's too nice a day to be indoors," I declined politely.

"True," he agreed, and planted a light kiss on my cheek before I ventured out alone. It was also too nice for my heavy riding habit, so I'd bypassed it in favor of my sprigged cotton shirtwaist, matching skirt, and a wide-brimmed straw bonnet with pink satin ribbons. The warm trade winds blew briskly. As I urged my horse down the beach I gazed across the rolling ocean to Molokai and Lanai. Both islands were clearly visible and I admired the gentle planes of their hills. Then I turned my attention to the sharp rise of the West Maui Mountains. What a spectacular backdrop for the landscape of this isle and the lavish Phillips home. The same was true of the multiwindowed cottage nestled beneath the palms, I noticed as my horse loped along the water's edge by the deep cove. As always the small dwelling kindled memories of my own home. Yes, the setting was different, but the size and the cozy look of the place were the same. I was about to turn the horse toward the big house when I saw Kalani on the path that led to the cottage. My lips parted as I followed her lithe movements. Even from a distance her grace and beauty were evident. Today she was more striking than ever in a bright native shift, her sleek dark hair loose and flowing. She knocked upon the door, just as I'd seen Jordan do mere days before. Once again the panel was opened. Only this time Kalani stepped inside and disappeared from my view.

chapter 13

I DIDN'T SEE Kalani again until the following morning, and when I did, the dark smudges were beneath her eyes once more and the wan look back in her face. Was she ill? I wondered anew. Or was she simply not getting a full night's sleep these days? The urge to ask if there was anything I could do for her swept back, but her distant expression made me suspect she might mistake my concern for prying. So this time, too, I held my tongue.

There was another concern in my mind: Jordan. He hadn't come home last night as expected. "I hope he hasn't met with any trouble on the road," I said when his name came up over Sunday breakfast.

Drew shrugged in nonchalance, though the contradictory frown that marred his brow made me think he was also worried about his brother. However, when Drew answered with a hint of what sounded like jealousy, I suspected that was not the case. "I'm sure Jordan is fine, Rachel. He was probably just detained in Hana."

Patience supported his statement with a firm nod and I was reassured in regard to Jordan. But what about Drew? Was that jealousy I'd heard in his voice. That question lingered at the front of my mind throughout breakfast then faded as the three of us left the house for church. There were more conveyances on the rutted road than I'd seen before. "People come from all over the area to attend the church my father founded," Patience told me with pride. When we arrived at the small steepled structure, that same quality—pride—shown in Drew's eyes as he introduced me

to the balding minister and the other members of the congrega-
tion.

I sat between Drew and his aunt in the front pew, the place of
honor, reserved solely for the Phillips family. The hymns we
sang filled me with the sense of peace and the minister was so
inspiring that I became wholly absorbed in his sermon. My attention remained riveted to him until he glanced up from the pas-
sage he was reading in the Bible and nodded at someone in the
rear of the chapel. Instinctively I looked around and a sharp in-
halation caught in my throat. Jordan! He must have just come in.
My gaze flickered over him. If he'd encountered any difficulty
on the way home from Hana, it didn't show in his face. Although, upon closer scrutiny, there were lines of fatigue about his
mouth.

Jordan glanced our way, and for one pulse-skipping moment
his eyes met mine and the all-too-familiar heat resurfaced. As he
sat down in the pew just inside the door, I forced my head back
around. However, not before I'd noticed he was still wearing the
dark suit he'd had on yesterday. Only now it wasn't as crisp. But
even a little rumpling didn't detract from the handsome fit and
the perfect cut of his trousers.

Just envisioning Jordan's long legs and lean frame intensified
the heat, and when Drew suddenly reached for my hand, I
glanced up and caught him looking from me to his brother.
Heaven forbid that the flush of heady attraction had stained my
cheeks as revealingly red as they felt.

At the end of the service Jordan was the first of the congrega-
tion to step back into the sunlight and he was waiting beside the
family carriage as we filed out with the others. I refused to let
my eyes lift to his, and if he sought my gaze, I didn't know.
"Jordan," Patience said, giving him a hug, "I'm delighted you
didn't miss the service. But you look weary, dear. Are you tired
from the long ride home, or did you keep late hours in Hana?"

"A little of both," he admitted. "The business was more involved than I'd anticipated. To make matters worse my horse
picked up a stone on the way back late yesterday and I had to
walk him several miles to town."

"How dreadful." She sighed in sympathy. "Rachel's concern
for you was well founded, then."

"Concern?" Jordan inquired, and I felt his gaze fix on me.

Still, I refused to meet it. I suppose that was rude. Nevertheless it was better than the embarrassing heat that would have suffused me had I looked at him.

"She was worried you might have had some trouble on the road," Patience explained.

"Oh?" Jordan sounded surprised and I could hardly blame him. My worry for him had also taken me a little by surprise. Now I didn't know what to say, or if a comment was even needed.

To my relief Drew changed the subject. "Where is your horse, Jordan? I don't see him anywhere."

"He was limping badly and I had to leave him in town. I picked up that gray at the livery."

"Why don't you tie the animal to the carriage," Patience suggested as Jordan handed her into the backseat, "and ride home with us."

Drew's lips parted to comment, but he must have had second thoughts, for no words came from him.

"Company and a comfortable ride would be welcome," Jordan said, and moved away. Drew helped me into the front seat, then climbed in beside me. Once again he reached for my hand, only this time with a proprietary air that made me uncomfortable. In what I hoped was a casual gesture I eased from his touch. To my dismay Jordan had turned back to us and I could tell from the flicker in his eyes that he'd seen me withdraw my hand. Drew shifted and picked up the reins. A minute later his brother returned to the carriage. Without looking at us, he boarded and sat down directly behind me.

"Did you stay at our hotel last night, Jordan?" Patience asked as we started forward.

A silent moment fell. "Yes, the hotel," he murmured.

Was that fatigue edging his voice? I wondered. Or was he being evasive? Drew's next comment, which held a trace of sarcasm, made me suspect the latter. "Well, of course, Aunt Patience, where else would he have stayed?"

Where else indeed? The rattle of a carriage moving briskly by drowned out Patience's reply. In any case, I told myself, where Jordan Phillips spent last night was none of my business.

Maybe it was just my imagination, but all the way home I had the feeling his intense eyes were boring into the back of my head. And it was all I could do to keep from squirming miserably on the seat and wishing my lace-trimmed bonnet were made of nonpenetrable steel.

Shortly after lunch Patience excused herself for her usual afternoon nap and Jordan left us for his workshop adjoining the carriage house. "I'm free to ride with you today, Rachel, if you'd like." Drew's offer was accompanied by a smile. But that expression was not reflected in his eyes and I knew his heart wasn't in roaming the countryside on horseback.

"I never pass up an opportunity to ride," I said softly. "But if it isn't your interest, Drew, I understand. We can do something else. A long walk perhaps."

"You are sweet, my darling." He bent and brushed my lips with his, then insisted again, "I want to share in your interests. Now, run up and change. I have a note to pen in my study, then I'll meet you at the stables in—oh, say—thirty minutes."

"Thirty minutes," I repeated with an appreciative smile, and hurried to my room. The sun was bright this day. Even so, the air was mild and I knew I would be comfortable in my riding habit. I changed into the green garment and secured the matching bonnet over my upswept hair. Then I descended the stairs to the entrance floor, left the house by the rear exit, and moved over the lava-stone walk. On my way past Jordan's workshop I saw the door was ajar, and when I heard him moving around, I automatically glanced in.

Before I could even focus on the interior, Drew called, "Rachel," and my attention swung to him. He was straight ahead, stepping through the wide doors of the stables and leading two saddled horses. "Hurry along, we don't want to waste a minute of this beautiful day." Considering his lack of enthusiasm for riding, his urging took me by surprise.

This was the first time I'd seen Drew in riding clothes and I was certain my expression conveyed approval. The sleeves of his linen shirt were rolled up and the collar open at the throat. Drew's superb-fitting trousers were tucked into tall leather boots, which were polished to a high luster. His eyes brightened as they met mine. Without a word he helped me into the saddle. Side by side we moved from the drive to the wooded path that zigzagged to the beach, then we cantered along the water's edge. The tangy aroma of the sea was especially invigorating, and well after we'd left the golden sand and galloped along the sugarcane fields, I could still feel the salt on my face. "I haven't ridden this far from the house before," I told Drew as we slowed the animals and loped along. This afternoon there was no smoke besmirching the sky, but the recently fired field on our right reeked of lingering fumes. My throat constricted as the heavy scent swirled by with the wind and I didn't know how the workers now harvesting the crop bore the aggravating smell. When I asked Drew about it, he merely shrugged and said, "I suppose they get used to it."

I doubted my lungs would get used to it, but thank goodness I didn't have to put them to the test. "Obviously working on Sundays isn't taboo on the island." My eyes widened as my attention fell on the lethal machetes being wielded by the Orientals cutting the canes, and a shudder coursed through me.

"The crop is harvested at its peak," Drew said, "whenever that happens to be."

"It looks like dangerous work."

"Very, those machetes are razor sharp. Injuries run high, and many men have been maimed."

My mind flashed back to the war. Swallowing, I cast out heart-numbing pictures along with the topic of injuries. "I gather your family is going into the sugar business," I said as we continued side by side up the road.

"Yes, at Jordan's urging. He thinks it would be profitable and I expect he's right."

"You'll be growing sugar, then?"

"I should say not." Drew laughed. "Farming isn't for us. If all goes well in my brother's dealings with the planters, we'll be their agents."

"In selling and exporting, you mean?"

Drew glanced up at a soaring sea gull and several seconds passed before he answered. "That would be part of the service we'd offer."

"You don't seem very enthusiastic about the venture."

"I can't say that I am. It's Jordan's interest, really. We each have our favorite areas of the corporation, which unfortunately causes a bit of friction between us on occasion."

"I should think such a difference would be beneficial to the company. You'd excel in your areas and Jordan in his."

"To a point that's true. But we don't always agree on what is of major importance in the business."

"If I may ask, exactly what is your prime interest in it?"

He hesitated. "Managing the grogshops. They're more lively," he added with the familiar devilish smile.

I wasn't surprised by Drew's answer. However, I did appreciate his honesty. "They also cater to vices." I tried not to sound sanctimonious.

"Ah, but vices are profitable, my love. And the men who patronize such places aren't going to become puritans if we should close up our places."

"True," I murmured, and knew it was pointless to press the issue. Especially when it was obvious Drew intended to carry on in his favorite area of the family business. The fact that he was openly discussing the dubious establishments afforded me the freedom to inquire at last, "Is that where you go in the late evenings, Drew, to the grogshops?"

He reined in and eyed me with sudden sharpness, though his tone remained even. "How did you know I leave the house at night? Did Jordan tell you? Or maybe Aunt Patience rambling during a flight of fancy?"

His reaction was a little startling and I pulled up short alongside him. "No, not them." I also kept my tone even. "I told you I've never witnessed one of your aunt's fancies."

"Then how?" he pressed, and I couldn't help regarding him with suspicion.

"I saw you riding out a couple of times." I hesitated, then asked slowly, "Is there some secret about your nightly outings?"

"Of course not."

"Then why didn't Jordan explain when I asked him where you were going?"

"I have no idea, although talking about grogshops with proper young ladies is hardly appropriate."

"So that is where you go after dark."

"Yes."

I waited for him to elaborate. But when Drew looked away, ending the discussion of what he felt unfit for feminine ears, I boldly reopened it. "Why do you go to those places at night?"

Drew frowned at my persistence, but at least he replied. "The answer is simple, Rachel. I haven't time during the day to tend to my duties there, so I see to them in the evenings. I'm sorry, I guess I should have told you about my unusual work schedule, but I didn't think it was all that important." ·

Obviously, telling me he was a widower hadn't seemed important to him, either. "You've asked me to be your wife, Drew. To me that means I need to know the total you."

A shadow fell over his face, but in an instant he laughed off the mystifying expression. "And the other way around, my sweet."

"Absolutely." I remembered the smudges I'd seen beneath his eyes and said, "I admire your dedication, but such long hours must be terribly tiring."

"I have no complaints."

"Your health could suffer."

"Not with you to watch after me," he teased, then leaned forward and gave me a long kiss.

On the way home I reflected on the side of Drew he'd just revealed. Clearly he was hardworking. So why then was I gaining the impression from Jordan that his twin was irresponsible? Actually, when it came right down to it, how could a man who volunteered for the war and fought to preserve the Union be irresponsible? Could it be that the subtle hints from Jordan were invented to discourage me from marrying his brother? I didn't want to believe Jordan guilty of such a despicable thing, any more than I wanted to believe his silent messages about Drew's irresponsibility. My mind whirled in a quandary and I prayed that coming to know the brothers better would reveal the truth.

As Drew and I moved back along the beach, I spotted an outrigger canoe some distance offshore and I pointed in that direction. Shielding his eyes from the sun, Drew glanced over the water. "That's Jordan," he said, then dropped his hand and looked away. "He and I used to race canoes almost every Sunday after church. But I lost interest in the activity a few years ago."

Before the boating tragedy with Claudia and Ellen? I wondered. Out of respect for Drew and his pain I let the subject drop.

Back at the house I thanked Drew for the pleasant afternoon. "It's wonderful being with you, Rachel," he said softly, "no matter how we spend the time." Then he excused himself to answer personal correspondence in his study.

His aunt was in the formal drawing room visiting with a friend who had come by. Patience introduced me to the silver-haired woman and invited me to join them for tea. They appeared to be having such an enjoyable time together that I didn't wish to intrude. So I politely declined with the excuse that I needed to freshen up after the long ride.

I went straight to my room, removed my bonnet, and rinsed my hands and face. I even opened the closet and scanned my meager wardrobe for a comfortable day dress. But I really didn't feel up to changing, especially when I would have to do so again for dinner in a couple of hours. Sighing, I closed the closet and looked around the room. The book on the night table caught my attention, but I wasn't in the mood to read. My thoughts were so scattered. What with trying to figure out the twins and then with coming to grips with the silent dictates of my heart, all I wanted was time alone.

The sound of the ocean drifting in through an open window beckoned. Without a backward glance I left the house by the rear door. As I moved toward the path to the beach, I saw Kalani leaving the one that led to the cottage in the cove. She was dressed in her gray servant's costume, with her dark hair primly secured at the nape. Her delicate features were set in a thoughtful expression as if her mind were a million miles away. Without a pause in step or a glance in my direction Kalani continued toward the house. I don't know why, but in those few seconds I watched her, I felt a tug of pity. I supposed it was triggered by the unhappy attitude of her chin and the sadness conveyed in the set of her slim shoulders. Had she received some bad news? I wondered as I stepped onto the beach and started up the sand. Or did the sadness have something to do with her occasional look of ill health? My mind was so intent on Kalani that nothing else registered until I glimpsed movement ahead. Then I stopped short and focused. One of the twins was sitting on the family dock a few feet away, fishing. My quickened pulse told me it was Jordan. The surge in my veins momentarily deafened me to the rolling surf and the sound of the wind that flapped my riding habit and blew tendrils of hair about my face. Jordan's dark-eyed gaze was upon me. Had he been watching me move up the beach toward him?

My initial inclination was to lift my hand in a friendly greeting and retrace my steps to the house. Anything to avoid the unwanted attraction and heat. But retreating was cowardly and I'd never turned and run. Besides, I reminded myself, it was imperative that I come to know both twins before I even seriously considered marrying Drew.

I inhaled a fortifying breath and went out on the dock. "Are the fish biting?" I inquired as I approached Jordan.

He glanced up from where he sat on the weathered planks. "I don't know yet, I just got here." Jordan was dressed in casual clothes similar to his brother's, only somehow this twin was more appealing. "Did you have a nice afternoon?" he asked politely.

"Very nice, thank you. Drew and I went riding, although I don't think he really cares to ride."

"Or any other outdoor activities, actually."

"Oh?" The word crooked out.

Jordan arched an inquiring eyebrow. "You didn't know that?"

"No."

"Does it matter that he doesn't enjoy the outdoors?"

The question was presumptuous, which made me wonder if Jordan hoped it would matter. In truth it did. I couldn't in all honesty envision sharing my life with a man whose interests widely differed from my own. But for now that was between Drew and me. So I lied a little. "No, not really. It's just hard for me to imagine someone who doesn't care to be outside volunteering for the army. To be tramping around the countryside in the dirt and mud and snow and the bitter cold."

Jordan turned back to his pole, clearly ending the subject.

I stepped closer. "May I watch you fish for a while?"

"If you'd like, but you might find it boring."

"Oh no, I love to fish."

His head came up and he regarded me with surprise.

"My brothers taught me, years ago." I sat down beside him on the dock.

"I can't picture you fishing."

"Why not?"

"Everything about you is so feminine."

Flattered, I smiled. "What's on the outside can often be deceiving."

"True, and not always pleasantly so, like now," he muttered grimly. "When was the last time you fished, Rachel?"

"Before the war. I don't suppose you have another pole with you."

He hesitated as if weighing his answer, and just when I'd convinced myself he was about to say no, he surprised me with, "As a matter of fact I do. I'm trying out this new pole. You can use the old one." He reached around to the other side of him, and for the first time I noticed the rest of his fishing gear. "I use worms. Do you bait your own hook?" The question was a challenge and I knew he was testing me.

I lifted my chin. "Of course I bait my own hook. Where are the worms?"

Jordan picked up a tin and held it out to me, the hint of amusement lighting his eyes. "This I have to see."

"Well, watch closely," I teased, "you might learn something." Without a squeamish blink I lifted a wriggling worm and secured him to the hook.

"Hmm, not bad," Jordan admitted, and happy memories of fishing with my brothers flooded back. Only with them my heart hadn't skipped an occasional beat.

I moistened my suddenly dry lips and threw in my line. "I saw you in your outrigger a while ago. Is it tied up at the end of the dock?" I looked past him, but all I really saw was his broad chest. My own rose and fell in response.

"I pulled it up in the cove."

"The cove?" My voice elevated a degree.

"Yes, is there some problem?" Without warning he glanced up the plateau to the house as if he sensed someone was watching us.

Instinctively I also looked around, but I didn't see anyone. "No," I said. "I just remembered I saw Kalani coming from there on my way here. Maybe you saw her, too."

Jordan shook his head. "She was probably visiting Mrs. Malo. I understand you haven't met her yet, Rachel."

"Unfortunately Drew hasn't gotten around to introducing us."

"Then allow me."

"That's very kind, Jordan, but maybe I should wait for Drew to—"

"You might have a long wait," he bit out. "My brother seldom visits Mrs. Malo. So if you'd like to meet her . . ."

"I would."

"Then it's settled. We'll go over as soon as we're done fishing."

Jordan's insistence brought a frown to my face. Why should he care one way or the other if I met the woman who helped raise him and Drew?

chapter 14

SO FAR THE fishing this day was poor; neither Jordan nor I had had even a strike on our lines and an hour had already passed. But more important our time together was amazingly peaceful and relaxing and at last it seemed the barriers to friendship that we had erected were beginning to crumble. "I've never fished with a woman before," Jordan said. "But maybe if I'd had a sister . . ."

"You probably would have taught her how to handle a pole the way my brothers taught me." I shifted my pole from one hand to the other. "Maybe one day, Jordan, you'll have a wife who will enjoy fishing with you."

"Maybe," he murmured. The light that had been in his eyes faded and I knew that I had inadvertently reminded him of his deceased fiancée, Ellen. Again I wondered what she had been like. I even felt a startling surge of envy that she'd been loved by this man and he'd asked her to be his wife. If it hadn't been for the tragedy, he and Ellen undoubtedly would be married. And in all likelihood I would not be sitting next to Jordan on the dock now.

I lifted myself from the dismal thought and tried to return the brightness to Jordan's eyes by asking him about his trip to Hana and of his new business venture. "Hana is the most beautiful place I've ever seen," he said, "with waterfalls and pools and spectacular valleys."

"It's hard to imagine any place lovelier than this," I breathed, glancing up at the West Maui Mountains.

Silent moments fell as Jordan reeled in his drifting line and threw it out again. Then he went on to tell me a bit about the sprawling sugar plantation he'd visited in Hana.

"It sounds a little like the cotton plantations in the South," I said when he'd finished, and I didn't allow myself to dwell on the destruction of countless Southern homes. "Drew told me you're hoping to become an agent for the planters."

"Yes. It's a bigger undertaking than I'd initially expected, but I'm sure we can handle it."

I had the feeling he could handle anything. "Aside from selling and exporting, Drew didn't say what else is involved in being a sugar agent."

"My brother has other interests." Jordan's jaw hardened.

"Yes, he told me." Just the thought of the grogshops similarly affected my jaw and I wondered if Jordan was also thinking of those places. In any case I wasn't about to inquire and chance straining the friendship that had only begun between us.

To my relief Jordan didn't pursue the question of his twin's business interest either. "To answer your question," he said, "as sugar agents we would arrange loans for the planters, buy supplies, keep books, and even recruit labor."

"That does sound like a big undertaking," I agreed. "Why can't the plantation owners or managers do all that for themselves?"

"They have their hands full with administrative and technical problems."

"I see." I reeled in my line, then frowned. "My bait is gone."

"We have plenty," Jordan reminded me lightly and lifted the bait tin. As I reached out, my hand brushed his. I tried to brace myself against the compelling thrill that swept through me, but my resistance dissolved, and my eyes automatically met Jordan's. In those deep, dark pools I saw my reflection. I also saw the revealing glitter of excitement our touch had produced in him. Time stood still, but my heart raced, and my mind brought forward the memory of our tantalizing kiss on the day of my arrival at the house. How long ago that seemed, and yet I could still feel the fervent pressure of Jordan's mouth on mine. The roar in my ears had nothing to do with the sound of the incoming tide slapping the wooden dock supports or with the trade winds blowing against us. My chest rose and fell and I became aware that Jordan's breathing had grown as ragged as my own and that he'd put aside the tin. "Rachel," he murmured huskily, and his free hand went to my chin.

His fingers were hot, scorching, and yet like teasing feathers on my flesh. As if compelled by invisible forces, Jordan lowered his head and I leaned helplessly near. His breath was fresh and warm and drugging, and that combined with the heat emanating from his strong body fueled the fire deep within me. Every thought vanished from my brain, every concern, and even the hopes and dreams I'd clung to. There was only now, only Jordan, his strength and overwhelming masculinity. His mouth was a whisper away and I closed my eyes in eager anticipation. Jordan's lips claimed mine, soft, yet hungry, and promising more as the kiss deepened, more than I could comprehend. My senses soared on a boundless plane and I reveled in the power we had over each other. I ached for these moments to last, to remain forever in the world beyond time. But in the next instant a wave on the incoming tide crashed resoundingly against the wooden pillars beneath us and we jerked apart, startled.

Jordan turned away. "Sorry," he muttered. But the lingering huskiness in his voice conveyed the opposite feeling.

"Me, too," I murmured, and wondered if my voice also contradicted my words. I wasn't sorry for the kiss, any more than he clearly was, but I was beginning to experience pangs of guilt. What must Jordan think of me for having yielded to him as if I had no ties to his brother? More important, how could I have let myself? True, I wasn't committed to Drew. Nevertheless, he had asked me to be his wife and I had come to Maui with that possibility in mind. If only he made me feel as Jordan did. If only, if only. Those words ran through my brain and I was more emotionally torn than ever.

"Damn," Jordan cursed under his breath, "our lines have become twisted together." Without a glance in my direction he slowly but surely straightened out the mess and even rebaited my hook. During those minutes neither one of us uttered a word and the continued silence grew unbearably awkward. To make matters worse I didn't dare look at him, not when my lips still burned from his kiss. So I divided my attention between the ocean and the brilliant orange Hawaiian sunset tinged with pink. Even so, my mind was on Jordan and every sensitive nerve within me still tingled. Good sense told me to excuse myself and return to the house. Just as I was about to reel in my line and obey the inner message, Jordan broke the silence. "Tell me a little about your nursing, Rachel?" he asked politely, his voice once again level.

I swallowed and forced my tone to match his. "There isn't much to tell. You already know what led to my taking it up."

"Yes, your mother became seriously ill."

"After she passed on, I cared for others in our small town."

"Then the war broke out."

I nodded.

"Is it hard for you to talk about?" He turned his gaze from the ocean to me.

"I haven't really talked about it with anyone," I admitted.

"Not even with my brother?"

"No, I'm sure Drew has his own torment to deal with. Maybe even plaguing nightmares." The memory of my own bad dreams sent shivers down my spine.

Jordan saw my lips twist and asked, "Do you have nightmares, Rachel?"

I hesitated. "Yes, although since I've come to this island, they haven't been as horrible as they were. Sometimes," I said without thought and in a voice that sounded far-off, "I can still hear the low rumbling sounds of the cannons. And always in those agonizing visions I see the faces of pain, and the endless stream of rattling ambulances that came and went."

"Drew told me about them."

"Most of them were nothing more than buckboards and the soldiers were stacked like cords of wood, sometimes even on their sides so more of them could be squeezed in." I swallowed again then continued in the distant voice. "So often the men who reached us by noon were gone by nightfall. And not just from wounds, but from malaria and typhoid and malnutrition. Sometimes I felt utterly helpless." Embarrassed, I brushed at the tear that spilled from the corner of my eye. "At other times I felt as if there were no God. I don't think your aunt would care to hear me say that."

Jordan placed a hand over mine, his touch now radiating comfort. "Aunt Patience would understand," he said softly, and gave me a handkerchief from his coat pocket. "I'm sorry, I shouldn't have pressed you to talk about things that could upset you."

"No, it's all right." I dried my eyes. "Somehow the talking has made me feel a little better. I know it isn't good to keep inner pain bottled up, but it's been so difficult for me to let go." I returned the handkerchief with a murmured thank you.

Jordan nodded. "We're almost out of daylight. Let's reel in and if you're still up to it, I'll take you over to meet Mrs. Malo."

"I'm fine, but I don't want to trouble you, Jordan." I followed his instructions with the line.

"No trouble, and I know she would like to meet you." He set aside his pole, then took mine and helped me to my feet. "We can leave the fishing gear. I'll send someone from the house to pick it up." As we moved from the dock and started up the beach, we once again fell into silence. Now, however, it was a comfortable quiet in which I marveled over how easy it had been for me to share some of the war memories with Jordan. Maybe in time I would be able to talk even more openly about my experiences and eventually come to grips with all the horror. Maybe then I would be able to meet the sights and sounds of each new day without being wrenched by memories of the past. Why, the sugarcane fire alone had knotted my stomach as visions had loomed of the billows of smoke I'd seen rising over Atlanta.

In the last rays of this day's setting sun Jordan and I entered the cove. The outrigger was pulled up, as he'd said. "Did you make that canoe?" I asked, noting how sturdy it looked, with its hull fashioned from a hollowed-out log.

"Yes, several years ago. I've been so busy at the office that this is the first I've taken it out in a while." We left the sand and started across the lawn that spread to the cottage. "I'd heard you'd been to Washington D.C., Rachel. I've often thought I'd like to go there." He'd changed the subject so completely that I suspected he didn't want to talk about canoes. But Jordan had his own horror to cope with, I reminded myself, even if his hand-crafted outrigger had had nothing to do with the tragic deaths. "I'm sorry," he said, "is Washington also painful for you to talk about?"

"No, but thank you for asking. I was there twice," I said in a quiet tone, "at the beginning of the war and then again about a month after President Lincoln was assassinated last spring. I went for the parade honoring the Army of the Potomac."

"There was a big write-up about the parade in our local newspaper. It must have been quite a sight."

"I'll never forget it, or the overwhelming pride I felt. It took two days for all of the troops to pass in review on Pennsylvania Avenue. Although," I grumbled, glancing up at the canopy of spreading palm fronds, "we could have done without General Custer and his theatrics."

"Theatrics?"

"The general galloped way ahead of his men, brandishing his saber," I explained. "And his yellow hair was whipping in the wind. He looked more like a showman than a soldier and acted as if he'd won the war single-handedly."

"Sounds like he has a bit of a bloated ego."

"Full-blown, I'd say."

Jordan nodded. Then he focused on the cottage ahead, his eyes growing thoughtful. "I seriously considered enlisting in the Union forces. But with Drew away on the mainland and then winding up in the army, I couldn't bring myself to leave Aunt Patience here alone."

"No, of course not," I agreed as we stepped onto the covered porch. As Jordan lifted his hand to knock on the front door, I reflected on "winding up in the army." That seemed a poor choice of words to describe a volunteer.

"Jordan," a feminine voice called, and we looked around. A heavyset older woman dressed in a flowing tapa shift came toward us from the wooded path. "I was just over to your place." Her attention swept to me, but the falling shadows of dusk prevented me from reading her expression.

Jordan held his response until she came to a stop before us, then he introduced me to Mrs. Malo. Her smooth bronzed skin was in stark contrast to the gray peppering her black hair. It was coiled in a neat bun at the nape and adorned with an enormous tropical blossom. She had a warm motherly look and it was easy to picture her helping to raise the twins. Somehow, though, I had imagined that anyone working closely with Patience in regard to her nephews would share her air of sophistication. "How nice of of you to come by," Mrs. Malo said to me. "You are as pretty as I'd heard."

I smiled. "You're very kind. I only hope Drew didn't exaggerate about me."

"He isn't the one who told me about you."

"Oh?"

Before she could even think to tell me who had offered the praise, and end my curiosity, Jordan asked, "Did you have a nice afternoon in town, Mrs. Malo?"

"Why, yes," she answered brightly. "It's always a joy to visit old friends." Without further ado she invited us into her home. It was as cozy as I had envisioned, and memories of my own home produced a lump in my throat. As the Hawaiian woman lighted the lamps in the small but airy parlor, decorated in cheery prints and shiny wood pieces of local koa, I noticed the handsome but unusual interior doors. In the upper panel of each was a carved cross, at the bottom an open Bible design. But then Patience's missionary parents had built this house and the family had lived here for many years. "Please have a seat." The other woman gestured to the sofa.

"It's almost dinnertime and we can only stay a few minutes," Jordan said as we sat down beside each other.

"Ah, yes, your aunt was changing for dinner when I was there." Mrs. Malo made herself comfortable in the chair across from us.

"You didn't visit with her, then?" Jordan inquired.

A frown marred the round bronze face. "No, unfortunately. But you know how it is now that I'm no longer employed in the big house. Your aunt and I seldom see each other anymore. I went over to give Kalani a gift I carved for her. Evidently my granddaughter didn't remember I was going to be away for a while this afternoon. So when I returned and found her note saying she'd stopped by, I called on her."

"Kalani is your granddaughter?" I said in surprise.

"Yes, I assumed you knew."

Jordan shifted beside me. "So did I."

"No one mentioned that fact. But how nice that she's close by, and following in your footsteps, Mrs. Malo."

"Yes," she said slowly, "I hope so."

What an odd comment, I thought, considering Kalani had already moved into her grandmother's former position in the Phillips household.

"Kalani is very considerate and visits here almost daily," Jordan told me.

Mrs. Malo confirmed the statement with a nod. "She is a blessing to an old woman and I do whatever I can to show my appreciation. That's why I carved the idol of Madame Pele especially for her."

A blank look must have crossed my face, because Jordan answered my silent question. "Madame Pele is the Hawaiian goddess of fire."

"She lives at Kilauea volcano on the island of Hawaii," Mrs. Malo elaborated, and in a voice that made the goddess sound as if she were a living being. "My granddaughter reveres Pele, who is the essence of feminine strength and power. You have that very strength, Miss Montgomery. I can see it in the straight set of your spine and the lift of your chin. Drew won't be able to keep you under his thumb," she finished with a chuckle.

Could Mrs. Malo see my spine suddenly stiffen? "I hope the thought never entered his mind." I managed a light tone, and prayed she was just teasing. Jordan's serious expression was hardly reassuring and I wondered if Drew had kept his wife under his thumb.

"Drew was such a devil as a boy," Mrs. Malo reminisced, "always into mischief. As fast as he got into scrapes, he was as fast to maneuver his way out."

"One day luck may desert him. It very nearly did this last time," Jordan muttered.

Last time? I wondered as the woman across from me sobered and nodded in agreement. I hoped one of them would explain what lay behind their exchange. Instead Jordan stood, ending the conversation. "We must leave now, Mrs. Malo. I'm sure Rachel will return for a longer visit soon."

Speaking for me was presumptuous and certainly narrowed down my response to her reply of "That would be nice." Yes, Mrs. Malo seemed friendly enough, and in all likelihood I would enjoy chatting with her again. But there was something behind her smile, a reserve, or maybe even a touch of the resentment I'd initially sensed in Kalani. Whatever the veiled emotion was, it made me wonder if her grandmother really wanted me to return. And why did I have the sudden and unshakable feeling that Jordan was pushing me to make another visit?

chapter 15

DREW WAS QUIET over dinner and I wondered if the message he'd received from someone in town minutes before we'd come to the table had affected his mood. The more I studied his face, the more convinced I became that he was worried about something. And that emotion was in his voice when he asked me distractedly, "How did you amuse yourself while I was in my study after our ride, Rachel?"

I regarded him over the rim of my water glass. "I went down to the beach. Jordan was there fishing and he kindly loaned me a pole."

"She handles it very well," Jordan complimented me.

"Really?" Patience said in surprise. "I had no idea you liked to fish, Rachel. Were you aware of that, Drew?"

He nodded, then asked me, "Catch anything?"

"No, not even a nibble on the line."

"Drew hasn't fished in years," Patience offered. "But maybe he told you."

I shook my head. If Jordan hadn't mentioned that his brother didn't care for outdoor activities, I might have been taken aback by their aunt's last comment.

"After the fishing," Jordan said, "I took Rachel over and introduced her to Mrs. Malo."

A muscle at the corner of Drew's mouth quirked. "Couldn't you have waited for me to take you over, Rachel?"

The sudden sharpness edging his tone brought my chin up in automatic defiance. "We were near the cottage and I couldn't see that it really mattered."

"The opportunity just arose," Jordan added in a casual tone.

"I'll bet," Drew snapped. "You're always stepping in, Jordan, always trying to control every situation."

I stared at Drew, trying to comprehend his anger.

Thank goodness his brother's temper didn't flare. "If that's what you choose to think," Jordan said, then regarded me apologetically. "I'm sorry, Rachel, I hadn't meant to trigger friction."

His expression was so sincere that I couldn't help but believe him. Although an inner voice issued the warning, his insistence upon introducing me to Mrs. Malo might have been rooted in a desire to cause trouble between his twin and me.

Patience fixed a steady gaze on Drew. "What difference does it make who introduced Rachel? It isn't as if Mrs. Malo is a dear family friend. She's a good woman. She served us well and has certainly earned our respect. But strict social protocol hardly applies to servants."

How cold that sounded. Snobbish! Yet the comment hadn't even raised the brows of the men. Was this the way of the wealthy, to look down on the help? In all fairness, though, how could I really fault these people? They provided generously for their former housekeeper. She didn't appear to want for anything. Moreover, her granddaughter now held the choice position in this household. Maybe that would have come to pass, anyway, for Kalani was competent. But maybe, too, the respect this family held for her grandmother had given Kalani a clear edge over the other servants employed here.

"No harm has been done," Patience insisted, and Drew let the subject drop. However, through the balance of dinner I sensed simmering irritation in him. Fuming over something as simple as an introduction seemed childish, and I began to wonder if there might be some basis to Drew's accusation about his twin. Did Jordan really try to control every situation? He had controlled me when it came to Mrs. Malo, but at least I'd at last met her. Drew hadn't made even the slightest effort in that regard.

Later, as he and I stood alone on the captain's bridge, he apologized for his behavior over dinner. "God knows I wasn't angry with you, Rachel. Jordan has always been the ruling big brother and sometimes his sense of superiority is more than I can tolerate."

I hadn't noticed that negative quality in him. But I was hardly an authority on Jordan Phillips.

"Can you understand, my sweet?" Drew lifted my chin and met my eyes.

As the youngest of three children, I definitely understood sibling rivalry. But to see it manifested in an immature outburst from a grown man was new to me and raised some concern. Was this typical of Drew, or just an isolated incident? Clinging to the hope that the latter was the case, I nodded.

Drew smiled and kissed me lightly. Then he wanted to know, "What did you think of Mrs. Malo?"

"She seemed very nice. And I was surprised to learn she's Kalani's grandmother."

"I'm sorry, I thought I mentioned she was. But their relationship has no bearing on us."

"True, but it is an interesting aspect of your household."

"*Our* household soon, I hope."

"Time will tell," I murmured.

Drew frowned at the vague reply. "How much more time?"

"I'll have an answer for you soon," I promised.

"I pray it's the one I want to hear."

And I dreaded the possibility of hurting him. That thought reminded me of the worry I'd seen in his face and I voiced my concern. "I don't meant to pry," I added, "but is there some problem, Drew?"

He expelled a long breath. "Something came up, a business matter. It's nothing I can't handle." My heart skipped a beat. Those last words were identical to the ones he'd offered when I'd asked him about the message he'd received during our visit at my home, the telegram that had prompted his abrupt departure for New York.

Thinking of that incident, I asked, "Will you have to leave the island to settle the matter?"

"No." Whatever the problem was, Drew clearly didn't wish to discuss it, because he switched the subject back to Mrs. Malo. He even lightened his tone. "Did she tell tales on me, Rachel?"

"Only that you were a devil in your boyhood."

"Well, thank goodness she didn't elaborate."

"Have something to hide, do you?" I also lightened my tone. However, on the inside I was dead serious, for his questions, verging on interrogation, made me wonder if there was something in his past he didn't want me to know.

"Only the typical youthful pranks, my love." Drew pulled me into his arms and I felt an unexpected heaviness in my heart and the sudden wish to be alone. Were the emotions linked to my growing doubts of him, or was I just tired?

"If you don't mind, Drew," I said, "I think I'll go up and turn in early." His brows knitted as I eased from his embrace.

"Of course, my sweet, it has been a busy day, and I know you still have my aunt to settle in for the night. Is she still off the sedatives?" he asked as he slowly escorted me up the stairs and to my room.

"She says she is and I have no reason to think otherwise."

He lingered before my door. "You are good for her. And even better for me. Sleep well, my darling." Once again Drew pulled me near, only this time he kissed me. The pressure of his lips on mine was urgent, and I yielded to his will, but my heart wasn't in this moment, either. As he lifted his head and gazed into my eyes, I had the uncanny sensation that he'd perceived the heaviness weighing on me.

The last thing I wanted was to hurt this man who had been good to me during such a crucial period in my life, and I managed a smile. It must have shown in my eyes because Drew returned the expression. "I truly enjoyed our ride together today," I told him softly.

"We'll do it again soon, Rachel," he promised, and turned away. About an hour later, as I lay in bed, I heard the familiar clip-clop of hooves drifting up from the drive. I assumed the rider was Drew and that he was on his way to the grogshops. Must he go to those disreputable places on the Sabbath, too?

That was the last thought in mind as I fell asleep and the first one to greet me in the morning when I awakened. Drew and the grogshops remained at the front of my brain as I dressed and fashioned my blond hair with side combs. On my way down to the morning room for breakfast I considered discussing my deepening concern about the taverns with Drew. However, one look at his aunt, seated alone sipping her prized sea-green morning tea, reminded me that she might be offended by talk of the unseemly places. So I rejected the notion, at least for now.

Drew was late for breakfast, and the moment he stepped into the room I saw the smudges beneath his eyes and noticed the worry was back in his face. My concern for him surely showed in my face. His aunt, on the other hand, verbalized her concern. "Drew," she said, "you look positively exhausted. You must get more sleep."

He shrugged. "I just had a restless night, Aunt Patience. It's nothing to fret about."

To me it looked as if he hadn't gotten a wink of sleep. "Maybe you should go back to bed for a while," I suggested.

"Not today I'm afraid. I have a full schedule." Drew downed a cup of the strong kona coffee, sampled a freshly baked cinnamon roll, then excused himself.

Patience watched him exit the morning room, her brow furrowed. Her lips parted and I assumed she was going to comment about her nephew's inadequate rest and touch perhaps on the late hours he kept. But then the familiar vague expression came into her eyes and it was as if she'd shut her mind against something unpleasant. A second later she pursued another topic. "Let's go down to the solarium after breakfast, Rachel." Her voice was distant.

Had she forgotten that we always went down there after breakfast? "As you wish," I agreed. "For any particular reason this morning?"

"Oh," she sighed, glancing around, "it just occurred to me that we haven't watched for whales lately."

"True, we haven't." So, shortly after the meal, Patience and I made our way down to the entrance floor and the solarium at the rear. She crossed to the huge windows overlooking the ocean. Thick clouds gave the water a silver-gray cast. For several minutes we stood side by side, staring out in silence. Then Patience stepped to the telescope, bent, and looked into the viewing device.

I wandered over. "See anything interesting?"

She hesitated. "Something is wrong."

"On the water?" I inched closer, fearful someone might be in danger.

"No, somebody shifted this telescope from where I had it positioned. Whales wouldn't be there."

I released a breath of relief. Then, since I had no idea of where "there" was, I asked, "May I see?" Patience moved aside and I looked into the instrument. My eyes widened. The dock! In a flash I saw myself sitting on those weathered planks with Jordan and a rush of guilt swept through me. Had someone watched as he'd kissed me?

🎐🎐🎐🎐🎐 chapter 16

THROUGHOUT THAT MORNING I couldn't shake the thought that someone might have spied on Jordan and me and my mind repeatedly reviewed everyone who had been in the house at the time we'd been on the dock yesterday. There were the servants, of course. As far as I knew, the only one of them who might have reason to watch us was Kalani and that consideration was based upon the eye contact I'd seen between her and Jordan. Maybe there was more behind those exchanges than I had imagined. Maybe Kalani had seen me going down to the beach yesterday as she was returning home from the cottage in the cove. Chances were she'd been there at the same time that Jordan was pulling his outrigger onto the sand mere yards away.

If Kalani had been spying on us, it could only be for one reason. She regarded Jordan as more than an employer. A romantic interest could explain her initial resentment toward me, which might well be simmering beneath the surface. If she'd perceived the attraction between him and me, that could also explain her unhappiness of late. In my mind those conclusions were logical, but my heart rejected the notion of an involvement between the pair. Hadn't I at one time suspected the same of Kalani and Drew? I firmly reminded myself.

As for Drew, he'd also been in the house late yesterday afternoon. He'd known his brother was out in the canoe and would be coming ashore before dark. Drew could have finished in the study early and gone looking for me. When I wasn't in the house, it wouldn't have taken him long to guess I'd probably gone to the beach, which he knew was my favorite place to walk. Had he repositioned the telescope?

On the other hand Patience with her tendency to absentmindedness could have repositioned it yesterday, or days ago, and simply forgotten. All in all that was the most reasonable conclusion. It was also the only one my heart and my mind agreed upon, and at last I refused to indulge in further speculation.

My third week at the Phillips home was busier than the first two weeks combined. To begin with I had to keep a close watch over Patience, for she had become so involved in the upcoming dinner party that she was overtaxing herself. I hated even to leave her for my fitting at the dressmaker's in town. "I promise to rest the entire time you're gone, Rachel." On that reassurance I kept my appointment with Madeleine. The silk gown she was fashioning for me was exquisite and the moment I slipped it on I knew it was already a perfect fit. "Ah," Madeleine sighed in delight, "no alterations to make. I'll just pin the hem." Her skill with measurement, color, and needle was priceless and once again I thanked her for making pleasant what I used to regard as tedious.

"Madeleine is a treasure," I said to Patience when I returned home, then told her my new gown would be delivered on Friday. And I could expect the second one by the end of the following week. But long before this week was out, Patience had a low spell and spent most of one day in bed. As fate would have it, that happened to be the very day Dr. Hawthorne stopped in on his regular monthly visit.

Dr. Hawthorne examined Patience and confirmed what I had suspected. "Too much excitement." He frowned down at her in the bed. "You are to stay right where you are through tomorrow. But knowing you, Patience"—he eyed her as if she were a disobedient child—"I expect you'll be up and around by then."

"Not if I have my way," I said firmly, and she scowled up at me.

At the conclusion of the examination the doctor and I left her to nap. On our way down the stairs he said, "If Patience insists upon getting up tomorrow, just see to it that she stays quiet."

I acknowledged his instructions with a nod, then said, "She seems so strong for someone with a heart condition."

He laughed. "I think it's her iron will that keeps her going."

"I know there's a lot to be said for determination," I returned lightly. "Have you time to join me for refreshments, sir?"

"Why, yes, that would be nice." Over herb tea and small sand-wiches prepared with an assortment of delectable fillings, Dr. Hawthorne asked me about my nursing background. I explained briefly, then listened in rapt silence as he told me a little about his practice and his periodic visits to the leper colony on Molokai.

"I had no idea there was one on the island." I put aside my empty china cup.

"I'm not surprised no one mentioned it. Talk of leprosy is a subject most people shun," he said, and I knew that was true. "Everyone who contracts the disease in the islands is sent there. The colony is a lonely and primitive place." He shook his head sadly. "I only wish I could visit more often."

"Is there anything I can do for those people?" The offer had scarcely spilled from my mouth when I remembered Drew's in-sistence that I give up my profession altogether.

Dr. Hawthorne flashed me a warm smile. "Spoken like a true, dedicated nurse."

"I hate to even think of people suffering."

He inclined his dark head in understanding. "Unfortunately the afflicted on Molokai are isolated in a rugged area from the others who live on the island, and getting in and out is extremely dif-ficult. The trip really isn't for a physician with a bad leg, which is why my visits aren't as frequent as I'd like. And it's certainly not for a young woman. Although such a statement sounds al-most ridiculous considering you were in the war and dealt with worse hardships."

Rugged terrain by comparison was nothing. But rather than chance agitating Drew, I didn't press the issue of helping in the colony. The doctor and I conversed for a while longer, then he left to complete his round of house calls.

From the drawing room I went up and looked in on Patience. She was sound asleep. Longing for fresh air and exercise, I asked one of the maids to keep an eye on her employer and I went out for a short stroll on the beach. As I passed the family dock I no-ticed the fishing gear had been picked up by one of the servants, in accordance with Jordan's instructions. Involuntarily I glanced up at the house, just as he had done yesterday as if he'd sensed someone was watching us. Had their been eyes on us then?

Frowning, I turned away. Without thought I followed the path

Jordan and I had walked on the previous afternoon. The changing tides had washed away our footprints, but it hadn't disturbed the outrigger pulled up in the cove.

I moved to the canoe and paused. The vessel looked heavy and decidedly sturdy. Considering that it was several years old, it was still in prime condition, right down to the paint. The outriggers, which extended from the hull, were secured with such obvious precision I couldn't imagine they would splinter. If the ill-fated canoe had been crafted with this same care— A screeching gull intruded on my thoughts and I reminded myself I must be on my way back to the house.

Instead of retracing my steps in the sand, I crossed to the lawn and headed for the wooded path. Palms dipped and swayed in the breeze and the sun glinted off the cottage roof. If Mrs. Malo was home, she was somewhere inside. Once more I paused, only this time I looked back at the beach. Jordan's boat was clearly visible. If Kalani had been here at the same time as he was yesterday, and she happened to glance toward the sea, she would have seen him. They might have even chatted together, or— Involuntarily my lips compressed and I broke off the thought on the reminder that Jordan said he hadn't seen her.

By the next day Patience was feeling better and she stubbornly insisted I not fuss over her. "I'll stay in bed," she promised, "but only if you go about your regular afternoon routine, Rachel. It's a beautiful one, go for a long ride. I only wish I could go with you."

She didn't have to twist my arm to get me out into the sunshine and in the saddle. On today's outing I avoided the road altogether and moved up the beach to an area I hadn't explored before. This part of the coastline was exceptionally beautiful and the cane fields on the right were nestled in the lap of the deep green mountains. As I slowed the horse to a canter I spotted a huge black rock jutting into the water up ahead. A woman dressed in a colorful shift sat upon the rock, at the base of which was a tethered horse. As I drew near I could see the woman's long dark hair was secured at the nape with a ribbon. Her head was bent, indicating that she was staring into the water below, and her shoulders drooped in obvious unhappiness. As I passed by, my lips parted. Kalani. My gloved hands tightened on the reins as sympathy constricted my chest. Clearly whatever was troubling Kalani hadn't as yet been resolved. If she had looked up and given any indication at all that she wanted company, I would have stopped and joined her on the rock. But Kalani did not look up, and I continued slowly along the beach. Later, on my way back, she and the horse were gone.

I didn't see Kalani again until dinnertime and then nothing in her face communicated that she'd seen me on the beach. She was preoccupied, however, and Patience scolded her once for clattering the silver salad forks on the plates as she helped clear the table for the main course. The noise she'd made was so slight it seemed unreasonable to make an issue of it. If the housekeeper was still in her employer's disfavor, why did Patience keep her on? Out of appreciation and respect for Kalani's grandmother, who had faithfully served this family for over thirty years? True, Patience Phillips was class conscious. But I'd also gained the impression she was devoutly loyal.

The days passed quickly, and between the hours I spent with Patience and trying to keep her quiet through all the dinner-party preparations, I didn't have time to go riding again. However, I did manage short walks about the grounds. One afternoon I even came upon Mrs. Malo working in her flower beds. She smiled when she saw me crossing the lawn from the beach and I went over and paid my respects. I hadn't planned to linger and I'd sensed she hadn't expected me to. But somehow we just naturally drifted inside and the next thing I knew we were chatting over tea. Maybe it was my genuine interest in her flowers that had dispelled her reserve and we were able to converse comfortably. Whatever it was, our visit was enjoyable and I delighted in her stories of the twin tricks Jordan and Drew had played as boys.

"Jordan and twin tricks," I said, "that doesn't seem like him."

"Oh, he outgrew them years ago. I don't know that Drew ever will. It's in his nature." She laughed, and something in the sound reminded me of Patience and the way she doted on Drew. Did this woman also dote on him? "Drew was a handful and a charmer," she added in a light tone.

"He still is the charmer," I pointed out, but refrained from mentioning that he'd employed his irresistible ways to persuade me to this island. The older woman bit her lower lip and I wondered if I'd kindled a memory she would prefer to forget.

"Yes, he is," she said quietly.

"Does he come to see you often, Mrs. Malo?"

"It's been a while. But I know he's been very busy since he's come home from the war."

Jordan was busy, too. Still, he managed to stop by here. If I were in this woman's place, that alone would make him the favored one in my eyes.

After tea I thanked Mrs. Malo for the pleasant conversation and warm hospitality. At her door I hesitated. A part of me pressed to mention Kalani's unhappiness, but again the other part insisted my concern might be mistaken for prying. So I left with no other words between us but "Good day." On my way back to the big house, I convinced myself that Mrs. Malo must know her granddaughter was troubled and was probably lending a sympathetic ear and maybe even giving advice.

As promised by Madeleine, one of the new dinner gowns I ordered arrived on Friday. "It is lovely," Patience said as I held it up before her.

"Yes," I agreed. "But this dress arrived with it. There must be some mistake. I commissioned a pale organdy."

From the drawing-room chair where she sat Patience's gaze shifted to the navy dress with figured flounces and border. "Do you like it, Rachel?"

"Why, yes, it's beautiful, but—"

"It's for you, dear, a gift for being so patient and caring of an old woman."

My lips parted. "But it's my pleasure and I don't expect any—"

She raised a silencing hand. "I know, and this is my pleasure," she insisted. "I knew the moment I saw that dress in the pattern catalog you and I were studying that it was for you. So I sent Madeleine a note and told her I wanted it in navy and to use her judgment on fabric. I hadn't expected her to have it finished this soon, though. The dear woman must have had her help working long hours. I must send a note of appreciation."

My eyes misted. "Thank you, Patience. This is the loveliest

gift I've ever received." I bent and gave her a hug. "I'm going right up and try it on."

"Wear it to dinner," she suggested, and I told her I would.

In my room I cast off my old dress and excitedly put on the new one. Then I stood before the full-length mirror and turned this way and that. The swish of quality satin made me feel elegant and ultra-feminine. The navy of this dress deepened the blue in my eyes, and the waist that dropped to a point in the front flattered my slender figure.

Drew's eyes gleamed in appreciation when I met him in the drawing room before dinner. Jordan's reaction was the same upon his entrance a short time later. Patience beamed. "Rachel is lovelier than ever, isn't she?" Her praise made me blush.

Smiling, Drew took my hand in his. "Absolutely," he said. "It was very thoughtful of you to present Rachel with the new dress, Aunt Patience."

Jordan arched an eyebrow and his gaze, which had dropped briefly to his brother's possessive hold on my hand, jerked up to my face. "Yes, very thoughtful," he murmured, and the hint of coolness in his voice made me wonder if he thought I'd cajoled his aunt into making this gift. In the past the possibility that Jordan regarded me as a fortune hunter had been irritating. Now what I felt was hurt, and with a sinking sensation I feared he was again erecting the barriers to friendship.

Drew was particularly cheerful and attentive over dinner, though perhaps it just seemed that way because his twin was quiet and an unsettling brooding expression had come into his dark eyes. I had never known that siblings who were identical on the outside could be complete opposites on the inside. And what I'd always heard about the close bond between twins didn't appear to apply to this pair. For the most part they were pleasant to each other, often laughed together, and sometimes even stood up for the other whenever their aunt was in one of her censuring moods. But always, just below the surface, there was the jagged edge of resentment. Actually, from what Patience and even Mrs. Malo had told me, the twins had been close as boys. Over the years what had brought about the change? I wondered. The boating accident? The fact that both older women, who had shared the responsibility of raising them, appeared to dote on Drew? That in itself could cause resentment. Then of course there were their different business interests, which Drew had said produced some friction.

I tossed in the bed, then stared into the darkness. If Drew and I married, how deeply would the sibling resentment affect our lives together? In my heart I knew the dismal answer. Just as I knew the physical attraction between Jordan and me could wreak disaster. And the one who would be hurt the most, I feared, was Patience.

chapter 17

ON SATURDAY EVENING the dining room table was extended to its full length and sixteen happy guests joined the family and me for a feast that surpassed anything I'd ever seen before. To be among this gathering of the elite seemed so unreal it was all I could do to resist pinching myself to see if I might be dreaming. The women were impeccably coiffed and dressed in the finest of fabrics, with glittering jewels at the ears and throat. And the men were outfitted in superbly tailored suits with velvet and silk lapels and imported shirts as white as freshly fallen snow. In my view, and admittedly I was a bit prejudiced, the twins outshone the other males in every respect.

At the head of the table Patience reigned supreme as hostess and was particularly attractive in an embroidered fawn-colored brocade, enhanced by a sparkling diamond-and-ruby necklace. Drew and I sat to her left and right. Jordan was at the far end in his usual seat—the spot Drew had once laughingly admitted he coveted, which probably produced a touch of resentment in him. But tonight there were no negative expressions. All the faces about me were wreathed in smiles. From the brightness in Drew's eyes each time he gazed upon me, I knew I looked as nice in the new violet silk as I felt. At my throat was a single strand of pearls that Patience had insisted I wear. She'd also loaned me her favorite pearl-encrusted combs for my hair and even sent her personal maid to help me arrange the luxuriant blond mass in cascading ringlets. I'd never felt more attractive or had so many admiring eyes on me. Two or three times I even caught Jordan watching me in that manner. However, on each occasion he quickly averted his gaze. In the instant before, though, the golden glow had flowed between us and the flutterings of my heart brought the familiar heat to my face. I prayed it didn't show in my cheeks. Just in case, I kept my head down and my attention focused on my plate until the warmth had subsided. Once, as I lifted my eyes, I saw Drew look from me to his brother. It seemed a casual gesture and I assumed the heightened unease in me was the result of my guilty conscience over my attraction to Jordan.

My brain whirled as I tried to remember all the guests' names, and I particularly delighted in chatting with Dr. Hawthorne and his lovely wife. She wasn't much older than my own twenty-two years and had also grown up in a family of modest means. From what I gathered her husband, on the other hand, was raised in the lap of comfort.

Later that evening, after all the guests had left, Drew and I went out on the captain's bridge for some fresh air. "You seemed to thoroughly enjoy yourself tonight, Rachel," he said as we stood alone at the railing.

"It was a wonderful evening. A little tiring for your aunt, though. For the sake of her health I was glad when she excused herself early and went to bed. I'm sure all the guests understood."

Drew nodded. "It was thoughtful of you to go up and help settle her for the night." An owl hooted in the distance. In the quiet moment that fell between us Drew and I must have been reflecting on the same guests, because he mentioned the couple on my mind. "I noticed you had quite a bit to talk about with Dr. Hawthorne and his wife."

"We have much in common." I hesitated, trying to think of a tactful way to approach a new concern that had arisen during my conversation with the friendly pair. "Drew," I said slowly, "I got the impression tonight that you've indicated to a number of people you and I are about to announce our engagement."

He lifted his shoulders in a vague gesture. "I may have. You can't blame me for being eager, my darling."

"You promised to be patient. What if it doesn't work out between us?"

"I don't view us in the negative," he said flatly. "If you would stop doing so, maybe—"

"Pressing for marriage isn't going to make it happen, at least not with me." I struggled to keep my voice under control. "Our relationship must develop naturally."

"And to think I was under the impression that you were a decisive woman."

"I was . . . until now. This is the biggest decision I'll no doubt make in my life and I want to be absolutely certain."

"So while you're considering, Rachel, I can't even dream about having you as my wife, is that it?"

My spirits plummeted to my toes, for he sounded like a spoiled little boy who was being denied a prized treat. "Of course you can dream, but for now I think talk of marriage should be a personal matter between you and me. Please try to understand." When Drew shrugged, I knew he did not, and I wondered if he understood anything at all about me. This was probably not the time to find out. Nevertheless my deepening doubts compelled me to venture, "As the doctor and I were talking this evening, Drew, he mentioned the shortage of medical help on the island. And he asked if I would consider training any interested women in a nursing capacity."

Drew's lips parted, and when he replied, his tone was sharp. "I hope you told him no!"

Because I'd braced for a negative answer, I managed to maintain my composure. "I told him I wished to discuss the possibility with you. I would only donate a few hours a week and arrange that schedule around your aunt's afternoon nap. She'd hardly know I was away from the house. You'd be at the office, so I wouldn't be taking time away from you, either."

Adamantly Drew shook his head. "I want you solely as my wife, Rachel. I don't share what I own."

"Own? Good heavens, I'm not a piece of furniture! If that's how you view marriage—"

"Of course it's not," he returned in swift defense. "Irritation compelled me to a poor word choice."

Had it really? I wondered. "Then maybe we should discuss this another time. For now I'd like to call it a night." I turned away.

Drew's hand flashed out and he caught me by the wrist. "Rachel . . ."

I twisted free. "Tomorrow, Drew. I'll see you at breakfast." I lifted my skirts and moved away. Own, indeed! I fumed over that word and its meaning all the way up the stairs.

In my room I paced, desperately trying to understand Drew and his views. In truth wanting me solely as his wife was a reasonable request. Even so, what harm was there in volunteering a few hours a week of my free time to a worthy endeavor? Many women gave of themselves to charitable causes; training others to assist physicians was no different. And how could Drew have even considered hinting that our engagement was about to be announced? Why was he in such a rush to marry? I asked myself for at least the twentieth time and reflected on how kind and thoughtful Drew had been on the mainland. Not once during our handful of days together had I gained the impression that he regarded a wife as chattel.

I stopped at the window and moved aside the curtain. The moon was bright and shadows danced over the landscape. Without thought my gaze dropped to the captain's bridge, and I was surprised to see Drew still standing there. Even though he was in the shadows, I could see his head was lowered, as if the weight of world were upon him. I'd never seen him looking dispirited before. Even during his worst days in the makeshift army hospital he'd somehow managed to project a certain sparkle. My throat tightened on those memories and I told myself that maybe I'd been too harsh on him tonight. What with losing Claudia, and then almost dying himself in defense of the Union, Drew had been through so much in the past two years. For the most part he was good and kind to me here, and I didn't want to hurt him.

On a twist of regret I swung about and went back down to the captain's bridge. My steps were quiet and Drew must not have heard me come up behind him at the railing, because he turned with a start when I said softly, "Drew."

His face was in the shadows, so I couldn't see his expression clearly. But when I placed a comforting hand on his, the current of awareness instantly told me this man was Jordan. I heard him swallow before he said, "I'm not the twin you're looking for, Rachel."

My heart and every other part of me insisted differently. "I'm sorry, I hadn't meant to startle you," I stammered. "I left Drew standing here and I—" I broke off, suddenly aware that my hand was still on his. I yanked it away as if I'd been scorched. "I'm intruding. I'm sorry," I said again.

"You're not really." He turned back to the moon-washed landscape. "Drew's probably gone up to bed." Silence fell. My brain told me to beat a hasty retreat, but my feet weren't receiving the message. Jordan glanced back over his shoulder. I couldn't tell if he was surprised to see me still rooted to the porch, or maybe even annoyed. When he spoke again, my concern over the latter was dispelled. "Did you enjoy the evening?" he asked politely.

I cleared my throat. "Oh yes, everyone was so warm and friendly."

"Most of the islanders are that way."

"I noticed one of the men this evening was alone. I assumed he isn't married." Without thought I stepped to the railing.

"You're right, he's not. There are a number of eligible men on Maui."

"I should think that fact would bring marriage-minded women flocking here."

Jordan shook his dark head. "There aren't many single Caucasian women to choose from in the islands."

"What about the Hawaiian women? I've seen some very attractive ones. Kalani, for instance." I held my breath, waiting for his answer.

For at least ten seconds all I heard was the breeze blowing in the trees and the surf lapping the beach. Then Jordan said, simply, "Some men do intermarry, but for cultural reasons many more do not." He paused as if weighing his words. "Some have even traveled to the mainland in search of brides."

Claudia had come from there, but then so had I. Surely a man of Drew's standing hadn't gone wife hunting. An unexpected chill dappled my bare arms and I hugged myself.

"Cool?" Jordan asked.

"A little," I replied, but wasn't certain if the night air was to blame.

"Here." Jordan removed his suit coat and I turned toward him as he slipped it around my shoulders. He was so near I could almost hear his heart pounding. The sound of my own was becoming a drum in my ears. Even though I avoided looking up into his mesmerizing eyes, I felt his magnetism. He brushed a finger along my cheek as if to assure himself that I was real, that I was truly standing before him. The night closed in around us like a warm cocoon and every inch of me ached for his embrace, his mouth on mine, and so much more that I didn't understand. A breath caught in my throat and I was powerless against his silent command to lift my eyes to his. Jordan was staring into my face with a yearning that turned my insides to sweet honey. "You are so beautiful," he murmured, and I could feel myself being help-lessly drawn closer and closer. Another second and—

"Oh, excuse me," Kalani said from the open French doors. Jordan stepped back and his attention shot to her. I was still too mesmerized to move. "I didn't know anyone was out here." She squinted into the darkness, to where he and I stood. "I was just closing up the house for the night."

Jordan released a slow breath. "We're on our way in, Kalani." He put a hand beneath my elbow and urged me forward.

As we stepped into the slant of light falling through the door-way, Kalani's gaze went over me and her lips parted when she saw the coat draped about my shoulders. "Mr. Drew is looking for you, Miss Rachel," she said in a courteous tone that held no hint of surprise or dismay. "I think he went down to the library to see if you might be there."

"Thank you, Kalani, I'll go down." The words had scarcely left my mouth when Drew glanced into the dining room and spotted his brother ushering me through the French doors.

Drew's eyes narrowed when he noticed the coat and I shriv-eled a little under its weight. "I felt a chill," I murmured inanely as I removed it and handed it back to Jordan with a thank you.

"I thought you were going up to bed, Rachel." Drew's tone was crisp.

"I did. I mean, I went to my room. But then there was some-thing I wanted to talk to you about, so I came back down. This time Jordan was on the captain's bridge."

"If you'll excuse me," Jordan said, "I'm going to turn in." I nodded. Drew moved aside, allowing his brother to exit. For a split second their eyes met and I saw emotion arc between them. Was it anger? Or resentment? I could understand both in Drew, especially if he was aware of the attraction between his twin and me. But what would have compelled Jordan to feel either emo-tion?

"May I close up now?" Kalani inquired.

"Yes," Drew told her, then frowned again at me. "Shall we talk in the drawing room?"

I inclined my head and neither one of us spoke until we were seated side by side on the sofa. "Why did you come down looking for me, Rachel?"

"I wanted to apologize for leaving you so abruptly. That was rude of me. I'm not usually so brusque. How did you know I wasn't in my room?"

"I knocked and you didn't answer."

"So you went down to the library looking for me?"

He hesitated, his eyes darkening with an unreadable expression. "Yes, to the library. I'm sorry, Rachel, for being so sharp and unbending. Can't we just forget that unpleasant episode ever happened?"

I felt my brows knit. Did he think forgetting would resolve our differences? I could only hope that in the days to come we'd be able to work our way through them. "For now I'll put it from my mind," I said quietly.

The hint of a smile touched his face and he leaned forward and brought his mouth down over mine. His lips were warm and persistent. But there was no fire in me, and after a few moments I withdrew from his embrace. "I really would like to call it a night, Drew."

"It's still fairly early, my sweet."

"I'm sorry, but I'm tired." I stood. "Thank you again for a lovely evening."

"I'm glad it made you happy."

As I turned away I heard Drew inhale a long breath and I wondered on another surge of guilt if he might have witnessed the kiss between his brother and me last Sunday.

In the week that followed Drew and I didn't mention the incident on the captain's bridge and I made no further comments about Dr. Hawthorne's offer to train women to assist local physicians. But the more I thought about it, the more enthusiastic I became, and I couldn't resist bringing up the subject to Patience. Her eyes brightened. "That sounds wonderful, dear. If that's what you'd like to do, then follow your dream. Heaven knows I'll always regret that I didn't at least try my hand at teaching. Only," she said in a warning tone, "do not allow your profession to delay marriage and children. My nephews are the only ones left to carry on the Phillips name and it must be carried on." She was so adamant that I was struck by the overwhelming feeling that if I didn't marry Drew and provide an heir, I would quickly fall into his aunt's disfavor. Had Drew's deceased wife felt the same? I wondered. In view of this woman's eagerness for an heir the numerous miscarriages I'd heard Claudia had suffered must have been doubly hard on her and the family. Could that be why Drew was in such a rush to marry? To put that pain behind him and move on with his life?

As for my life I'd come to love it on this wonderful island where I could indulge in the joy of nature. Whenever the weather allowed—less often now that the fall rains were becoming more and more frequent—I continued to enjoy long walks. For those times my favorite place was the cove where I could gaze upon the charming cottage that reminded me of home. I had visited there again with Mrs. Malo. As I was leaving, Kalani stopped by to visit with her grandmother. A day later I saw Jordan heading over after an outing in his canoe. If he spotted me, he didn't look my way and I'd made no move to attract his attention.

My favored place for riding was the pristine beach where the big rock jutted into the ocean. On my third ride that way I saw Kalani sitting atop the rock again, staring into the water as she had before. There was such a melancholy look about her that this time I couldn't help reining in. She must have glimpsed me in her peripheral vision, for she glanced around. "Would you like some company?" I called up to her. If she'd replied in the negative, I would have moved on. But when she simply shrugged, I dismounted and left my horse beside hers. Feeling a little like the tomboy of my youth, I climbed up the huge rock and sat down beside Kalani. "The view is even more beautiful from here than it is from the house," I said. Except for the smoke rising from a cane fire a short distance ahead, the sky was clear.

"Yes," she whispered, and I could see the pretty Hawaiian was mesmerized by the water swirling around the jagged coral in the tide pool below.

"How breathtaking." I also stared down.

"That is a sacred pool." Her voice now sounded distant.

"The kahuna told me of ancient legends, is there one surrounding this place?"

Kalani nodded, and several seconds passed before she said,

"The warrior chief Kahikili repeatedly showed his courage by jumping from this very spot."

My eyes widened. "How did he make it past that protruding rock shelf?"

"That is what made him so brave and skilled. Kahikili ordered every one of his warriors to jump . . . and they obeyed."

"They all cleared that shelf?"

Kalani shook her head. "Many did not, including my great-grandfather."

"How sad."

"No," she insisted, "those warriors were not truly lost. That is why this pool is sacred. In its depths the spirit is released from the body and soars to join the gods." Her voice had grown reverent and I knew without even looking at Kalani that she believed the legend. She fell silent again, and a few minutes later she excused herself to return to her duties at the house. And I continued up the beach.

When I saw Kalani later over dinner, the melancholy still showed in her face and even in the way she carried herself. What was troubling her? "Rachel," Drew said, drawing me back to reality, "you're very quiet and thoughtful tonight."

"I'm sorry if I haven't been good company."

"You must have a lot on your mind, dear?" Patience said quietly, and I nodded. "By the way did your second dinner gown arrive from Madeleine?"

"Yes, this morning. It's lovely."

Drew smiled at me from across the table. "I can hardly wait to see you in it tomorrow night, Rachel."

Jordan shifted and glanced up at Kalani as she supervised the serving of the soup. Patience frowned at him, then returned her attention to me. "What about Dr. Hawthorne's offer, Rachel?" she asked. "Are you going to take him up on it?"

Drew's jaw hardened. "You told Aunt Patience?"

"I mentioned it."

"Mentioned what?" Jordan inquired, looking puzzled.

"Dr. Hawthorne asked if I might help train other women to nursing."

A muscle at the corner of Jordan's mouth tightened and even Kalani's features set. What objections could they possibly have to my helping out in the community? "Have you come to a decision?" Patience pressed.

"No," I returned, and Drew's unyielding expression told me his view on the matter had not changed. Rather than chance another heated discussion I switched the subject by inviting Drew to join me for a ride the following morning. It was Saturday, and as far as I knew, he planned to be home most of the day. "I thought I'd ride up to the cane fields," I added. "I haven't been that way since you and I last rode together."

"If I can," he said after a moment. "I brought home a stack of work and I have no idea how long it will take me to get through it. The afternoon would be better for me, though."

"The afternoon is fine," I agreed. But when that time came, Drew was still up to his eyebrows in the paperwork.

"I'm sorry, Rachel," he said. I nodded in understanding and left the house alone. On my way to the stables I heard Jordan pounding on something with a hammer in his workshop. But I didn't stop or even look in.

It had rained heavily all night and there were lingering puddles here and there. The air smelled fresh and white clouds sailed the azure sky. As usual I avoided the road and moved up the beach. As I approached what Kalani had told me was called Black Rock, I was surprised to see her sitting there. With all the scurrying about the house for tonight's dinner party, I had expected her to be too busy to venture out this afternoon. But perhaps the supreme position in the household afforded her some free time during the middle of most days. Once more Kalani was staring into the sacred pool as if drawn by a mystical force. But then she clearly believed in the power of the legend. Today she didn't glance around and I didn't stop.

As the cane fields wound closer to the beach, I urged my horse up to the narrow road. On the ocean side were scatterings of trees and shrubs. To my right the thick clusters of tall stalks still smelled faintly of the fire that had burned away the dry leaves. Scores of men labored beneath the sun, cutting the sugarcane. And once more the mere sight of the razor-sharp machetes sent a shudder through me and my mind turned back to the war.

As always the painful memories brought a lump to my throat and I told myself I shouldn't have come this way during the harvesting. I tugged gently on the reins, and just as my horse swung about, something whizzed past my head. A resounding thud set my teeth on edge and lifted the hairs on my nape. With a tight rein on the horse I glanced toward the sound. The blood froze in my veins. A machete was quivering in the tree just a few feet away.

chapter 18

IF I HAD waited a second longer to turn toward home, that machete would be embedded in my head instead of in the tree. Trembling, I swung my horse back to the cane field and my mouth fell open. The plantation workers were still hacking away at the stalks as if none of them had even glimpsed that nearly fatal moment for me. But one of them had hurled that knife!

Rising anger overrode my fright and that emotion was in my voice when I called to the nearest worker and demanded to know if he'd seen what had happened. The man's eyes grew wide in his bronzed face and he shook his head emphatically as I pointed a rigid finger at the tree. "Not me, not me," he insisted, and called over several other workers. Every one of them gaped at the machete and all I heard were swift denials of guilt as they held up their knives as proof of innocence.

I stiffened in the saddle and all but shouted the primary thought in my mind, "Someone threw that knife!"

The commotion must have caught the attention of the man on the road up ahead, because he swung his horse around and hurried our way. "Why has work stopped here?" he demanded, reining in.

"Are you in charge, sir?" I met his eyes.

"I'm the overseer."

Once more I pointed a rigid finger at the machete. He also stared and I bluntly told him how it had come to be in the tree. Frowning, he urged his horse over and pulled out the knife. "The handle is gone," he said, returning to my side. "It must have somehow broken loose during the cutting." The sun glinted off the razor-sharp blade.

Chills raked my spine. "And that just came sailing through the air, is that what you're implying?"

"That's how it appears to me, miss."

"Do handles break off very often?"

"I'd never heard of it happening before. But how else can this be explained?"

How else indeed? "And where is the man who was using that machete?"

His jaw set. "I'll find out."

"And I'll wait here until you do."

He nodded and turned away. I watched as he questioned the rest of the workers nearest the road. All of them also had their knives in hand, and again I saw head after head shake in negative response. The overseer came back to my side. "I'm sorry, miss, I have no idea who this machete belongs to. Whoever the worker was, he could be hiding in the heavy growth, frightened, or have even run off, fearing punishment." He apologized for the terrifying incident and promised to have all the machetes on the plantation examined that night.

There was little else I could do but accept the apology and thank God I had not been killed. Reaffirming my vow to stay clear of the cane fields during harvest, I turned my horse back to the beach and urged him to a gallop. As we passed Black Rock I saw that Kalani and her animal were gone. She must have left a while ago because there wasn't a soul ahead of me on the beach. Although she could have taken one of the many paths up to the road and be following it home.

As for me and home I was still shaking when I arrived. And my legs nearly buckled beneath me when I dismounted in the stables. My horse tossed his head and whinnied as I clutched a stirrup to keep from falling. I hadn't seen anyone about as I'd entered, and I started when a familiar masculine voice called, "Who's there?"

I caught my breath. "Rachel." I looked around as one of the twins poked his head out of a stall.

"Rachel, good God," he rasped, eyeing me still clutching the stirrup, "are you ill?" He rushed forward.

"Just wobbly. I'll be all right in a minute." I wasn't clear-headed enough to identify the twin immediately. But when he put an arm around my waist to lend support, the surge in my veins told me this was Jordan. He helped me to a chair in the corner, and when I was seated, I told him what had happened.

His lips parted in disbelief. "I've never heard of a handle breaking loose from a machete."

"The overseer said the same. Still, the handle was gone."

"I guess that's what you'd call a freak accident," Jordan murmured.

"Yes," I gulped. "I suppose."

"Thank heaven you weren't harmed." He gave my hand a comforting squeeze and insisted, "I'll help you to the house. Just give me a minute to turn your horse into a stall." As he moved away I noticed that he was dressed in casual clothes and dark leather boots. He unsaddled my horse. After putting him in a stall, Jordan closed the gate on the one he'd stepped from moments ago. Beyond it was the gelding he always rode. The animal's coat glistened. From sweat? I wondered. "Have you been out riding, Jordan?" I asked as he crossed back to me.

"No, I was currying my horse. I like to take care of him myself, although I don't always have the time."

"And I shouldn't be taking you away now. I can make it to the house on my own."

"Well, at least let me see you safely to the backdoor." Before I could say another word, Jordan helped me to my feet and tucked my arm in the crook of his. As always his touch was lightning, and his heat and strength were a whirlwind on my already jumbled senses. I inhaled a long, fortifying breath and tried in vain to shut my mind against his silent power.

As we were leaving the stables the Hawaiian hand came in. His rich brown skin reminded me of the pretty housekeeper and I focused on her, grateful to have my thoughts diverted. Curious, I asked Jordan, "I saw Kalani out riding on the beach, has she returned yet, do you know?"

"I haven't seen her. But I don't think the horse she generally uses is here. Did you want to talk with her?"

"No, I just wondered if she was back." Why had I even mentioned the housekeeper? Good heavens, I thought wryly, was Patience's drifting mind contagious?

Jordan instructed the stable hand to tend to my horse, then we continued to the house. At the rear door he inquired politely, "Are you sure I can't see you up to your room, Rachel?"

"I'll be fine, thank you."

He nodded, and a second later he was on his way back to the stables.

I entered the house and climbed the stairs. On the second floor the maids were preparing the formal dining room for tonight's dinner. The bright-eyed one carrying a fragrant floral arrangement nodded in my direction. "Would you like bathwater right away, miss?" she inquired.

"Yes, please," I responded, and started up the last flight. The moment I entered my room I noticed the porcelain tub had been brought in. I crossed and tapped lightly on the connecting door. When Patience didn't answer, I gave a gentle twist to the knob and peered into her quarters. She was on the bed, still napping.

I turned back to my room and was slipping out of my riding habit and into my wrapper when I heard a horse on the drive. I glanced out the window, expecting to see Kalani returning home. Instead my eyes widened as Drew came into view. I'd assumed he was still in his study slaving over the paperwork. Where had he gone? And after he'd told me he couldn't spare the time to ride today. If he had joined me, I might not have been on that critical spot in the road when the machete went sailing by within an inch of my head. I shuddered at the memory and could hardly wait to rid myself of the deep chill in a nice hot bath.

I had just released my hair from the constraints of combs and pins and was brushing it about my shoulders when a knock sounded on the door. Certain this was the maid with the bathwater, I hurried and opened the panel. "Drew—" His somber expression caused my heart to skip a beat.

He crossed the threshold. "Jordan just told me what happened to you in the cane fields, Rachel. I had to see for myself that you're all right."

"I'm fine now," I murmured as his gaze traveled down the front of me, and I felt a flush at being caught in my lightweight wrapper.

"Thank God." Without warning he hauled me into his embrace.

"Drew, please, I'm not properly dressed."

He muttered something unintelligible under his breath, then reluctantly stepped back and looked me over again. The gleam of reassurance came into his eyes along with another emotion. The latter he verbalized. "You are so beautiful, my love."

"At the moment I'm just grateful to be in one piece."

He sucked in a sharp breath. "I don't even want to think—"

"I'm sorry, I shouldn't have been so literal. Where were you? I mean, I just saw you coming home."

"I was out looking for you."

"Oh?"

"After you left for your ride," he explained, "I realized being with you was more important than any amount of paperwork, or even the business."

"How sweet." I spoke past the lump of emotion that had risen in my throat.

The hint of a smile touched Drew's lips. "Unfortunately you and I must have taken different routes to the cane fields."

"No one there said anything to you about—"

"I didn't stop to talk with anyone. When you were nowhere in sight, I came straight back to the house. But I promise you that tomorrow I'm going up to the plantation and confront the owner. Nothing like that will ever happen again."

"That isn't necessary," I said softly. "The overseer has already assured me in that regard. But please, Drew," I entreated, "don't tell your aunt what happened. There is no need to upset her."

"I won't, my darling, and I'll pass your request on to my brother. Drew brushed my lips with his, then turned away as two maids came in bearing buckets of hot water. The minute the tub was filled, I climbed in, lay back my head, and closed my eyes. Slowly but surely the heat and rising rose-scented steam eased the tension within me. Most of it was from the fright, the balance from the ever-present attraction to Jordan and my deepening feelings for him. Just to be near him fueled desire, and every sensitive nerve in me ached for some mysterious fulfillment. A tremor of delight escaped my lips as I pictured Jordan in the casual clothes, with his shirt sleeves rolled up and his long, muscular legs in the trim trousers. Most days, of course, he dressed for the office, which usually included Saturdays. This was the first time he'd been home at this time since my arrival at the house. All in all, though, Jordan was virile and appealing in everything he wore. And Drew, too, I reminded myself as a loud warning voice told me to keep a safe distance from his twin.

With that warning firmly in mind I left the tub. After toweling dry, I began to dress for the evening in the lovely patterned gown that matched the blue in my eyes. By now I could hear Patience moving about in her room and I assumed she was also readying herself for dinner. I didn't see the older woman until we met in the grand drawing room. Her cheerful smile reassured me that she was unaware of my horrifying experience with the machete.

Once I had managed to shove that incident to the farthest reaches of my mind, this night's party became even more enjoyable than the previous Saturday's. But that was primarily because I heard no comments in regard to an engagement between Drew and me. And I let him know with my eyes that I appreciated the fact that he'd yielded to my request to keep that subject to ourselves for now. The evening ended on a happy note, and when I crawled into bed, I even complimented myself for steering clear of Jordan.

There wasn't any personal contact between us on the following day, either. For after church Drew insisted upon teaching me how to play cribbage. At the mention of cards Jordan excused himself and went out to his workshop for his fishing gear.

"I guess your brother doesn't care for cards," I said as Patience moved away to take her afternoon nap.

Drew's brows knitted. "We're different in that respect, too."

And every other one, it seemed to me. "I'm afraid I've never been good at card games," I confessed.

"Not to fear, my darling," he teased, "I'll teach you everything I know."

In all honesty I would rather have gone fishing. But I didn't want to hurt Drew's feelings. Besides, if he could ride with me, then the least I could do was learn to enjoy his amusements. But the longer we sat across from each other at the table in the informal drawing room, shuffling cards and moving pegs in small scoreboards, the more I longed to be out wandering the beach.

"You're doing fine, my sweet," Drew tried to reassure me.

"That's easy for you to say," I grumbled. "I haven't won a game yet." He inclined his head in a sympathetic gesture. Even so, I had the feeling he didn't really want me to win. But I'd at least made an honest effort to learn the game, and somehow in the process Drew and I had regained a bit of the closeness we'd shared on the mainland. The gleam in his eyes told me that this made him happy. For me the closeness was comforting.

I focused on that renewal of warmth as I slipped between the sheets that night and snuggled down. But when I drifted off to sleep, bad dreams haunted me. This time I saw Drew and me in the makeshift army hospital. He and I were playing cards with scores of wounded soldiers and cannons rumbled all around us. This was the first nightmare I'd had in days and it, too, shook me awake. Or had the light but persistent tapping done that? Where was the sound coming from? I rose on one elbow. The door! Before I could sit all the way up and blink the sleep from my eyes, one of the maids called softly, and yet with an urgent note in her voice, "Miss Rachel."

"Yes," I called back just as softly, lest Patience be disturbed.

A young Oriental girl came in. Guided by the moonlight falling through the windows, she stepped to the bed. Even in the semidarkness I could see her brows knitted in worry. I sat bolt upright, pushing the hair back from my face. "What is it?" I choked out in a whisper.

"Mrs. Malo was just here, she needs your help at her place. Hurry, please, miss, there's been an accident . . . it's Kalani."

chapter 19

IN A SECOND I was out of bed. "What happened?" I asked quickly but quietly as I darted to the closet for my clothes.

The maid lighted a bedside lamp. "Mrs. Malo didn't say." The girl kept her voice low. "But it must be bad; she was very upset."

"Is she still here?" I pulled on my dress, caught up shoes and a wrap.

"She ran back home."

A minute later the maid and I were hurrying down the stairs. As we rushed along the entrance-floor hallway I cautioned over my shoulder, "Don't let Miss Phillips know about this and upset her."

"I won't say a word." When we reached the rear door, the maid hauled out a lantern. "You might need this."

As she lighted the lamp I asked, "What time is it?"

Just past eleven-thirty. Let me know if you need anything, my room is next to the kitchen on this floor."

I nodded, took the lamp, and stepped out into the night. The moon was bright, but little of its glow fell through the trees flanking the path between the houses, and I was grateful for the lantern that lit the way. As I hurried along the path I wondered what kind of an accident could have befallen Kalani in the dead of evening.

Mrs. Malo must have been watching for me from a window because the door was swung open as I approached the porch. "Hurry, please," she cried. "Kalani is in terrible pain."

"What happened?" I questioned as she ushered me quickly into a small bedroom and took my wrap.

"She was thrown from her horse. He stumbled in soft sand on the beach."

My heart lurched at the sight of Kalani lying in the bed, pale and doubled up in pain. And there was blood on the covers. "It hurts so bad," she wailed.

In an instant I was at her side. Her unbound hair was tangled and flecked with sand and her brow was wet with perspiration. I touched her cheek. No fever. Then I eased back the covers. More blood. Kalani was hemorrhaging. "She needs a doctor, Mrs. Malo." I kept my voice under control. "Someone from the big house can go for one. Dr. Hawthorne is a friend, he'll—"

"No, no." The old woman's voice was shrill. "No one must know."

"But I haven't the training—"

Kalani cried out, "Please don't let my baby die."

"Baby?" I stared down at her, stunned. Why hadn't I guessed? The signs of morning sickness had been there.

"Please," she implored, only this time Kalani's hand went to my sleeve, clutching.

"You must lie quiet," I urged, and examined her. Her right shoulder was bruised, but thank goodness there wasn't a broken bone in her body. I couldn't tell, though, if all the blood was from the threat of miscarriage or if there were other internal injuries. "Bring warm water, Mrs. Malo." Then I insisted once more that a physician be summoned. But the women still would not listen.

"Our shame is great enough," Mrs. Malo said as I wet a cloth from the basin that had been brought in and began to bathe Kalani. "No one must know about the baby."

"Your granddaughter's life could be in danger." But even that did not make a difference to either one of them. In the end there was nothing I could do but call upon all my nursing skills to try to save Kalani and her unborn baby. As Mrs. Malo and I worked feverishly my heart grew heavier and heavier as memories of my mother's many miscarriages flooded back to me. Once, during a particularly agonizing moment for Kalani, my eyes misted. The tears were for her, and for my dear mother. It was then that I took the older woman aside and questioned, "Where is the baby's father? He should be here for Kalani."

Mrs. Malo's jaw hardened. "He does not want my granddaughter and the baby." She wheeled and went back into the small bedroom.

Anger burned in me. No wonder Kalani had been so unhappy, despondent, actually. What kind of man would abandon the woman who carried his child? That anger simmered, then flared anew when Kalani, in her third month of pregnancy, lost the baby. Sobs racked her already tortured body and she was inconsolable. "I wanted the baby conceived of my love. I wanted a part of—" Through all the crying and pain, she never once said the man's name. Her grandmother never let it slip from her lips, either.

I stayed at Kalani's side all night, struggling to keep her quiet, to keep the blood from flowing heavily again. By early morning, as the sun was coming up, the weakness had at last compelled her to sleep. And her grandmother and I dropped into chairs in the kitchen. Over cups of steaming tea I asked, "What was Kalani doing out riding so late at night?"

"She's always liked to ride on the beach in the moonlight. She never had any trouble before. Is she going to be all right, Miss Rachel?"

"Yes, I think she'll be fine."

Fresh tears brimmed in the dark eyes. "Thank God. And Thank God for you. But please," she begged again, "don't tell anyone."

"I won't," I promised, and we agreed that I would simply inform the Phillipses that Kalani had suffered a fall from a horse and would be away from her duties for several days. Perhaps even longer. "I'm going home now and get some rest, Mrs. Malo. Please try to do the same. I'll be back to check on Kalani later. But if there's any problem, a fever, anything, come for me." Again I longed to urge that a doctor be summoned, but I knew the words would still fall on deaf ears.

At the door Mrs. Malo hugged me, and for an instant I felt as if I were in my mother's embrace. Quickly I turned away, blinking back tears. Upon my return to the big house I sought out the Oriental maid who had awakened me last night. I explained briefly about the accident and reassured her that Kalani would be fine. This woman's reply was identical to Mrs. Malo's. "Thank God."

"If I'm needed at the cottage, please send someone for me immediately."

She nodded, and I continued along the entrance-floor hallway. I had hoped to make it to my room and freshen up before I informed Patience of the accident. But we met on the stairs as I was ascending the last flight and she was heading down to breakfast. Shock widened her pale blue eyes. "Rachel, there's blood on your skirt."

"Blood?" one of the twins rasped as he approached the third-floor landing. "Are you all right, my darling?" The endearment told me this was Drew. But I should have realized that right away. Jordan was an early riser and would have left for the office by now.

"I'm fine," I said, and held my explanation about Kalani until Drew joined his aunt and me on the stairs. Then the pair stared at me in a moment of stunned silence. What a strong reaction, I thought, considering I'd merely said the housekeeper had been badly shaken and bruised. But maybe I was just too tired to gauge expressions properly.

"Is there anything we can do for Kalani?" Patience inquired.

Convince her to consult a doctor. I bit back the words, fearing they might generate questions I wasn't at liberty to answer. "Nothing at the moment, Patience."

A muscle in Drew's face tightened. "Maybe I should go over and look in on her."

His aunt waved what looked like a warning hand. "I don't think that's necessary, Drew," she said. "I'm sure Rachel will maintain a close watch over Kalani and keep us informed."

"Yes, of course," I said slowly. "Right now she isn't up to seeing anyone. If you don't mind, Patience, I'm going to try to get some sleep."

"Go ahead, dear, I'll be fine."

"Sleep well, my sweet." Drew gave me a tender hug. Then I continued up the stairs. I changed back into my nightdress and returned to bed. I was so weary I could scarcely keep my eyes open, yet I tossed and turned. Kalani's deep sadness was like a vise on my senses, and when I wasn't envisioning her grief-stricken face, I saw Patience's hand raised in the warning. Drew's offer to call on Kalani had been thoughtful and I couldn't imagine what had motivated his aunt to respond with the negative gesture. But Patience's eccentric mood swings were always mystifying and I usually gave up trying to figure them out. In the end I also gave up on this one and within minutes I was asleep.

When I awakened in the early afternoon, I enjoyed a light meal while Patience kept me company, then I returned to the cottage. "Kalani's still very weak," her grandmother said. "But when she woke up a while ago, I managed to get a little broth down her. Then she went right back to sleep."

I looked in on the pale woman. Her breathing was normal and there still was no sign of fever. That was a blessing. Once again I returned to the big house and I did not retrace my steps on the wooden path until just before sunset. Then I was surprised to come face-to-face with Jordan. He was dressed in a business suit, so I knew he wasn't on his way home from fishing or an outing in his canoe. Besides, those pastimes usually had a positive effect, and Jordan's expression now was almost grim. "Were you over at Mrs. Malo's?" I asked what seemed the obvious.

He raked a hand through his thick dark hair. "Yes. Drew told me what happened. It's a good thing a nurse was close by." He managed a small smile.

Somehow it had grown so easy for me to share things with Jordan, to take him into my confidence, or at least partly into my confidence where the housekeeper was concerned. "Kalani suffered quite a bit of pain," I said, "and really should see a doctor. Maybe you can convince her, Jordan."

He lifted his shoulders in a helpless gesture. But I knew there was nothing helpless about this man. "If you couldn't convince her, Rachel, then I'm sure I can't. In any case she said she's feeling better. There's probably nothing to worry about."

Then why were his eyes narrowed in worry? Obviously his concern for Kalani ran deep. Why, though? As Jordan moved past me my mind stubbornly went back over the brief exchanges I'd seen between him and the housekeeper. Had he known what was troubling her? Had she told Jordan about the baby?

Over the next three days those questions plagued me, and the more tight-lipped the Hawaiian women became about Kalani's lover, the more I focused on her and Jordan. Has those silent messages between them risen from intimacy? And what about his visits to the cottage? Had he gone there to see Mrs. Malo, or her granddaughter? Repeatedly my mind fixed on that day Jordan and I had fished from the dock. Just before then he'd been in the cove. Kalani was there at the same time. Might she and Jordan have rendezvoused in the cottage while her grandmother was in town that afternoon? As I recalled, Jordan had known the old woman was going to be visiting friends. Maybe Kalani hadn't forgotten that fact, as her grandmother had assumed.

A knot formed in my stomach and I told myself that even if Jordan had known about the baby, that didn't mean he was the father. Maybe the whole Phillips family had been aware of the pregnancy. That could explain why the very proper Patience had suddenly turned cool toward Kalani.

All through Kalani's convalescence Patience was solicitous and generously offered any needed assistance. But once Kalani returned to her duties in the big house, the cool regard gradually returned. However, Kalani didn't seem to notice, or perhaps she just didn't care. Her body had healed but her spirit was not rallying. "I wanted that baby so much," she said one afternoon as we sat atop Black Rock. "Even if everyone around would have scorned me."

She knew I'd done everything possible to save her baby and my earnest efforts had formed a bond between us, a growing friendship. I didn't want to pry into Kalani's personal life, but one particularly nagging question surfaced and spilled from my mouth before I could even try to stem the flow. "Kalani," I said quietly, "did Mrs. Phillips and the family know about the baby?" My heart pounded so loudly I feared I wasn't the only one who heard the beats.

Kalani stared dully into the sacred pool and seconds passed before she answered. "No, and you mustn't tell them."

Relief washed through me. Jordan was not the father. Although maybe Kalani wasn't being truthful about the family. Maybe she was trying to shield them from scandal. I expelled a helpless breath. "Of course I won't tell them," I promised.

She leaned forward, her gaze now fixed, as if she could see something in the depths of the water. When she spoke, her voice sounded miles away. "I'd hoped that when the baby's father learned I was pregnant, his family would accept me and he and I could marry. But the baby didn't make a difference. I still wasn't good enough for them. I kept hoping and praying they

might change their minds, though. Now," she choked, "there is
no hope. I will never have him. Never have his baby."

Her unhappiness was wrenching and all the words of comfort
that came to mind seemed inadequate. I knew how to help heal
the body, but healing the mind was beyond my depth. "You are
young, Kalani," I said, "with a whole life still ahead. I know that
isn't much consolation, but time does heal."

"Maybe," she murmured, never lifting her eyes from the tide
pool below. "He and the baby were my life."

I didn't know what else to say. At one point I even thought of
suggesting that Kalani turn to her idol Madame Pele for strength
and solace. But that smacked of paganism. Or at least Drew
would think so and I didn't want to do or say anything that might
get back to him and raise his ire. As it was, he was already annoyed with me for spending so much time with Kalani. "It isn't
proper, Rachel," he insisted. "Kalani is a servant."

"Yes, but I can't stop caring just because her station in life
isn't equal to yours. Mine isn't either!"

"That's different."

It wasn't different and I didn't know why he had convinced
himself otherwise. Because he loved me? Whatever the reason, it
was not the issue at this moment. "Kalani needs someone right
now, a sympathetic ear. I wish I could explain, Drew, but I
can't." Of course I could, if he knew about the baby. But to come
right out and ask if that was the case would be a betrayal to
Kalani.

"You can't lend a sympathetic ear to everyone you come
across who is feeling low, Rachel. If you're starved for feminine
companionship, accept the invitations to call on some of the ladies you met at our dinner parties."

"I'm not starved for anything," I retorted, annoyed by his lack
of understanding and compassion. "I will accept some of the invitations. Even so, I don't choose friends based upon bank ac-
counts and the social register."

Drew's lips thinned and he dropped the subject. Still, I had the
feeling I hadn't heard the end of this. Did he intend to shape my
life? To keep me under his thumb as Mrs. Malo had hinted?
Where was the man who had once delighted in my streak of in-
dependence? Obviously I hadn't seen the real Drew back on the
mainland. If it turned out he wasn't the one for me, I told myself,

then I would have to leave this house. The thought alone added more weight to my heart. I'd come to love this place, the tropic island, and dear Patience. I would miss her terribly. And ... I would miss Jordan. I didn't even want to consider what that silent admission meant. After all, if he was involved with Kalani and had refused to do the honorable thing by marrying her, then he was a scoundrel.

My heart rejected that loathsome word. At the same time my brain rebelled against the very real possibility that I was in love with Jordan.

I tried to bury the ton of concerns that cluttered my mind by immersing myself in the *Canterbury Tales*, which I'd selected from the family library. But thought after thought resurfaced tormentingly and I finally put aside the classic and went out for a ride on the beach. The day was as gloomy as my spirits and it looked as if the brooding sky was about to release a torrential downpour. Somehow I didn't really care if the dark clouds opened up on me and I continued along the windswept sand. As I neared Black Rock I saw Kalani's horse standing at the base. But I didn't see her anywhere. Odd! I couldn't imagine she would go off and leave her horse, especially when it was a long walk back to the house. I cupped my hands around my mouth and called her name. Again and again. The only sounds that came back to me were the wind, the rolling surf, and the screeching gulls.

As I once more glanced up the rock sudden chills prickled my flesh and my heart thumped. That rock was slick in places and she might have fallen. Hurriedly I dismounted and climbed to her favorite spot. My gaze swept one way, then the other. A strangling breath caught in my throat and I blinked, refusing to accept what my eyes had focused upon. When I looked again, a muted scream escaped my mouth. Kalani was in the sacred tide pool below, floating facedown. Her arms were outstretched and her hair fanned out about her shoulders in a black cape of death.

chapter 20

THE PHILLIPSES AND I attended Kalani's funeral, along with her family and friends. Thick dark clouds hung low in the sky, which cast an even heavier pall over the senses. Most people believed Kalani had accidentally fallen from Black Rock. Others who had been aware of her recent depression feared she might have jumped into the sacred pool, to set her spirit free to join the gods. If the legend of Black Rock hadn't been so real to her, I wouldn't have even considered the possibility that she had taken her life. Deep in my heart I didn't believe she had done such a thing, but I supposed a little doubt would always linger in the back of my mind.

Patience was more shaken by Kalani's tragic death than I had expected. Even her nephews were somber and unusually quiet. And the brooding expression had come back into Jordan's eyes. If he had been romantically involved with the pretty Hawaiian, then what must he be feeling now? What must the whole family be feeling? Kalani's death in the ocean had surely returned the painful memories of the ladies who had drowned when their outrigger capsized two years ago.

The Phillipses watched over Mrs. Malo through the hard days before and directly after the funeral. It was heartwarming to see them rally around the woman who had been in essence a part of their family for such a long time. She accepted their concern graciously, yet for all her show of appreciation I sensed underlying bitterness. I couldn't tell, though, if it was aimed at them, or if it was just a part of her grief.

Mrs. Malo's family also watched over her and I paid daily calls. Sometimes I only stayed a few minutes; at other times, when she particularly needed comfort, we chatted over tea in her kitchen. She never talked about the miscarriage that had deepened her granddaughter's depression, yet I knew the pregnancy was to remain a well-guarded secret and I reaffirmed my own inner vow never to tell anyone.

Through all our conversations Mrs. Malo didn't once mention if she thought Kalani had taken her own life, but the old woman's bitterness made me suspect otherwise. If she believed this, then she must despise the man who abandoned her granddaughter. Not only him, but his family, who had refused to accept her. That nagging thought kept taking me back to the Phillipses. The class-conscious Patience and Drew would vehemently disapprove of taking a servant into the family. I had no idea of Jordan's feelings in that regard, but out of respect for his aunt he would, I suspected, bow to her wishes. Had he been Kalani's lover? Was that even any of my business? My heart told me yes. It also told me that if Kalani had leaped to her death, the decision had been her own. No one had stood behind her and pushed. No one else could really be faulted.

Still, for my own peace of mind, I had to know if Jordan was the one who had enjoyed her complete love and then turned his back on her. I doubted that Mrs. Malo would ever identify the man, especially if he was Jordan. After all, she owed the Phillips family a certain loyalty, along with appreciation for the privilege of living in this comfortable home. The only way I could find out if they were at the core of Mrs. Malo's resentment was through our casual conversations. She did like to reminisce about the twins and their boyhood days on the island. When she went back through the years, it was as if she were really in that other time. "Those were the happiest and most rewarding days of my life," she had told me. The stories she related of the brothers painted vivid images in my mind, their Sunday-afternoon canoe races and the countless fishing competitions they had arranged with their friends. "Jordan was always better than Drew at the outdoor activities," Mrs. Malo said over tea late one afternoon.

"When I first met Jordan, he didn't impress me as the kind who liked to be outside," I admitted. Then I added what was clearly true, at least as far as the brothers were concerned, "Obviously I'm not good at first impressions." But of course my initial impression of Jordan had been governed by anger over the embarrassing kiss. "What activities did Drew excel in as a boy, Mrs. Malo?" I sipped from my cup of tea.

"Chess and similar games. Then later . . . cards."

"He's trying to teach me how to improve my skill at them. Actually, lack of it." I laughed. "I'm afraid cards really aren't for me."

"All for the better," she murmured, and appeared to be lost in thought. "Drew has given too much time to that pursuit, all those nights at the—" She broke off abruptly as if she suddenly realized she'd said more than she should have.

"All those nights at what?" I prompted gently, my mind on the grogshops. Heaven knew Drew spent plenty of evenings in those places.

"Oh, nothing, just an old woman rambling." She rose and began to clear away the tea service, ending the conversation.

If it truly was nothing, wouldn't she have explained what she'd meant by "all those nights"? Over the next twenty-four hours those words ran around in my mind. The more I considered them, the sharper became the pictures of Drew playing cards with the other soldiers in the army field hospital. He'd always been the one to gather the men for the daily games. All along I had assumed he'd done so out of the goodness of his heart, to keep their minds off the war. Now, as I reflected on the brilliant sparkle that had been in his eyes as he'd played those games, and his glee every time he'd won—which had been most of the time—I began to wonder if his motive had been noble. Drew was good at those games. Maybe too good for someone who claimed he played just for the fun of it. Were cards more to him than mere amusement? Might that be why he was in charge of the grogshops, the establishments his aunt and brother rarely mentioned? Their reticence alone showed they didn't approve of the unsavory places any more than I did. It could also explain Jordan's hints about his twin being irresponsible. Maybe there was nothing to Mrs. Malo's comment concerning Drew and the cards. But I had to know for sure. How could I uncover how deeply his interest ran in the games of chance? If he was addicted to them, he certainly wouldn't admit it—especially not to the woman he hoped to marry. And I doubted his family would tell me; their loyalty was to Drew.

There was only one way I could think of to find out if he was a gambler. It was sneaky, and I hated being underhanded. Still, my future was at stake and I had promised Drew an answer to his proposal soon. So one evening, when I was certain he would be going to town, I changed into dark clothing that would help me blend into the night and crept out to the stables. To my good fortune no one was around. Quickly I saddled the horse I always rode and quietly urged him up the drive and toward Lahaina. Just this side of the city I maneuvered the horse into the thick growth of shrubs and trees lining the road. Since I didn't know which taverns the family owned, and dared not inquire around town, I waited for Drew. Twenty minutes must have passed before he came into view and I held my breath as he passed by. When he was far enough ahead not to notice he was being followed, I urged my horse back onto the road.

In Lahaina Drew tied his horse to the hitching post before a tavern and went inside. I tied my animal to the post in front of the funeral parlor a few doors down. Except for the noise coming from the scores of grogshops it was quiet and only a few coarse-looking men were moving about. Thank goodness none of them appeared to notice me. That blessing I attributed to the faint moonlight and my dark clothes and bonnet, which made me part of the shadows.

I stepped onto the boardwalk and all but tiptoed to the tavern Drew had entered. Raucous music and loud masculine voices assaulted my ears. At the window I glanced around, making certain no one had caught sight of me. Then I flattened myself against the wooden building and peered through the panes. The smoke-filled room beyond was crowded with men. All of them were drinking and many were playing cards. My heart soared when I didn't see Drew. Maybe he maintained an office behind one of the closed doors at the back and he was indeed tending to business. Just as I was about to make my way around to the windows at the rear to see if that was the case, one of the doors was opened and Drew crossed the threshold. A shaggy-bearded man at a nearby table signaled him over. "Come on, Drew," he bellowed, "give us a chance to get back what ya won off us last night." The others at the table nodded and made comments I couldn't hear above the din.

My spirits slid to my toes and I felt my shoulders sag. Smiling, Drew crossed to the table. He also said something that was lost to me in all the noise. Then he sat down and shuffled the deck of cards he'd been handed. I don't know how long I stood there, or how many games I watched Drew play, before I finally turned away and started back to the house.

I slept fitfully that night and by morning I had decided it wasn't fair to judge Drew a gambler based upon what I'd seen on one occasion, and had heard about his winnings on another. So at the end of this day I followed him again. Only this time he went to a different grogshop, which I assumed the Phillips family also owned. Once more Drew played cards, but not with the same good luck I'd observed before and worry gradually tightened his clear-cut features.

The same emotion tightened the muscles in my face. I dreaded telling Drew I could not marry him and explaining what lay behind my decision. And I hated to think of Patience's disappointment when she learned the marriage she'd hoped for wasn't even a remote possibility and I would have to leave this house.

The fact that I would have to leave produced an ache in me and I pondered my decision throughout the day. But in the end it was the only one I could make. So after dinner I invited Drew to join me for a stroll in the flower gardens. The worry I'd seen in his face at the grogshop on the previous night still touched his features. I supposed this wasn't the best time to broach the gambling and to respond to his marriage proposal. On the other hand I doubted there could ever be a good time. After we admired the colorful blossoms in the wash of moonlight and had commented about the scented air, I said in a quiet voice, "Drew, if I may, exactly what is it you do at the grogshops?"

"See to the running of the places," he answered simply. "There's quite a bit involved. But I've told you that before."

"Yes. I was wondering, though, do you ever gamble with the other men?"

He eyed me in surprise. "On a rare occasion, just to be social."

"You mean, like once or twice a year?"

My persistence turned his expression to a frown. "I don't count the times, Rachel. But yes, around that. Why the odd questions, has someone been talking to you about me. My aunt, with her tendency to twist facts? Or Mrs. Malo, who long ago lost patience with me because of my boyhood pranks?"

"I've never heard your aunt twist facts, Drew, and Mrs. Malo dotes on you." I released a long breath. "I'm just concerned about the grogshops and what I remembered of you and your card playing in the army hospital."

"That was just a diversion, you know that, Rachel."

"I think it was more."

"Why would you say such a thing?"

I hesitated. "I saw you playing cards . . . last night and the one before."

"You went spying on me?"

I nodded. "I'm not proud of it. But I had to know if you indulged in gambling and I doubted you would tell me if I asked."

"A man is entitled to his amusements," he said flatly.

"If they don't affect his family. Gambling can cause such misery. I've seen and heard of men losing everything. I don't want to live under that threat." I softened my tone. "I'm sorry, Drew, but I can't marry you."

The color drained from his face. "There is no threat," he insisted. "I win more than I lose. Besides, this family has plenty of money, Rachel." He reached for my hand, but I stepped back.

"I'm sorry," I repeated, "but living with a gambler is not for me."

"Don't make a hasty decision," he begged. "Give my proposal more thought."

"More thought won't change my mind."

But Drew wouldn't listen. "Take all the time you want, and please, Rachel, don't say anything about this to my family until you and I have talked again."

There was nothing more for us to talk about. But out of respect for Drew and all the kindness he'd shown me, I agreed to his request. "Remember, my darling," he said, "I need you."

The desperation that had come into his voice and expression was wrenching. Did he really love me that much? Although he hadn't said love, but rather need. To him, were those emotions one and the same? When I crawled into bed, I felt as if the whole world had crumbled around me. Drew surely felt the same, but at least he had his family, his home and work. I had no one. My life was back in limbo and I wasn't certain which way to turn.

Drew came home early from the office the next afternoon, which was not unusual for a Saturday. What was unusual,

though, was his invitation to ride with him. We'd only been on
one ride together and I knew he hadn't really enjoyed roaming
the countryside on a horse. Moreover, he'd even gone out of his
way to avoid the subject of another such outing. "Thank you for
asking me, Drew," I said softly, "but I really would like to be
alone." He looked so dejected I almost changed my mind and accepted the invitation. I didn't want to hurt him, but I couldn't encourage him, either. I placed a gentle hand on his arm, then I
turned away and left the house for the beach.

Deep within me I guess I'd known all along that Drew was not
the man for me. He had many fine qualities and he'd been good
to me. But there was no sparkle between us, no sense of the
magic I now knew could exist. However, even if both had been
there, the gambling, and Drew's views on marriage, would have
still come between us.

As I wandered along the beach I refused to let my mind focus
on the magic I felt with Jordan. But when I came upon the cove
and saw him fishing in the surf, the instant fluttering of my heart
overrode the message in my brain. I stopped and gazed on Jordan. The bright sun highlighted his dark hair, which was tousled
by the brisk trade wind. His skilled hands and strong arms
worked the fishing pole he held. Jordan stood in the foamy water, his trousers rolled up and the waves gently breaking about
his legs. A rush of emotion overwhelmed me and at long last I
admitted to myself that he was the man I wanted. I had known
that from the first moment I'd seen him and had sensed his inner
strength and confidence. But my loyalty to Drew had kept that
truth sealed away in my heart. What difference did my feelings
make, though, if Jordan didn't love me? And I had no reason to
believe his interest ran any deeper than the physical attraction
between us. Besides, there was Kalani, and if he had abandoned
her . . .

Once again I felt my shoulders sag. Just as I was about to retrace my steps in the sand, Jordan glanced my way. Our eyes met
and held as the familiar current flowed between us. My quickening pulse warned me to return to the house, but the overwhelming ache just to be near Jordan scattered every shred of good
sense in my brain. My throat dried. Even so, I managed to ask
politely, "Are the fish biting today?"

Jordan moistened his lips and replied without averting his eyes from mine. "I've caught three already."

"Three. How wonderful." I moved closer, but I wasn't certain if it was under my own power, or from his magnetic pull. "Mind if I watch?"

For the first time since Kalani's death I saw Jordan smile. "As I recall, you've asked me that before."

"Yes, that day on the dock."

"I remember."

The gleam coming into his eyes told me he was also remembering our kiss that afternoon. I swallowed, then said without thought, "I also asked if you had an extra fishing pole."

He acknowledged my reminder with a nod. "This time my answer is no, which is probably just as well. You aren't dressed for surf fishing."

"Oh, I wouldn't say that, all I have to do is throw off my shoes."

"But your skirts?"

"Water won't harm them."

"You love fishing that much, to get your skirts all wet?"

I loved him much more, but I couldn't confess to that truth. "Yes, although I don't know the first thing about surf fishing." I'm not really sure how it happened, but the next thing I knew my shoes were sitting on the sand near Jordan's and I was standing beside him in the water. It was cool and my skirts were quickly soaked to my knees. But I hardly noticed or cared. I was with Jordan and that fact made me blissfully warm and happy. He showed me how to cast the line. Unfortunately I couldn't quite manage to get it far enough out into the ocean.

"No, no," he said, moving to stand behind me, "like this, Rachel."

My heart leaped as he leaned forward, his body touching mine as his hand slid down my right arm and he instructed me to bring the pole up and then back over my shoulder. His voice had grown a little husky, and that along with his touch and radiating warmth threw my senses into a heady spin. As I reacted blindly to Jordan's instructions our bodies moved as one and every sensitive nerve within me responded to the moment. "That's the way, flip the line forward." His voice was even huskier than before. Quickly he stepped back to my side as if a warning inner voice had shouted at him.

During the next hour Jordan didn't touch me again and I told myself I was grateful. But the stirrings deep within conveyed the truth my mind stubbornly refused to accept. Once again I didn't catch any fish, but that might have been different if a storm hadn't suddenly blown in, causing us to scramble to catch up the gear. "It'll be pouring any second," Jordan said. "I'll take all of this; grab the shoes and head for the house." The words had scarcely left his mouth when the heavens opened and a deluge pelted down on us. "Take cover, Rachel," he urged, forgetting about the house. We ran to the thick cluster of palms that formed a near-perfect umbrella, with its surrounding shrubbery that would protect us from the howling wind. I glanced up. "Something wrong?" Jordan asked, settling beside me on the ground.

"I just wanted to be sure there were no coconuts that might come sailing down on us."

"Good thinking." He grinned. "Are we safe?"

"It looks that way."

"You're soaking wet, Rachel."

At least my hair hadn't come loose from the pins and combs and fallen around my face like hemp, as it had on that day of my near drowning. "So are you," I pointed out, and didn't dare let myself stare at the shirt clinging to his virile chest. I prayed my clothes weren't as revealing as his.

"Are you cold?"

With him sitting so near I was stifling hot. "No, but I can't find my other shoe." I tried to distract myself. "Oh, there it is, I must have dropped it in the rush to get here." I reached past Jordan just as he leaned forward to hand me my shoe and we nearly bumped heads. "Sorry," I murmured, and my gaze automatically came up to meet his eyes. The rain beat a deafening staccato, but all I heard was the drumming of my heart. The flames of desire that flickered in Jordan's eyes fueled the fire within me and my attention dropped to his mouth. His lips were soft and inviting and I leaned helplessly closer.

He lifted my chin, his fingers warm and provoking. "You are so beautiful," he rasped, "so exciting and vital, Rachel. You're all a man could ever want."

Euphoria encompassed my brain and I felt as if I had been

lifted to heaven. "Do *you* want me, Jordan?" I asked, with a boldness I had never dreamed was in me.

He lowered his head and answered with a deep kiss that rocked my senses and my lips parted as I yielded to his sweet pressure. In an instant Jordan's tongue slipped between my teeth and darted tormentingly. I'd never been kissed like this before, never known such delicious sensations, yet the hunger in the core of me begged for something I couldn't define. Jordan's hands were tantalizing irons on my flesh, branding, claiming, driving me mad with the weeks of pent-up longing. His mouth was at my ear, his tongue sending shivers of pure delight over every inch of my body.

With practiced ease Jordan laid me back and lavished kisses on my face and throat. I didn't want him to stop, yet I whimpered in a moment of shock when his mouth blazed a trail to the sensitive flesh at the scooped neck of my dress and lingered. Somewhere in all the heat he'd eased up my wet skirts and every part of me responded to his gentle, yet fervent touch. My mind was awhirl with the thrills that were rapidly building. Vaguely I heard the wind and the rain. But both were in the everyday world we'd left behind. In this one we lay in our secluded haven, our paradise, where we weren't apt to be seen by anyone.

Jordan's mouth was back on mine, his tongue more persistent, my own equaling his ardor. "Oh God, Rachel," he moaned when he lifted his head. "Can you feel what you do to me?"

How could I not feel the heat and strength of his passion? It had been a little startling at first and I'd almost recoiled. Now I regarded the outward show of his need with wonder. "Yes," I breathed, and kissed him with the passion that flowed hot in my veins.

Jordan's hand went to the hooks of my dress, then he paused and muttered with the agony of one who could not bear to be denied what he so desperately wanted, "I can't let this happen. Drew . . ."

Drew? The name floated in my brain. I could hardly think for all the excitement in me, for the need to have Jordan's mouth back on mine. "It's all right," I murmured, delirious. "I told Drew I couldn't marry him."

Jordan's head shot up. "You don't love my brother?"

"No. I tried to, but . . ."

For a split second happiness overwhelmed the desire in Jordan's eyes, then he kissed me again. "I love you, Rachel. I would have told you sooner, but I thought you and Drew were—"

"You love me?" I stammered, fearful that my ears had deceived me.

"As I have never loved another." His voice was a sensuous whisper. "Do you love me?"

I nodded, my throat clogged with emotion. "My heart has been yours from the moment I first saw you, Jordan, from our very first kiss."

"Then we both knew in the same instant." The world spun crazily as Jordan pulled me close. This was euphoria, the incredible realm in which time and shame were replaced by boundless longing and the need to pleasure Jordan as he was pleasuring me. I will probably never remember when or even how we shed our clothes. But then all that really mattered was the joy we were discovering in each other's arms. I hadn't known what to expect at that moment when we became one, and I winced at the sting of pain. Jordan kissed away the hurt, then all I felt was his strength and the breathtaking sensations of our bodies moving together in perfect rhythm. Every stroke lifted me to a higher plateau, every kiss prolonged the deepening thrills. The rain that still pounded down sounded as if it were miles away and the crashing, wind-driven waves more distant yet. Crashing, crashing. I quickened the rhythm. How would this joy end? Did I want it to? I tossed my head as I twisted and turned and maneuvered. I had never known there could be anything like this. Jordan's mouth on mine was fierce, his darting tongue a whip on my sharpened senses. My heart beat so fast I feared I might expire, but I didn't even care. I clung to Jordan as he maneuvered, his heat searing and his solid strength catapulting me to a delirious summit I could never have imagined. I shook convulsively on the heady crest and Jordan moaned low in his throat in the throes of his own ecstasy. Now I knew true euphoria! The world crashed around us. For a fraction of a second as we soared together I opened my eyes. The rain had stopped and a brilliant rainbow shone in the cloud-dappled azure sky. So beautiful, and yet hardly that in comparison with what I felt in these cherished moments.

By the time Jordan and I had floated back to reality, the sun was bright and the rainbow had begun to fade. As we lay in each other's arms, he asked me about my decision regarding Drew and marriage.

I hesitated. "I promised your brother I wouldn't speak of this to anyone just yet and I've already said more than I should have. But if I hadn't—"

"We wouldn't have declared our love for each other this afternoon, Rachel. We wouldn't have—" Jordan finished his sentence with another long kiss. "Can you just tell me briefly what made you decide against my brother? There's a particular reason why I ask."

I couldn't imagine what that reason was. But in view of what Jordan already knew it seemed pointless not to answer. So I told him why I'd decided against marrying Drew. "A husband who gambles is not for me," I concluded firmly.

Jordan expelled a long breath. "That's what I wanted to know. I was hoping you'd find out about the gambling, Rachel. For your sake I'd wanted to tell you. But if I had, Drew would never have forgiven me and I just couldn't bring myself to betray him. I was hoping you'd catch my little hints and figure it out for yourself. Just as I also hoped Mrs. Malo might have a slip of the tongue."

"Is that why you were so determined that I meet her?"

He nodded. "She's a wonderful woman and would never intentionally say anything against our family. But she is also worried about Drew. He's ruining his life, Rachel. In the process he's making everyone around him miserable."

"The gambling is that bad?"

"Beyond control. He's lost a great deal of money. I'm afraid he spends more time at the grogshops than he does in the office."

"I don't suppose selling off the shops would make a difference."

"No. But I can tell you Aunt Patience rues the day she let Drew talk her into buying those places. He's always been able to charm what he wanted out of her. You're shivering. Come, let's get you back to the house and into a hot tub before you catch your death." Jordan helped me to my feet and we pulled on our wet clothes. Then he kissed me lightly and murmured near my ear, "I love you, Rachel. No matter what might happen, don't ever forget that." He caught up my shoes, said he would return for the fishing gear later, and we started up the beach.

On the way back to the house I asked, "Just what did you mean by 'no matter what'?"

The brooding expression returned to his eyes. "I'll tell you one day soon, Rachel, when we have plenty of time to talk."

In essence Jordan was asking me to trust him. I loved him and wanted to. But I'd trusted Drew, who also said he loved me, and he had let me down. How could I be certain now his twin wouldn't do the same?

chapter 21

JORDAN AND I left the beach. As we neared the house the backdoor opened and Drew came out. "Rachel, where have you been for such a long time." His gaze raked over me and I felt myself flush. "You're soaking wet, and where are your shoes?"

"I have them right here with mine." Jordan held them up. "We were caught in the rain."

"So I see," Drew muttered, his gaze now raking his brother. "I didn't know you two were out together."

I took my shoes. "I came upon Jordan on the beach and he was showing me how to surf-fish when the rains came. If you'll excuse me, I'm going up for a bath." As I moved past Drew I could feel him watching after me and I prayed he couldn't tell that surf fishing wasn't all his brother had taught me this afternoon. But of course how could anyone tell? At least I didn't have to worry about prying eyes at the telescope. For even its keen lens couldn't have penetrated the foliage in the cove.

When I entered the house, I asked one of the maids to please bring me up bathwater. She nodded, eyeing my wet clothes with open curiosity, then told me Patience was still napping. Moments later, as I set down my shoes on the floor in my room, I remembered that I had once thought Jordan had probably never even run barefoot in the grass with a girl. True, he and I hadn't run in the grass, but the beach was the same. How wrong I had been about him.

As I undressed I was horrified to find traces of sand still clinging to my dress. And when I looked into the mirror, I saw the fine particles there, too. Had Drew noticed and guessed what had transpired between his twin and me? I didn't regret what we had done. But Drew had enough troubles and I didn't want to hurt him any more than I already had by rejecting his marriage proposal. Now that I knew he had a gambling problem and money could be crucial to him, I wondered even more why he'd asked me to be his bride. In his place I would have looked for a woman of substantial means.

The tub and hot water were brought in. As I soaked in the scented bubbles, then washed from head to toe, I relived every moment of the lovemaking. Jordan had been so tenderly determined to satisfy the hunger that had tormented me from the moment we'd met. "No regrets," I murmured, then reflected on Kalani. She'd probably felt the same until she learned she was with child and her lover turned away from her. He couldn't have been Jordan, I told myself again. He wouldn't turn away from me if I . . .

I poured water over my head as if it would wash away the unsettling thought. Since I'd guessed wrong about the kind of man Drew was, mightn't I have done the same with his twin? I swallowed the painful lump that had risen in my throat and left the tub. My plum-colored percale had been laid out. After I toweled dry, I dressed and brushed my hair. Then I sat down before the open window so the warm air would dry the golden tresses. The rainbow I'd seen earlier had long ago disappeared, but the sun still shone brightly and the palms swayed in the brisk breeze. In the distance smoke from a cane fire swirled up to join the scatterings of billowy clouds.

With so many thoughts and concerns crowding my mind I was too restless to sit quietly for long. A glance into Patience's room confirmed that she was still asleep. I fastened my hair at the nape with silk ribbon and went down to the rear flower garden. It was so peaceful among the lush greenery and riotous blooms, though once I glanced up at the house, sensing someone was watching me. But I didn't see anyone at the doors or windows. I must have circled the lava-stone walk several times before I moved to the path canopied by tall trees. Branches creaked in the wind and leaves rustled. Footsteps sounded behind me. Startled, I whirled. There was a second of pain in my head, then the world went dark.

I don't know how long I was unconscious, but as the darkness receded I felt myself being caught up in strong arms and something in the air made my throat burn. Smoke! Racking coughs overcame me and my eyes watered. My lashes fluttered. But before I could see where I was and who held me near, the man opened his arms and I thudded painfully to the ground. Every bone in my body shook upon impact and my lungs were growing heavier from the smoke. Panic-stricken, I forced open my eyes and blinked back the moisture. Smoke! Everywhere. Thick and black. Tall canes looming. Fire! Oh God. The words screamed in my aching head. Instinctively I reached up. There was a bump on my temple. The man must have struck me. But how had I gotten here? I tried to push myself up, but the strong hands came down on my shoulders, shoving me back down. For the first time I saw my captor. One of the twins. Which one? His eyes were venomous. I screamed, and he clapped a hand over my mouth. "If I can't have you, Rachel," he ground out, "then neither will my brother." Drew? I clawed at him and tried to roll away. The sugarcane leaves poked at my flesh and every breath I took seared my throat and lungs.

"Why . . . you doing . . . this?" I choked, scrambling forward.

He caught me by the hair and jerked me back. "I saw you on the dock kissing my brother." His words also choked out. "I failed to get you with the machete, but I won't fail now. You have no family to question your death, like Claudia and Ellen did."

The horror of his words shook every fiber in me. "You killed them?"

"So easily, my love. Just a little sawing on the outrigger and then that storm conveniently came up. I'd hoped to spare you for a while. After the machete it seemed we were getting closer again and I felt renewed hope. Now, though—"

"But your wife," I gasped. "And Jordan's fiancée. Why?"

"I couldn't let him father the first legitimate heir. But I couldn't harm him either, my own brother. Claudia"—he spat the name—"with all her miscarriages was useless to me. Just as you would have been worthless once we'd had a child." The racking coughs that overcame Drew caused him to loosen his hold on my hair and I scooted forward. "Rachel," he shouted through the spasms.

I scrambled to my feet and darted forward. The cane was so tall and thick and the choking smoke hung low. I crouched, keeping my head below the dark fumes. I ran blindly between the clusters, zigzagging this way and that, stumbling. Sometimes I was sure I heard running feet behind me, but I never looked back. My lungs felt as if they were about to explode and my eyes burned and watered so badly I could hardly see. I didn't know where I was and Drew's warning about never finding the way out of a cane field screamed repeatedly in my thumping head. The sheer fright and panic kept me going. I pushed at stalks, fell, scrambled back up, and pushed onward. All the while I feared Drew's hands would suddenly come down on me.

I zigzagged again and again and then, as if by some miracle, I stumbled onto the road. I paused just long enough to catch a breath, then ran as far as I could from the licking fire before the smoke and exhaustion swooped down over me and the darkness fell again.

I awakened, coughing. "You're going to be all right, Rachel," Jordan said softly, and gave my hand a gentle squeeze. "You're home and in your own bed." As my eyes fluttered open I saw that he sat beside me, and I remembered in a rush of visions the horror in the cane field. "Drew," I gulped, and tears streamed down my face.

Jordan shook his head and dried my tears. "A plantation worker found you on the road alongside the cane field. Later they found . . . Drew. Somehow he'd wandered in and apparently couldn't find his way out."

"He's gone?"

"Yes," Jordan murmured sadly, then helped me sip from a glass of water. "What were you and my brother doing up at the cane fields yesterday and in the old wagon we haven't used in years?"

"Yesterday?"

"You've been in and out of consciousness ever since you were found. There were no saddle horses with you, just the wagon. Can you talk about what happened, Rachel?"

I didn't want to tell Jordan what his brother had done. But I couldn't carry that horror alone. Memories of the war were bad enough. So in a soft voice that didn't irritate my throat I explained what I knew. All the color drained from Jordan's face when I told him Drew tried to kill me in the sugarcane fire and that he'd made an earlier attempt with the machete. "After he knocked me out in the flower garden here, he must have driven me to the cane field in the wagon," I murmured, then related what Drew had said about the outrigger and the two lost ladies.

"My brother killed Ellen and Claudia." The words choked from Jordan's lips.

I nodded slowly. "All because of something to do with the first legitimate Phillips heir. Why should that matter?"

Jordan expelled a ragged breath and seconds passed before he explained. "In the last few years Aunt Patience has grown more and more determined to have the family name carried on. In her will she has stipulated that the first one of her nephews to father a legitimate heir will inherit control of her estate."

My mouth fell open. "Are you saying Drew's primary reason for marrying was to have a child and gain the wealth?"

He hesitated. "I'm afraid so, Rachel. He went off to the mainland looking for a bride."

My brain ran in circles, trying to sort everything out. "But why would such a callous man, a murderer, risk his life by volunteering for the army?"

"Drew didn't volunteer. He gambled himself in by losing a bet. My brother had gambling debts from here to New York, and the people there have been pressing him heavily to pay up in the past few months."

"Maybe that's why he left my home in Ohio to go there."

"Probably. Drew was so afraid you'd find out about the gambling. I knew he worried that Aunt Patience might inadvertently let it slip out in the course of your conversations with her."

"That brings back a question I've been puzzling over. Drew told me your aunt suffers from flights of fancy and that she sometimes twists facts. But I've never seen her like that."

"With good reason. It isn't true."

"Then he must have tried to convince me of that lie to protect himself in case she revealed more than he wanted me to know."

"My brother played all the angles of deceit."

In the days that followed Jordan and I talked at length and confided more and more in each other. He even told me that Drew had fathered Kalani's illegitimate child. I was more relieved that Jordan hadn't been the man in her life than surprised that Drew was her lover. "Couldn't he have married her," I asked, "and gained the family wealth?"

"Aunt Patience will only accept a Caucasian heir. She was furious with Drew and Kalani. But he always managed to smooth our aunt's ruffled edges. There was nothing Kalani could do. But at least I was able to convince Patience to provide financially for the child. I was finalizing those arrangements with her when Kalani lost the baby."

I suppose we will never know if Kalani had taken her own life. But in talking more with Mrs. Malo, Jordan and I suspect Drew might well have been responsible for the pretty Hawaiian's death, too. For her grandmother said Kalani had hinted to Drew that she was going to warn me about the kind of man he really was so that I might never be hurt by him. "After the way you befriended my granddaughter," Mrs. Malo said to me, "she would have done anything in her power to protect you. Unfortunately, when you first came to the island, she felt the complete opposite. She was jealous and so certain that if you weren't here Drew would marry her." The old woman paused. "Just to irritate you and make your life miserable, Kalani put the gecko in your bed and some of Miss Patience's sedatives in the fruit punch you took to the beach."

"Kalani?" I sat back in my chair, stunned.

"Yes, she told me right after she lost the baby. She said when you came so close to drowning, she knew how dreadfully wrong her jealousy was. It wasn't long afterward that she finally accepted the fact that Drew would never marry her."

"Considering what he'd done to your granddaughter, you didn't seem to be angry with him, Mrs. Malo."

"No. I knew how he could charm the women and I warned Kalani about taking up with him, that he would never give his heart to a servant. But she chose not to listen, she brought the grief upon herself. I hope you can forgive her for what she did to you, Miss Rachel."

"Kalani became my friend, that is how I will remember her."

As for Patience I wonder if she will ever forgive herself for what happened to Drew and what he'd done to the ladies. "If it hadn't been for that stipulation in my will about an heir, he and the others might be alive today."

"You can't blame yourself for all the terrible things Drew did," Jordan tried to comfort her.

"The stipulation didn't have the same effect on Jordan," I pointed out, and gradually she began to accept our reassurances.

Late one evening, as Jordan and I strolled the garden, he said, "I worried about telling you of Aunt Patience's will, Rachel. I was afraid you would think I said I loved you simply because of the stipulation. Yes, I want children one day. But what I want more is you." He pulled me close and gazed into my eyes.

"Why didn't you trust me in the beginning, Jordan? I hope you didn't think I was after the family money?"

"In spite of my immediate attraction to you I was afraid you might be like Drew. That's why I once asked if you were a night person."

"Because he was out most nights, in the taverns?"

"Yes, I was afraid you might go gallivanting, heaven knew where. Anyway, Patience and I agreed to sell off the grog-shops. Now, something more important." He brushed my lips with his. "Will you marry me, my darling Rachel?"

My heart leaped out of rhythm. "Yes, oh yes, Jordan. Except . . ."

His expression sobered. "Except what?"

"I'd like to continue with my nursing for a while. At least take Dr. Hawthorne up on his offer to help train others in the field. Would you mind?"

"Would you reject my proposal if I did?"

"Well . . ."

"Never mind." He laughed. "I don't think I really want to know."

"Then I have your approval?"

"Whatever it takes to make you happy." He gave me a long and thorough kiss that left us both trembling.

Shortly after Christmas Jordan and I were married and I delighted in being part of a family again. Through all my growing-up years my brothers had been the heroes in my life. In my heart they always will be. But the hero I treasure the most is my beloved husband.

421